SLOCUM HAD HEARD ENOUGH. NOW HE HAD TO GET OUT BEFORE HE WAS CAUGHT.

He slid up the sash and went over the sill, landing on ice and going to one knee, with both hands spread out to break his fall. The snow wasn't piled here. He heard the window begin to close and then an almost silent, whispery kind of *swish*—that sort of barely heard sibilation, signaling danger by no more than the noise of air being cloven nearby. Slocum reversed his movement, starting to go flat instead of standing up, and something very hard took him alongside the temple and blotted out all his senses, plunging him into a black silence that could well have been death.

JAKE LOGAN

OUTLAW BLOOD

PLAYBOY
PAPERBACKS

Published simultaneously in the United States and Canada by Playboy
Paperbacks, New York, New York. Printed in the United States of
America. Library of Congress Catalog Card Number: 77-79430.

Books are available at quantity discounts for promotional and indus-
trial use. For further information, write to Premium Sales, Playboy
Paperbacks, 1633 Broadway, New York, New York 10019.

ISBN: 0-872-16979-0

First printing November 1977.
Fifth printing December 1981.

1

The town of Retch squatted on a miserable scrap of desert in the southeast corner of the Arizona Territory, dirty brown hills speckled with cactus and greasewood on its skyline, rimmed with uncut thickets of cholla. The town was as ugly as its name and even uglier than its countryside. Every time that Slocum walked out of the Earthquake Saloon to suck in a few breaths of genuine air, he'd wonder if the place had been named Retch because the miserable, forbidding landscape had made somebody air his paunch just to see it, or if maybe the founding fathers just hadn't been able to spell *wretch*. Either way, the name fit.

Daily, for most of a week, he'd made up his mind to light out for Tombstone, which wasn't so far away: he'd heard that it now bragged of a population of close to a thousand people. But the luck was running good, there was an astonishing amount of money floating around in the godforsaken hole, and Slocum had ridden away from his luck too many times before. Damned if he'd be spooked by nothing more than a rotten eyesore of a view!

He spat into the street. He could smell the first big snow of the winter coming, and halfway made up his mind again—but knew that he'd likely still be here this time tomorrow night. There was silver-mine money and buffalo-hunters' money and smuggling money in Retch, a sight of which was steadily finding its way into his pockets and saddlebags. He hadn't counted it—that was

5

bad luck—but he knew it was more than he'd held for a fistful of months. He'd had a streak like this only once before that he could call to mind, at the Casino in Santa Fe. And that had lasted a much shorter time.

He gulped the chilly air, a last enormous lungful, and turned away from the moon-chalked deformity of a town. He mused, so long, Retch. Now back to the wretches.

The first thing he looked at was his private bottle of double-bonded bourbon. There'd been some jokes about Slocum importing his own whiskey from the Palace of Mirrors down the street. But, after his first taste of the tornado juice served here in the Earthquake gambling hall, he'd refused to take another. The wonder was that it didn't rot the corks and eat through the bottles. He'd gone out for a case of the best in town. And nobody that frequented this ramshackle joint had shown himself worthy to share in Slocum's good liquor. Retch's male residents were a cultus, snaky bunch of scrofulous buffalo hunters, bullwhackers, mule skinners, prospectors, thugs, down-at-heels cardsharps, Mexicans, louts and a few war-hands who'd drifted in between jobs—every man jack of them with wool in his teeth. If they were so cheap that they'd drink the throat-searing tanglefoot whiskey here, when most of them were ass-deep in cash, then John Slocum wasn't about to be charitable with his bourbon.

Even in Dodge and Deadwood he'd never come up against such a haired-over set of curly wolves as this pack. A man's life hung in the balance at any particular minute in the Earthquake Saloon. Slocum kind of enjoyed that, and besides, his luck was running deep and long.

The bottle of whiskey at his place on the seven-player table looked to be exactly as full as when he'd left it to take in some fresh air and sit out a hand. Still standing, he lifted it to his lips, and was two hairs

6

away from swallowing when an acrid stench stopped his hand. Even in this atmosphere of flaming coal oil, stogies, cigarettes, booze, and the accumulated sweat of twenty or thirty years, he could tell what had been substituted for his double-bond.

He lowered the bottle slowly and looked them over. Half a dozen smirks came back to him.

Slocum said in a calm, reasonable, quiet voice that carried over the roar of the den, "What louse-bit son of a whore drank my whiskey and pissed in the bottle?"

Nobody answered. Someone stifled a snicker. Slocum eased back the flaps of his elkskin jacket with his elbows, freeing the butts of the heavy Peacemaker .45s on his hips. "I asked you nice, who did it?" he shouted. And suddenly the place was so hushed that the lonely howl of a distant coyote was clearly audible through the chinks in the walls.

One by one he watched them, and they responded variously: the two buffalo hunters with belligerent glaes, the tinhorn with a slight shake of the head, the aging cowhand with a level, blank stare, the Mexican nightrider with a "No, señor," and the fellow in black broadcloth, who looked like an undertaker and was certainly a gunny, with a tight grin as cold as a two-day corpse in a snowbank.

Slocum decided on the last one. Several times during the week he'd tried in a desultory way to goad Slocum into a fight. "You," said Slocum, his dark eyes flat and hard.

"If I'd thought of it," said the pistolero, "I might have. But I didn't."

Slocum took his word. Next best guess was the bigger of the pair of buff hunters, whose mean streak could be smelled almost as far as the stench of his unwashed carcass. "You," said Slocum, whispering now. "You mangy bastard, you done it."

"What you intend to do about it?" The great lum-

7

mox pulled out a big old dragoon revolver, slowly so that Slocum made no answering draw, and laid it on the table.

"Why, nothing," said Slocum easily, "except to return it to you." He reached over and upended the bottle. The urine splashed over the hunter's mop of greasy hair and trickled down his face into his beard. For a long instant he sat motionless, eyes squinted against the filthy stuff. Then with a raging bawl he snatched at his gun. Slocum, whose enormous hand still gripped the whiskey bottle upside down, jerked his wrist in a half-circle and smashed it on the side of the man's skull. The thick bottle broke, the joker's eyes flew wide open and then shut convulsively, and he went limp and collapsed to the filthy sawdust of the dirt floor in a reeking heap.

Slocum's hand hovered over his Colt. "You want to make this your fight too?" he challenged the second buffalo skinner.

"Me? Hell, no!" The man shook his head vigorously, both grimy paws waving peacefully in the air. "He ain't no friend of mine, mister. He's only my partner. If I'd been you I'd of blowed his brains into the spittoon where they belong."

"That's what'll happen to anybody else that figures me for a patient humble man," said Slocum. He raised his voice. "Hey! Room for one more at this table. Seven makes the best game."

At first no one answered directly. There were mutterings and muted arguments. Then the door swung wide, cracking loudly against the wall, and a slight, almost frail young fellow stepped inside. He was dressed in a thick bearskin coat, black Levi's that must have started out blue, boots worn down at the heels and an ancient Stetson that had lost its original shape and drooped down both sides of his head. He was clean-shaven, but his face was so smeared with trail

8

dust and grime that a razor obviously hadn't touched it in the last week. It crossed Slocum's mind that the kid was maybe too young to shave.

Somebody gave a nasty horse-whinny of a laugh and said, "Ain't he the cute one!"

"He sure is," said the black-clad gunman, his voice more serious. Slocum threw him a glance. The newcomer might be in trouble. He was fresh meat in a dive where no woman, not even the most raddled harridan in town, ever dared to come. Not all of these savages were partial exclusively to women, either. Slocum stayed on his feet, a little way from the table, and waited to see which way the wind would blow.

The kid gave the crowd and the den a long look of contempt, then shouldered his way to the bar, which was made of a stiff old buffalo hide that had been pulled tight, when it was fresh, over a pole frame. It was just as sturdy as wood and plenty big enough for the Earthquake, which was primarily a poker house and not a saloon.

"Whiskey," he said. The bar-dog grinned and drew a shot from the bung of the keg. Everybody watched to see how badly the kid would strangle.

Slocum almost spoke: there was a kind of innocence in the youngster's face, visible even through the dirt, that made Slocum feel sorry for him. He kept his mouth shut, though, We all need to learn our own lessons. A cub who tries to grow up too fast and too tough has to collect his lumps. And, in this case, his raw throat.

The kid downed it in one gulp. Nothing happened. He didn't even wince. He just stood there smacking his lips and staring thoughtfully at the wall. Then he said, "Well, I expected tarantula juice, but that is *something*. Let's see. The rawest alcohol you can find, cayenne pepper, tobacco juice and a little gunpowder to give it a tang. Then you pour in enough Arbuckle's,

9

boiled a couple of hours, to color it up like real whiskey." He switched his bright blue eyes to the bar-dog's astonished face. "Right so far?" The man nodded dumbly.

"Then, by God," said the kid, "you throw in some rattler heads!"

There was an angry growl from the throng, and somebody yelled, "Sam, you been selling us snakehead whiskey, you dirty old cuss?"

"No! I swan on my mother's grave I never," said the bar-dog, beginning to sweat. "Not the heads, that's a fool stunt to pull. I just give 'er a cup or so of side-winder blood to the barrel. That helps keep out the cold from your bones." When this seemed to satisfy the customers, he nodded to the kid and said, "Sonny, I don't know how you could tell all that, but you hit it on the nail. You ain't as green as you look."

"You got the same poison in those bottles?"

"Yeah."

"Gimme a bottle and a glass." He turned to survey the room again. "There a seat open in a game?" he asked in his adolescent's voice.

"An answer to prayer," said the hardcase in black. "Right here, boy. Don't step on the corpse."

The crumpled-up buffalo hunter groaned. "I ain't dead, I'm resting a minute."

"But you're out of the game," Slocum told him. "Never mind that bottle, just bring a glass," he said to the kid, and was a mite surprised at himself for it. "I've got some still-made whiskey with no tobacco juice in it, and you're welcome to a share. Anybody with a sense of taste like yours ought to pamper it."

The kid stared at him with eyes like chips of sun-warm Indian turquoise. Then he gave a short jerk of the head, like a shrug; the bearskin coat was so big and bulky that Slocum couldn't tell whether his shoulders moved inside it or not. "Right." He came across the room, stepped over the skinner, and sat down in the empty chair beside the gunny. Slocum tipped a generous drink from his second bottle into the glass. "Thanks," said the kid, and sipped at it. "Better. I'm obliged."

Slocum sat down and the Mexican nightrider began to deal. They were playing five-card stud, the American variety. Slocum got a king up and an eight in the hole, both diamonds, and decided to see one more card. There was a round of betting, and Slocum got a low spade and folded. So did the gunny in black. The kid raised on a pair of eights. Eventually he took the pot, about a hundred dollars—they played with money in the Earthquake, the owner being too cheap to furnish chips.

The big buff hunter stood up, grunting and wheezing and patting his temple. His partner chortled. "You got a bump there would take a roach three minutes to run around. Was telling this feller I was amazed he didn't blow your head open."

The bigger lout glared at Slocum. "I dunno why you didn't, but I'm glad. Rather have a scalp full of piss than a face full of lead." He scratched his nose. "Reckon I was drunk to do that. I better have some booze to sober up by." He lurched to the bar.

"You know what that jasper did to your friend with the fancy liquor?" the pistolero asked the kid. "He drank up his—"

"Get your goddamn hand off my knee," said the kid, looking out of the corners of those brilliant eyes and casually unfastening the front of his thick coat.

"No harm intended, sonny. When he'd drunk it all up, he took out his—"

"Get your fucking hand off my leg," said the kid a little louder.

Slocum pushed slightly farther away from the table. The gunman grinned over at him. "I seen you was

11

taken too, tough guy, when he came in. Don't make any funny moves, there's a sleeve-gun looking at your guts under the board. This one's mine. First, anyway."

Slocum cursed himself for a pea-brained jackass. He'd been on the watch for a sudden movement toward the holstered Starr double-action .44, and never even thought of a derringer. In the space of a breath, he considered all the possibilities. He could throw himself sidelong while slashing up with his right-hand Colt, and no matter how fast he did it, he could get himself shot in the belly. The sleeve-gun was certainly big-bored; at this range it could do as much damage as either of his own .45s. He was in a bind and nothing made sense but surrender. He laid his hands on the table.

"You got a stingy gun looking at him," said the kid quietly. "Mister, before you pull your trigger, you ought to check on what's looking at *you*."

The black-suited pistolero flicked his gaze off Slocum for what he must have expected would be a split second. The kid's hands moved like well-oiled lightning: one yanked back the furry coat, the other came up with a sawed-off shotgun in a sling that had been so camouflaged by the enormous bearskin that even Slocum hadn't suspected it was there. The muzzle centered on the gunny's chest. "One," said the kid, "two—"

The derringer clattered on the poker table, rattling among the cartwheels. "Jesus," gasped the other, "don't, don't."

"Then put your Starr beside it."

"Sure thing, sonny." He did, delicately but fast. Nothing on earth terrified a man who knew weapons like a sawed-off shotgun at point-blank range. "I purely hope you know how to handle that thing without accidentally shooting it," he said, sweating and trembling.

"Lay down your knife, too." The kid was cold as ice, thought Slocum, still a little shaky himself.

"I got no knife."

"It's in a sheath down the back of your neck."

The gunny's eyes popped. He reached up and drew a lean, heavy-bladed throwing knife from behind his head. It joined the two guns.

"And the boot hide-out too."

He hitched up a leg of his pants and drew a short-barreled revolver and tossed it down with the rest.

"*Santos!* The man is an arsenal," exclaimed the Mexican.

"Don't forget the Winchester up his ass," said the tinhorn, and whooped with laughter. "Never saw so many popguns and stickers on one man before. Think we ought to lynch him on general principles?"

"Let him go," said Slocum. "He's leaving town anyway." His dark eyes turned ugly and flat for the second time that night. "Soon's he can saddle his horse. Ain't that right?"

"Sure is," said the depleted gunman. "I'm in a hurry. Got to have breakfast with a girl in Tombstone."

"You mean a boy, don't you?"

"All right, a boy." He stood up slowly.

"Think I'll just walk along with you for a spell," said the middle-aged cowhand, picking up his rifle from behind his chair. "Make certain it's your own horse you saddle." He levered a cartridge into the chamber. "Night, gents. That was interesting."

"Not half as much to you as it was to me," said Slocum. He looked at the blue-eyed youth as the two left. "I'm beholden."

"We're even. I drunk your whiskey."

"Have some more," said Slocum, pushing over the bottle. He scooped up his money and jammed it into his pocket. "Game's over for me. I'm hungrier than a fresh-woke bear in the spring."

"Some place open this time of night that has a griddle?" asked the kid.

"Other towns it's late night," Slocum told him. "But

13

in Retch this is just about the middle of the afternoon. There's a place."

"Care if I come along?"

"I'd like that," said Slocum, unfolding himself, grabbing his Spencer .52 carbine, looping the buttons shut on his elkskin jacket. "It's on me."

"I pay my way."

"Don't go all stiff-necked on me. You just saved my life. That's worth a breakfast."

The kid considered. "Well, this one time."

"Tarnation!" said Slocum. "You got hell's own pride in that little frame of yours."

2

They took the middle of the street and walked side by side past the livery barn and corral, the outfitting store, a couple of saloons, where the light spilled out in flashes as the batwings swung, the two-story hotel, the crib that called itself a parlor house, hide-and-pole shelters of no conceivable utility, and the big Palace of Mirrors, a casino as far above the Earthquake as New York was above Deadwood. Slocum noticed that the kid kept eyeing him. "What is it?"

"Do you hire out your gun?"

"No."

"But you're a gunfighter."

"A man has to protect himself in this world. Learned to shoot when I was a tad, brushed it up considerable in the War, and got good afterwards because I knew I was a natural target."

"Why?"

Slocum sighed. "Because I can look awful mean! That satisfy you?"

"You aren't a professional slinger, then," said the youngster, persistent.

14

"No."

"You've killed men, though."

"I don't enjoy it but I do it when it's necessary. And I don't lose any sleep over it, because I never killed a man who wasn't aiming to do the same to me."

They walked on a little farther in silence. Then they saw the cowhand coming toward them, slinging his rifle carelessly like a dude with a cane. "Gents," he said, nodding.

"You see off that shark all safe?" the kid asked him.

"Well, in a manner of speaking I did. He reached inside his coat and I cut him loose. He's explaining himself to Ol' Nick this minute." The fellow shook his head, mock-sadly. "Turned out he was only going for a handkerchief, but was I supposed to know that?"

"You did right," said Slocum.

"That was the shot we heard," said the slim young fellow in the big bearskin. "If you want to haul his remains to the sheriff's office, there's a reward posted on him."

"Reward? Then why in suffering blazes didn't *you* gun him?"

"It's only $25. Not worth it," said the kid shortly.

"Right now 25 bucks looks like six months' wages," said the cowpoke with fervor, "after that game tonight." He wheeled and trotted away toward wherever he'd left the dead gunny.

"Here's the eating house," said Slocum, turning in to a shack built of used lumber. "Not much to look at, but the cook's good." They went in and took seats. A large greasy man saluted Slocum and looked at the kid.

"Nuts and brains," said the latter.

"Got any of that salmi left?" Slocum asked.

"Enough for one big bowl."

"It's mine."

"Coming up." He turned away.

"How do you want to be called?" asked the kid.

15

Slocum eyed him. It was the polite Western formula. Between the shotgun, the ability to drink sidewinder whiskey without gagging, and now the correct question, it was plain to him that the kid, however young he might be, was no tenderfoot. "By my right name," he said. "John Slocum."

"They call me Brandy." The kid fidgeted a little. "Not that I'm so fond of drinking it," he said defensively, "but my name's Brandywine, see?"

"Even so, I'll bet you could tell Napoleon from 3-Star Hennessey," Slocum said, "with your sense of taste."

A short sound emitted that might have been a grunt of amusement. "You fell for that pepper-tobacco-coffee business?" The bright eyes in the grubby face slanted over at him. "That's just the standard recipe for the forked lightning you get in those dives. I took a guess at the snakeheads."

"Came close," Slocum acknowledged. "It was a bang-up performance. Scared old Sam shitless."

"You mind a personal question?"

"Seems that's all you've chucked at me tonight. Go on."

"You don't like boys, do you?"

"You mean the way the late pistolero did? No!" said Slocum. "Why?"

"Figured to ask you if you'd share your bunk with me. I stopped at the hotel when I hit Retch," said Brandy. "There's so many men in town that there ain't a room left, not even space in the livery loft. I left my saddlebags and gear at the hotel, in case."

"If you were my size, you'd have to spread a pallet on the floor. As it is, you're welcome to part of the bed." Slocum took off his jacket; the huge wood stove threw more heat than all the bodies that sweated up the Earthquake. "The skinners and hill rats and the

16

fellows from the silver mines are hustling in ahead of the winter. I could smell snow coming tonight."

"Yeah, me too. You intend to wait here for spring?"

"Wait in *this* festering sore?" he burst out. "Like some poor vinegarroon stuck in a privy? I've traveled in the winter before this. Besides," he added, turning morose, "my luck ran out tonight. No sense in staying now."

"Why do you say that?"

Slocum ticked off his reasons. "So now," he finished, "if I'd keep playing in the Earthquake, where you may have noticed the tempers are shorter than a tomcat's pecker and twice as hot, there'd be one yack after another who'd try to bait me—I'm the poor soul that let a man live who'd tried to make him drink urine, and had to be rescued from some two-bit hombre by a kid that don't even shave yet! Besides, game splintering up that way, it's sure to snap my luck."

"There's another gambling place in town," Brandy reminded him. "The Palace of Mirrors."

"Nope."

"If you washed up and shucked off those moldy pieces of rag and leather you call clothes, they'd let you in." The kid grinned.

Slocum thought about that. Maybe the boy was right. A gambling man tended to fall into patterns of thinking that didn't really have much basis in fact. And Slocum was a gambler from the days just after the War Between the States. He made up his mind. "I'll give it a stab. Spruce up and try the Palace tomorrow."

The cook set a bowl of rich-smelling, thick stew before Slocum, and a big plate of calves' brains and buffalo testicles in front of the kid. "What's in that?" asked Brandy, sniffing at the salmi.

"Prairie dog roasted and mixed into a sauce that

17

tastes like gold looks." Slocum tossed a double eagle on the counter. They ate fast and ravenously until it was all gone. "Got any pie?"

"Sorry, I been et out of pie tonight. Got some spotted pup."

"That'll do fine. Enough for two."

They inhaled the rice-and-raisin pudding and had seconds. Slocum leaned back and sighed. "I reckon this place is half the reason I stuck to Retch so long." He shoved the coins across the oily wood. "Keep the change," he said. "That meal deserves it."

"Your luck still running good?" asked the cook, scooping up the cartwheels and making them vanish sleight-of-hand fashion.

"I hope so," said Slocum cautiously. He shrugged into his elkskin; Brandy hadn't even unbuttoned the big coat that hid his shotgun. They got up. "Your sweat's gonna freeze the minute you hit the air. Don't you ever take that grizzly off?" When the kid didn't answer, he said, "This isn't the kind of town where they stick you in jail for carrying a shotgun, you know."

"Hey," said Brandy, pointing as they walked through the streets. "Somebody dropped a silver dollar."

It lay there in the grit of the road, winking at them with reflected moonlight like the eye of Lady Luck herself. "Pick it up, kid," said Slocum, "bring you good luck."

"You're the one who's full of ignorant trust in omens and signs. You pick it up."

Slocum bent down to reach for it, and heard the mellow, heavy boom of a Sharps buffalo rifle. He flung himself prone, thrust his Spencer .52 into position, raked the opposite side of the street with narrowed eyes, spotted a fringe of powder smoke reaching out from the black shadow between two hide-and-pole houses, threw the lever down to drive a cartridge into the chamber, levered back and thumb-cocked the big

18

side hammer and fired into the dark. The echoes of the heavier rifle were still sounding as the sharp crack of the Spencer cut in and drowned them. Slocum rolled over once and shot again. A bawl of pain—or was it anger?—rocketed out of the night, and Slocum heard the thud of big feet pounding away. He leaped upright and ran across the road.

Brandy was beside him as he knelt to pick up something for the second time in a quarter-minute. "That was a Big Fifty," the kid said. "You can tell 'em by the deep roar."

"I appreciate the information," said Slocum meagerly, and carried his find into the moonlight. It was a Sharps, ancient and rickety but well kept. and its stock had been shattered by one of his bullets. The chances were that the buff hunter hadn't any worse than a tingling shoulder and hand, he thought, examining the angle of the slug.

"I knew I should have killed him," he muttered. "Now I won't get shet of him till I do blow out his lamp." He reached over and gripped Brandy's wrist hard: it was about as thin as a hoe handle. but wiry, and the kid tried to pull it away. Slocum exerted a mite more force. "Come on, I want to show you something," he said. tugging him across the street. The hole in the lumber of the restaurant was just where Slocum's head had been the instant before he leaned down to reach for the cartwheel. "You see that? A buffalo hunter don't miss. I knew that's where it'd be." He opened the door and called, "Anybody hurt in here?"

"No," said the cook, "but I got a new peephole in the front and one to match it in the back. Sharps, was it?"

"Yep. Likely still traveling, too." Slocum shut the door. The ball of lead had had a hell of a charge of black powder behind it in the three-inch-long shell, because a bison took a lot of killing; it would range

19

better than a mile, even after tearing through a pair of heavy planks.

"Now," he said to Brandy, "you see what omens and fortune can do?"

The kid stared at him. "He should have aimed for your belly."

"And my luck ain't gone," said Slocum happily. "I've come closer to passing in my chips, but I don't like to think about lying forever in Boot Hill." He retrieved the silver dollar he'd gone for, and this time got it and stuck it into his pocket. "I'm gonna keep this one. Lucky charm. Maybe have it mounted in gold and hang it on a watch chain."

"You're incurable," said Brandy.

They went down to the hotel. Slocum stopped by the desk, which was nearly two feet wide, and said to the sleepy-eyed clerk, "He's sharing my room. I want a bath, and so does he."

"Use the same water?"

"Of course."

"Four bits, and the Injun will bring the warm water in ten minutes."

"Hot water."

"Hot water in half an hour."

"We can wait." Brandy picked up his saddlebags and blanket roll from beside the desk and followed Slocum to the first-floor room. Slocum lit the fat coal-oil lamp with a lucifer he'd struck on his thumbnail, and he motioned to the kid to shut the door. His own belongings lay where he'd dropped them five or six hours before. He shucked his jacket and leaned the Spencer against the wall, took off his two gunbelts and stretched mightily.

John Slocum was one hell of a big man: lean, but wide in the shoulders, with a rock jaw and, under his wool shirt, muscles that didn't bulge much but rippled flat and hard like limber razor strops up and down his arms. The planes of his face were flat, creased and leathered by all the kinds of weather that had ever been invented. He looked like a man built for fighting, a man who knew it and was faintly amused by the fact. He grinned at Brandy, his deep-set dark eyes catching glints from the flicker of the lamp.

"You may's well take off the grizzlyb'ar overcoat, son. This is as warm as it'll get till you're piled with blankets, and if there's one thing we don't need in here it's more sweat."

"Don't give me orders, Slocum," said the youngster.

"Only suggesting. At least for sweet Pete's sake, kid, unburden your shoulder of that sawed-off. It's bending you sideways."

Brandy glanced at the single window, which was covered by an old rat-nibbled colorless tatter of a curtain. It shut out the sight of the raw, jerrybuilt town, but did it conceal this room from any curious eyes out there on the street? He hadn't given that an instant's thought before the kid had opened the door and disappeared. Slocum gaped. "What the sam hill?"

In a minute the kid was back. "It's safe," he said.

"What is?"

"The window. You can see light in little dots and slits, but you can't see in at all. Even if they know where you're sleeping, they got to bust the window and shove back the curtain before they take a shot at you—an aimed shot, anyway."

"Damned if I thought about that," said Slocum admiringly. "You got a noggin on those skinny shoulders, Brandy."

"Even a flathead snake sees to it that he's in a safe hole when he's going to sleep. And a wolf's even more careful, or he don't live to wake up," Brandy said, looking pointedly at him. "For a fellow who walks the center of the road, you sure take some fool chances, Slocum." He shook his head. "It's a powerful wonder

21

how you lasted this long. You don't sit with your back to a wall even in a pigpen like the Earthquake, and you carry two guns but let yourself be almost dry-gulched by a lousy sleeve-gun. Then you don't check the openings to your cave. Holy murder! You're close to making *me* believe in luck, watching you operate."

Slocum sat down in the room's only chair, which had come West in some homesteader's wagon a long time ago, and built a smoke. He offered it wordlessly to Brandy, who accepted it. He made another for himself and lit them both. "Now, boy," he said slowly, "you need to be filled in on a couple things. I've been winning steady for nigh a week. I'm loaded to the horn with cash, and everybody knows it. But nobody in that joint was about to shoot me in the back in front of thirty witnesses, because they'd have sworn it was murder and divvied up my fortune—except that they'd never find where I've stashed most of it." He gestured for the other to sit on the bed. "Anyone, anyone in the world up to Curly Bill and Hickok and Tilghman themselves, can be outfoxed by a derringer under the table. I cat-eyed this whole town every time we stepped out o' doors tonight, but again, nobody on earth can come from a bright-lit place and spot a man who's hiding in a shadow as black as last year's underwear. If the skinner had cocked his Sharps, I'd have heard it and gone to the ground; but he already had it cocked before we showed ourselves. And last, as to that rag across the windowpane, I'd have got around to thinking about it sooner or later!"

"Sure you would," said Brandy, heavy with sarcasm. He started to unload his pockets onto the heap of his belongings in the corner. Out of various places came a derringer, a throwing knife, a short-barreled gun and a Starr .44. Then he shrugged out of the bulky coat, facing away from Slocum and slung it over his shoul-

22

ders. He unbuckled a cartridge belt that carried a holstered single-action Army Colt and laid it gently on the pile. The sawed-off greener, with its sling. followed. Then. buttoning one hole of the coat. he turned.

Slocum chuckled. "I see you retrieved the pistolero's armament. You intend to wear all of that stuff, plus your own?"

"Hell! I'll sell it to Easterners for souvenirs. Carve some scallops on the guns and swear they belonged to Jesse James or Fighting Ben Thompson or somebody like that. That gunny was wanted. you know. Saw a flier in Tombstone. Told about all the guns and the knife. I recognized him soon's I came in."

"Pass the jug." Slocum gurgled a long thirsty swallow, leaving about two ounces of the quart. Now the fine prairie-dog taste was gone, but he felt better.

A tap on the door brought him to his feet. "Yeah?"

"Hot water ready." It was an old squaw's voice.

"Thanks. Here," he said, opening the door and putting a coin in her hand. She looked at it and nodded and left.

Slocum dug into his war-bag, grubbed around in the whang strings and cartridge boxes and tobacco sacks, and found the brown lye soap-nut he always carried. Often a sleazy hotel offered soap that would put holes in armadillo hide. "Me first," he said. "You're dirtier."

"I can't argue that with you."

Slocum stared. "Godalmighty," he said, "that's about the first time since we met that you've agreed with what I said."

He found a clean pair of long-handles and left the room, grinning. For half an hour he scrubbed and lolled in the steaming water, shaved. then poured in another copper bucket of fresh hot water that the squaw brought him on top of the used bath-water, dried off, and pulled on his long-handled underwear. He gathered up the dirty clothes he'd been wearing for

23

weeks, held them at arms' length and padded down the hall barefoot to his room. It was locked. He rapped and spoke; it opened.

"Why the hell—"

"I'm carefuler than you," said Brandy, "and I aim to live longer." He brushed by Slocum and vanished. Slocum closed the door, deliberately didn't lock it, hung his newest Peacemaker beside the bed on a nail thoughtfully provided by the management for that purpose, noticing that Brandy had done the same on the other side with his Army .44. Wild kid *was* cautious.

Slocum reached for his last full bottle, stretched back on the bed, crossed his legs at the ankles, extracted the cork, and guzzled.

That weird little tad had worn his bearskin coat to the bathroom. If he figured to wear it to bed, he could think twice. It smelled like a bear who'd been rolling around in a well-used stable.

Slocum adjusted his hanging holster so that his hand could close on the butt of his gun without his having to thrust up his whole frame to reach it. He sighed, drank, and began to doze.

A knock on the door brought him full awake and reaching for the Colt. "It's open."

The door swung wide, and a tangle of Levi's, Stetson, wool shirt and big thick dirty coat flew in and landed on the pile of Slocum's trail duds. Then a girl stepped inside and closed the door and turned the key.

"Bejesus!" said Slocum, feeling as though a mule had whacked him in the guts.

She was tall and, so far as could be seen under the sparkling white cotton nightgown, slim, but she had the greatest, most upstanding, fullest, most mouthwatering set of breasts he could have dreamed up on a lecherous night. Her hair was cut short, almost like a man's, but it suited the long, oval, feminine face in an odd, a *different* way from any Slocum had ever seen.

24

Her eyes glowed brilliantly in the coal-oil flare, her nose was narrow and perfect, and her mouth was nearly as tall as it was wide, her lips were that full and ripe and luscious. She smiled at him, a soft flash of heaven of a smile.

"Hi, John Slocum," she whispered.

It was only when he took a second squint at those blue eyes that he realized the girl was Brandy.

3

"Pussy got your tongue, John Slocum?"

She stood there smiling at him. She'd shown him a couple of mocking grins before; now she was all woman and this smile was not the tight one of Brandy the kid, but an open, inviting delight of a smile from Miss Brandywine the woman. Her eyes had subtly changed too, from the blue of hard turquoise to the warm friendly blue of a summer sky.

In the ordinary way, if a lovely girl had walked in on Slocum like this he'd have been off the bed and grabbing her off her feet and toting her across to the bed as quick as he could draw and fire his revolver. But this—this boy who'd turned into a princess— she purely immobilized him.

"Where do you suppose the cat hid it?" she asked.

He cleared his dry throat. "Hid what?"

"Your tongue."

"Oh. Ah," said John Slocum, who'd had more women that he could remember and had considered himself full-grown and mighty handy with words ever since he'd been seventeen. "Uh, yes, my tongue. Good God, you are prettier than an Indian pony in a meadow full of buttercups."

"Thank you, John." She drifted toward the bed sedately and came to a stop on the opposite side. "How many blankets do you think we'll need?" she asked, like it was the most serious question in her mind.

He'd wrenched his gaze from her face down to her bosom. The nightgown hadn't been sewn yet that could disguise that pair of tits. The nipples pushed out the white cotton material, big brazen nipples that meant to be noticed. He felt his manhood stir and throb and lift, and hastily bent up his near leg to hide the bulge. "I been sleeping with three soogans," he husked out, "but I guess two will be plenty, since there's two of us to throw heat." He stared at her big full breasts. "They weigh about four pounds apiece."

"More than that," she said, with a quick flash of Brandy the kid, watching his eyes.

"I meant the soogans! Matter of fact, I reckon one ought to be enough." He blinked. "Brandy, you are the best thing that ever eventuated in the Arizona Territory, but what in thunderation are you wearing that saddle string around your neck for?"

She laughed. "I went down to the sheriff's office while you were bathing. Figured they'd be burying that gunman around sunup, and maybe I wouldn't want to get up that early." She pulled the rawhide over her head; dangling from it, hidden before down her back, was the throwing knife in its sheath. "Damn sheriff charged me two bits for it, and I know he was going to plant it with the corpse. Wanted four bits for the Starr holster, so I told him to go milk an elk." She chucked the knife and scabbard across the room onto her stack of gear. "Shall we try one soogan and see if we stay warm?"

"Sure, sure," he said, rolling hastily off the bed. She was here in her nightdress, she was going to sleep in his bed, she was pretty obviously ready for anything, and still he felt embarrassed about his pecker shoving out his long-handles like a damn flagstaff. They rolled off two of the blankets, Brandy as demure and innocent

26

as a bride, her eyes downcast, and Slocum sticking out in the middle as if he'd been some carnival attraction. He realized why he felt this way. It was the transformation. He'd been thinking for two hours that this vision was a tough kid permanently on the prod, and now she was a girl and what was worse, she looked like a nice, decent, goddamn virgin of a girl. She couldn't be, he told himself ferociously, not when she'd walk into his room in her nightgown—but the incredible cleanness and whiteness of that garment suggested chastity—and he'd had nothing but lacquered whores in so long—oh, hell! Double-bonded triple-distilled hell! He stood back and faced her.

"You intend what I intend?" he asked her.

The blue eyes focused on his randy erection. "I think I do," she said thoughtfully, "if I read your intentions right." She smoothed the cotton down over her breasts, thus extending him by another quarter-inch. "There's no sense in rumpling this, though," she said, and reached down and pulled up the skirt and worked the gown over her tits and yanked it off her head. She walked leisurely across the room toward a couple of clothes hooks on the far wall. The undulations and ripplings and bouncings of that trim but utterly female ass drove Slocum clear over the brink. He ripped off his long-handles so insanely that he lost a number of the buttons, and while she hung up her nightgown he flung his mutilated underwear onto the chair.

"My, that was quick," she said in the up-and-down voice he'd been accepting as a boy's. She came to him and stood nearly toe to toe, so that the end of his pecker barely touched the softness of her belly. "John," she said soberly, still mocking him a little but pleasurably and without offense, "before we do anything else—"

"Yes?" he said, as close to strangling as he could get without passing in his chips.

27

"Let's fuck."

He gripped her by the shoulders and let out an old-fashioned rebel yell that must have wakened the entire hotel. He bent and picked her up, but gently, gently, unlike his usual manner, flipped back the remaining blanket with his toes, and laid her as tenderly as a child on the feather tick. Then he went around and lay down beside her, his cock aimed as ready as a Winchester. She took it in one hand.

"I wouldn't hold that too long if I were you," Slocum said in a tone he hardly recognized as his own. "You're liable to get splattered up prematurely." He began to fondle the marvelous breasts. He may have touched better, but he couldn't imagine when. Of course they were why she always kept that bearskin on. Nothing but bear fur or heavy buffalo hide would disguise such prominence as theirs. The nipples were broad and pink-brown and gorgeous mounted on the expanse of the sleek white flesh, pointing toward him as she rolled onto her side.

She tugged him to her, using his erection for a handle. Her right leg came up and over both of his. "In," she said eagerly, closing her eyes, "in, in, in!" Slocum went in.

It was over too quick, he thought at first, and then he looked into half-opened blue bits of summer sky and a slack mouth and realized that all the racket and yowling and groaning while he was spurting into her hadn't been entirely his. She had climaxed at the same moment. That was good. That was fantastic for the first time. She'd been as ready for it and as close as he had.

"John Slocum," she said, panting, unable to control the after-effects of what must have been a whopper, "I like you. Don't take it out yet. Oh, I like you!"

"You sound a little sad about that," he said, panting himself.

28

She said something in a foreign language, and smiled lazily at his bafflement. "That means that all animals are sad after a really good pronging," she told him.

"I'm not. I feel just fine."

"Female animals, I suppose it means."

He slid limply out from between her legs. "I sure wouldn't want to make you mournful, honey," he kidded her.

"It's gone already, the sorrow. My God," she said, fondling him until he rose again with renewed lust, "I don't think I can get it all in."

"Lady, you may not know it, but you just *had* it all in, clear up to the hilt."

"I mean in my mouth. I want to try everything with you. But, well, you may have noticed I don't have the widest lips in creation. Oh, hell," she said, writhing around on the sheet and gripping the soaking wet organ, "let's find out!"

And she'd been right. She managed half of it, which after that first hoorah of a time was plenty for Slocum, and she worked at it while he milked her tits gently where they hung heavy beside his belly, and bejesus if this one wasn't even better than the beginning of the frolic, for it took longer and the sensations were so protracted and lingering that he thought he'd lose what was left of his mind. After she knelt upright and swallowed slowly, as though she'd been tasting old, old whiskey, she said, "Was that bearable?" and giggled, because his face must have been showing that it had been damn near matchless.

"You made a snotty kind of a boy," he said, "but as a girl you're nickel-plated and gold-engraved and shined to a high polish. Let's have a belt of bourbon and smooth each other down a while and then maybe you'd like another little death yourself."

Brandy put her arms around his neck and stared at his face, all flushed and corded with veins and beating

29

a tom-tom rhythm like what remained of his temporarily expended rod. "You're an odd one, John. How many drifters would use a term like 'little death,' I wonder?"

"Was a time when I spoke English. Now I usually talk Cowhand. Comes easier. As you found out."

"Yes."

"How long have you been passing for a boy?"

"On and off, quite a spell. How long have you been a drifter?"

"An even longer spell." There'd been a day when he'd taken the term *drifter* as an insult; not any more. It was what he was. An other-side-of-the-ranger. Too soon impatient with a region where nothing was happening. Perpetually moving on, flowing with the rivers, breezing down the wind. He accepted that now. It was Slocum's way. There were worse ways.

"You're a beautiful woman, Brandy," he said suddenly. He did not pass out compliments like that often, but she demanded it with the lithe marvelous body and the big ripe mammae and the loving face, so he said it, and was glad. "What's your honest first name? I can't go on calling you Brandy."

"I wish you would, John. I was christened Minnie."

" 'Minnie' fits you like a hog's snout on an antelope. I'll stick with 'Brandy,' then." He petted her smoothly, marveling at the flawless white skin. Only her face and hands were sunbronzed, and the palms a touch leathered from doing a man's work with horse and guns. Yet they were like satin on his body, her stroking and brushing along his limbs and chest like a delicate unending kiss. "Brandy, sweetheart, how do you pass for a male in hot weather?" he asked, tonguing her nipples luxuriously, hefting the considerable sphere of one breast after the other.

"Mostly I don't. There are places where they know me and what I do, and they accept it 'cause they know me."

"What do you do? Besides make love like Cleopatra on a tear."

"Man's work. This isn't the time to pow-wow, Johnny—if we start spilling our life stories, the words'll get in the way. Lots of time later."

"True." He kissed her, slow and deep. "Your brains match your frame," he muttered. "Why in tunket did I have to meet you in Retch? We ought to strike out for New Orleans, where you'd get the appreciation you deserve."

"Strolling down past the Cabildo on the arm of big Kid Slocum," she said. "I'd be the envy of every wench in town and every Creole highborn cat."

"Nobody ever called me 'Kid' even when I *was* one. It's John."

Leisurely they fondled each other, like two children playing with marvelous, unfamiliar toys. Their styles of lovemaking fitted like a bow on a fiddlestring, like a woman's fingers on the keys of a piano, like a metal disk against the ratchets of a music box. Music, that was it.

They were silent for a moment, and then after sharing several long pulls of bourbon, Slocum said, "I'm sorry you don't enjoy all this, ma'am, but it's a necessity for me. You just close your eyes and think about something else, and after a while you can go to sleep, for I'll be tuckered out."

She giggled quietly. "It's horrible, but you did buy me a dinner. I'll survive, and feel I've paid my debt to you."

He kissed her on the cheek. Her cheeks were high flat planes, much like his own. "You purely do please a man, Brandy. I think I've lost five pounds since you finished your bath."

"Half of it's in me," she said. She twined her long lean fingers in his chest hair and tugged till it smarted. "You're a man, John Slocum. Is it always like this with you?"

31

He was mute for so long that she said, somewhat sharp now, "If you're working up a lie to please me, it isn't necessary. I never figured I was your first woman."

They played with each other for a quarter-hour or so, and when the squaw Slocum had sent out earlier for whiskey tapped discreetly on the door, he had to cross to it with his masculine weapon at full attention. The squaw caught a glimpse of it as she handed him the bottle and he tipped her another cartwheel. She said something in Navaho and this time gave him a great broad unmistakable grin. He locked the door and returned.

"What did she say?"

"Oh, just thanks."

"The bloody hell she did," said Brandy, punching him in the iron-hard gut. "She said, 'You should be an Indian, although you're too much man for any one squaw.'"

Slocum uncorked the fresh bottle in his usual manner and spat the cork halfway across the room. "Well, it ain't true. And either you didn't hear her plain, or that's one dialect you don't savvy. Because she said, 'If my man had owned such an organ, I would never have left our hogan for months at a time.'"

"I know how she feels," said Brandy and had a drink.

They sipped the good whiskey turn and turn about, resting quietly and speaking a few words occasionally. The night grew colder, but the one soogan was enough. And after a while they made love again, very slowly and comforting this time. About dawn they slept, still in each other's arms, so deeply that they never heard the terrible, bitter cold rain begin to fall.

4

They had smelled snow on the night air, but when it came it was rain, one of the coldest rains in the memory of even the old Indians who lived in brushwood wicki-ups outside the town. The frigid dampness of it came into the hotel room and tried to climb in bed with them, and Slocum flung on another blanket and huddled smack up against the warmth of that arrow-lean body with its glorious pillows of bosom and thought about how hungry he was as the storm rattled and crashed outside. He went over and pulled back the curtain to stare at a gray-black day all slanted with silver sheets of rain. He mentioned his rumbling gut.

"I'm starved," Brandy agreed. "We could send the squaw for a couple of meals."

"Damned if I'll let an old woman go clear to the end of the street in that frostbit waterfall, not if I starve for it." He stared at her in the gloom of their dank den. "But a lady's got to eat, and a man too, especially after a night of jubilation. I'll go."

"John, you can't flounder through that downpour!"

"If I can't walk, I can swim. What you figure I'm made of, sugar?" He began to dress. "Whatever it is, there'll be plenty of it. I'm not leaving this building again till the rain's played out." He grinned at her. "Lock the door," he said, and left her thumbing her nose at him.

He found the hotel squaw and asked if she had a basket for carrying food that she could lend him. She said that he must not go outside. He said patiently that his own squaw had just told him the same thing, and that women in the old days recognized their men's ability to walk through a little water without dying of it, and that she, a Navaho of a certain goodly number of years' experience, surely did not see in him a frail child? She smiled and grunted the Indian equivalent of *Hell, no*. Slocum said it was certainly a dreadful day but it was necessary that they eat, and asked where did she herself get food—here?

She told him that the timber restaurant was the only source of cooked food in town, but she had a little attached shack in the rear of the hotel where she could fix some scraps of meat and vegetables when she was able to get them, and had a small store of jerky and Indian bread. She fetched him a big wicker basket, Hopi-woven, that would keep anything dry even if it sank in a river. He set his mind to the business and plunged out into the rain to the restaurant.

Upon entering the restaurant, he set the basket on the counter and said, "You got a ragout of something that a person without any teeth could manage?"

"Sure. Buffalo stew, simmered a long time. Maybe the tripe's a speck chewy, but the rest of it's just this side of drinkable." The cook frowned. "That isn't for you, Slocum? You got your teeth!"

"Slocum!"

The shout came from down toward the back of the room. He whirled and, out of the gang of men lounging in the warmth, spotted a squat, squinty-eyed fellow whose arm was moving backward; even though his hand was hidden behind another man, Slocum recognized the gun-draw motion. The bastard was a total stranger to him, but there was only one possible reaction to that move, and Slocum made it. The right-pocket Peacemaker flashed out as sharply as though from a greased holster. He hesitated the fraction of a

second—an inexperienced witness would have said that
he didn't hesitate at all, but he did—and as the stranger
shoved the other one sideways and his gun showed, its
muzzle looking straight at Slocum's chest, Slocum shot
him in the face. At the impact of the heavy slug, the
man went ass-over-tea-kettle to the floor, his pistol dis-
charging into the roof.

"Who in blazes was he?" Slocum asked of the crowd
in general. The only response he received was shrugs
and spread hands and cocked eyebrows. Then someone
said, "He seemed to know you all right."

"I got a fine memory and I never seen him before
this minute."

"He hollered out your name," said somebody.

"He heard me say it," the cook told them. He looked
at Slocum. "Maybe some gal's brother?" he suggested.

"I wouldn't touch a female who'd have him for kin,"
said Slocum. He surveyed the room, thick with steam
and powder smoke and the stink of wet wool inter-
larding the fine cooking odors. "Anybody else don't
like my name?" he asked loudly. The gun was still in
his hand. Its front sight had been filed off, or he'd
never have cleared it from his pocket so slickly. "Or
figure I didn't give him a fighting chance?"

"Mister, nobody ever outdrew a leather slapper who
had a longer start on him, and won," said an old
gristle-heel, and cackled. "He must of had two seconds'
leeway of you. Nicest fight I seen this year."

"Except, Slocum, dammit," said the cook, "every
time you show up here I get another hole or two in
my place, and this one's dripping!"

"Stick a pan under it," said Slocum, "it's likely the
cleanest water in town. Look, I'm gonna tote that carcass over to the sheriff and try to find out about him."
He pushed the basket across the counter. "You fill
this up while I'm gone. First I want a big jar of that
buffalo stew, with as little tripe as you can manage.

35

Then I want two hot dinners, whatever you got today that tastes best. Plenty of it. And a can of peaches for afterwards. Then put in whatever else there is—grub that'll taste all right even when it's cold. Some spotted pup if there's any, and two or three bottles of hot coffee. Any space left, you can fill with surprises."

He grabbed the corpse by one boot and dragged him to the door and went out into the repulsive curse of a town, being buffeted and all but bruised by the torrent of gelid rain.

At the sheriff's office and jail, a handsome man, blond, gray-eyed, maybe twenty-four or -five, said from behind his battered old desk, "Must be almighty important to bring a man here through that weather."

"Just want to report a killing," said Slocum, drying his face on a wet sleeve. "Shot a short-trigger gink who was making a try for me, and damned if I know why." He explained briefly. "There's a whole eatery of men who saw him draw first," he finished.

"So you brought him here to get him off your hands," said the sheriff. "Do you think anybody's going to bury him in this rain? The ground's pure ice already, and getting worse."

"Where ought I to of drug him, to a saloon?" Slocum got sore. "Or left him to stink the restaurant into bankruptcy?"

"Why couldn't you have carted him to the undertaker? Judas Priest," said the sheriff, looking glum, "this is the second one in twelve hours. The first is barely underground."

"Well, that one threw down on me too," said Slocum. "But he had a reasonable excuse."

"You didn't kill him."

"No, I left that to another hand. The one that collected the reward." Slocum chucked the dead man's belongings on the desk. "That's what was in Number

36

Two's pockets. See those 'wanted' fliers? Dozen or more of them. I figure him for a bounty hunter. Thing is, there sure as hell ain't a bounty on me. So how come?" Slocum felt confident there were no wanted posters on him ever since he was reported killed in an attempted hold-up in Wyoming. He took off his John B. and slashed a long, broad stripe of rainwater across the office floor. "No undertaker's equipped to answer that, is he? And you bitch about me bringing the fucker here. You ought to be thankful I left him outside. He'd have shit up your atmosphere for a month."

"Please watch your language," said the sheriff.

Slocum gaped at him. He wasn't a prissy-looking fellow, maybe not exactly a hardcase, which you'd have expected for Retch's lawdog, but sure not a goody-goody. "I didn't mean to offend your ears, son," he said politely. Maybe the man was a member of some really strict faith. "But I got to tell you," he said, unable to repress it, "sometimes I spit in the street too."

"You don't offend *me,* you blame fool," said the sheriff, standing up; he was a head shorter than Slocum. "It's my fiancée. She's back in one of the cells."

"This day gets crazier by the minute," Slocum said, his dark eyes widening. "You mean to say you got your betrothed in a jail cell? What'd she do?"

"She's cleaning it!" The officer sat down again, looking helpless. "I don't like her to do it, but she says it's woman's work. And my Indian's off on a hunt—he's my deputy and handyman."

"I wouldn't have cussed if I'd known that." Slocum raised his voice. "I do apologize, miss."

"No need," said a very young soprano voice, "I've heard worse."

"Where?" shouted the sheriff.

"From my pa, silly," said the invisible girl, laughing. She had a laugh like a narrow brook full of smooth

37

pebbles, running fast and with birds singing in the trees overhanging it. Slocum wished that he could see a girl who laughed that nicely.

"Slocum," said the sheriff, who had begun to go through the wanted notices. "You said your name is Slocum, and the man drew on you when he heard it?"

"He yelped it out like a da— like a dern jackass the minute he heard it. If he hadn't, he'd be alive and I'd be shi— I mean, I'd be lying dead out in the rain instead of him. Best bet to my mind is that he was a bounty hunter just starting out in the profession. Otherwise he'd have kept his head shut."

The sheriff held up one of the fliers and slowly turned it so that Slocum could see it. It was crumpled and damp, but the smeared ink was plain enough. There was a picture on it, a drawing that might have been John Slocum.

Above the picture it said, "$2000 Reward," and beneath, "John Slocum, alias Kid Slocum," and "Dead or Alive," and in smaller type, "Wanted for Bank Robbery and Murder," and then in regular newspaper print, "In Tombstone, November 24, robbed bank and killed two tellers. Slocum is well over six feet tall, has dark hair and skin, carries two revolvers, and is extremely dangerous to approach, perhaps insane. If seen, wire nearest Federal Marshal or Sheriff of Tombstone," and some other stuff that Slocum didn't bother reading.

"That ain't me," he said flatly. "And don't go for your gun, friend, because it's a lead-pipe cinch I'm faster than you are."

"It looks like you."

"It also looks like about twenty other guys I could tick off to you." Slocum shook his head. "Sweet spirits of turpentine!" he exploded, even now keeping in mind the girl in the cell back yonder. "Kid Slocum? I never been called that in my life." Then he recollected that he had, just last night; but that hardly seemed important enough to mention. "I've bent a law now and then and gunned me a few gazebos that asked for it, but I never robbed that bank, sheriff, and never murdered anybody!"

"You shot a man about ten minutes ago."

"And come straight here with him! Would I do that if I was wanted? He-heck, that was a *killing*, not a *murder!* Don't you know the difference?"

"I've learned it since I came West," said the sheriff a little sadly. "Can't say I agree with its logic, but I know it. Why would you think he was a bounty hunter because he threw down on you, unless you're wanted?"

" 'Cause he had a pocketful of posters is why! I never gave any thought to why he'd try for *me,* unless there was another Slocum wanted. He never heard but my last name, and didn't take time to check. Amateur!" said Slocum with immense scorn.

"Were you in Tombstone on November 24th?"

Slocum thought. "No, not in maybe six months. Went to Tucson from Globe and then came here along about the 25th."

The sheriff read the notice again. "Your name. Sounds like you. Looks like you. Give me a reason not to slam you in a cell."

"First, that is not me!" Slocum yelled, jabbing the paper with a forefinger. "Second, there's not a slinger in this town can outdraw me, and even if you are the law and got that flier in your mitt, I won't allow you to arrest me—plain, son? Because I am not any damn fool Kid Slocum. Now look," he said more peacefully, eyeing his man, "you've been thinking it over, and you doubt the whole thing too. Shows in your face plain as print. No wanted man hauled a corpse through that ice and rain and pulled out a bunch of fliers and just brought them in here without going through them, did he? Not after being yowled at and shot at. Or do I look like I ain't got the sense to pound sand in a rat hole?"

"I can't simply let you leave town."

"Nobody's going anywheres for a while. This rain will be snow pretty soon, coming down on ice. A man would have to be off his mental reservation to strike out for anywhere short of El Dorado till it clears some. I'll be at the hotel whenever you want to talk to me. Meantime, you can telegraph the Tombstone law and find out about this. I'll want it cleared up myself, more'n you do."

"Willie," said the voice like a young pretty brook, and Slocum turned his head quick because he did want to see the owner. "I believe this gentleman. The paper says he is possibly insane. He doesn't sound crazy to me." She was short, inclined to an attractive plumpness, with green eyes in which even by the flicker of the lamp he could detect little flecks of swimming gold; she was very fair, a pale ash blond, her hair worn in a bun that when loosened must have floated down to her waist, and her face was the lovely round dimpling kind that was occasionally born into Eastern farmers' families of German descent. Under a thick knitted wool scarf of white she wore checkered gingham that allowed her figure to assert itself modestly. "How do you do, Mr. Slocum," she said. "My name is Amelia Schmidt. The sheriff's name is Willie—that is, William McGunn. His manners are better when there's not so much on his mind."

"Amelia, dang blast it," the lawdog protested unhappily, "you hadn't ought to come in here when—when—"

"When there's a dangerous criminal loose," said Slocum. He grinned. "Pleasure, Miss Schmidt." He sat on the edge of the desk, trying not to undress her with his eyes. She was very young, and she was the sheriff's affianced lady. But she sure was a dainty, blooming little nymph. She took him back, a long way back, to before the War, to when he was a virgin, trying to spark the country girls, and didn't have any idea whether to put it in the front or in the rear.

"Willie," Slocum said, switching his gaze, "you're a lucky man. Your fiancée's got sense as well as beauty. I'm not a lunatic. Can you get onto the Tombstone wire and find out the straight of this pickle?"

"You know anyone in Tombstone?"

"Drifters, gamblers, cowhands, and barkeeps. I been through a few times, never for long. Don't know any respectable citizens, I'm afraid. But there's got to be other details, facts that aren't written down here." He picked up the flier. "It could be me," he said, half to himself. "It could be Jack Tompkins, too, and Pete Evans, if one of the eyes is glass."

"Do you carry two guns?"

"Not ordinarily. Just happens that I am now."

"Could you explain why?" The sheriff was being tremendously polite—whether by nature or with an intense effort of will on account of the girl, Slocum couldn't say.

"How long have you lived here?" Slocum countered.

"Seven or eight months. Why?"

"Then you must realize something about Retch. It's a mean, rough town. You'd never call it exactly hell with the hide off, like you might a few places in Texas, or a honkytonk town, like Dodge. But it's mean. Mind you," he put in quickly, as the man's face darkened, "I don't claim there's no decent element. Miss Schmidt is quality, and you seem like a nice boy yourself. Somewhere there's got to be good folk going about lawful business. But in the main, Willie, this Retch of yours is a big unhealthy lump of a fester, a suppurating sore on the face of the territory. It's jammed with bad animals, wolverines and alligators and weasels and Gila monsters and grizzlies. Thunder, it's like an animal itself! It squats here in its ring of mountains like a broken-backed toad, as ugly as sin. There's a spooked feeling to it, as if—" Slocum groped for a second—"as if the dregs of all the Boot Hills in the West had climbed out of their graves and trudged into Retch."

"My heavens," said the girl faintly. "You make it sound hideous."

"To my mind it *is*. I've been in towns where the wickedness blew up in your face at regular intervals. Where they'd gun a man for the boots he wore, or just out of high spirits. But Retch hasn't any high spirits. It's just got low, crawling, venomous poison in its blood. Lord knows why! Maybe there's a disease in the land here that draws the slugs and vipers from their holes out beyond the hills."

"I admit that you put into words a lot that I've felt myself," said McGunn slowly. "There's a good element —Amelia's father owns one of the silver mines, there are a few decent storekeepers—but in the main, yes, I agree. However, that's atmosphere, that isn't fact. We don't have any more killings here than in any other town this size. But," he said with weary patience, "what has all this to do with you carrying two guns?"

"Kind of a preliminary," said Slocum. "I carry, by ordinary, one good sidearm and one good rifle. But I take my weapons as I find them, same as my horses and women and whiskey. I like to tote one good Peacemaker .44 and a Winchester rifle of the same caliber, so's my ammunition is just one size. However," he said, taking a deep breath and trying to remember the sequence, "I lost my Winchester in a Comanche raid near the Texas border and bought a Spencer .52 because it was the best rifle that come to hand just then. My old .44 cutter got stepped on by numerous steers when I was dumb enough to interfere with a stampede, and I borrowed a .45 Colt that was almost new from a gambler who hadn't any further use for it after he dealt himself a flush from inside his vest. I was en-titled to it, because it was me he was flushing and me that put him to bed with a shovel.

"Then in Globe, before I took out for Tucson, there was this varmint in a saloon. He must have been a fixture there for days, wearing calluses on both elbows and finally on his chin from standing at the bar night and day. He run out of money and was pleading with the crowd for somebody to buy his gun for the price of one more drink. There was hell's plenty of offers, but I couldn't see him lose a good weapon for a price like that, so I bought his gun for a double eagle and he was so grateful he threw in the belt and holster. It wasn't as new or in as good condition as my own, but it wasn't bad—had a lot of firing left in it—and I stuck it in my war-bag and forgot it. Then after Tucson, when I'd heard a little about Retch, all bad, and had a hanker to look it over, I slung it on my left hip."

"So you were a two-gun man at the time of this bank robbery," said the sheriff pointedly.

"Yeah, but I wasn't near Tombstone! I was on my way here, through the mountains."

"How did you kill that crooked gambler?" asked Amelia. Slocum thought her eyes sparkled with excitement.

"Amelia!"

"It's a proper question, Willie. Mr. Slocum had no pistol at the time, according to him."

"That's true, miss," said Slocum, looking at her ginghamed chest and flicking his eyes up at the ceiling to shuck the temptation. "I only had my rifle, which was leaning against my chair. A dumb thing to do, but it was a respectable house." He didn't think it neces-sary to add that the house was a fancy whorehouse with a piano and a gaming room as well as eighteen girls and a bouncer. "When I mentioned the brace game he was trying to pull, he drew on me. Well, with a gun

43

coming up from a waistband, a fellow don't have time to argue or to reach for his carbine, so I just leaned over as quick as I could and threw a straight right. Meant to catch him on the chin, but he jerked backward and I hit him in the throat."

"And what happened?" she asked, breathless and leaning forward. It was easy to see that despite her residence in Retch, this sort of wild detail was new to her.

"The gambler died," said McGunn sourly. "That's what usually happens when a man the size and toughness of Kid Slocum hits a man in the Adam's apple."

"Crumpled it right up," Slocum agreed. "I'd be obliged if you wouldn't call me 'Kid,' sheriff."

"Sorry. The fact is that I tend to believe your story. I've seen a great deal of the malignancy you were speaking of just now, Slocum, and you're a different breed. I honestly don't think you'd shoot down two helpless bank tellers in cold blood. I'll let you go if you'll promise to stay at the hotel until I get more particulars out of Tombstone."

"If I'm not there, I'll be playing at the Palace of Mirrors."

"Leaving the Earthquake?"

Slocum gaped. "How'd you know that?"

"That's where the late Knots Barker, the gunman last night, was hanging out when he was disarmed and marched halfway here." William McGunn regarded him levelly. "I hope it isn't known all over town that you're a wanted man. Or your namesake, anyway. One thing I don't hanker for is another carcass dragged up to my door."

"I played in the Earthquake near a week," said Slocum. "In that time there were at least seven killings. Did you hear of any of 'em except this Barker?" The sheriff shook his head. "Thought you wouldn't. They either drag 'em out for the coyotes and buzzards, or

44

plant 'em up northwest in Boot Hill. They don't bother you with anybody that hasn't got a pricetag on him."

"I'll be damned," said McGunn. "Sorry, Amelia."

Amelia looked as though she'd have more respect for a man who didn't apologize for such mild cussing, thought Slocum. This country girl had spunk in her and might be tougher than her betrothed.

"Get on the wire, before this norther ices it so bad that it snaps and we're out of communication," said Slocum.

"You think it'll be that bad a storm?"

"All-fired right I do. It's about ready to turn to snow. By tomorrow it won't be safe to cross the street without snowshoes, Willie."

"All right, Kid."

They glared in mutual cussedness at each other. Then Slocum laughed. "Sorry! How's 'Bill'?"

" 'Bill' is just fine, John."

"Be seeing you." He hunched down into the jacket, took a deep breath, and plunged into the icy rain, slamming the door behind him.

He made cautious, fast tracks for the restaurant, his boots stabbing straight down at the ice so he wouldn't slip. The basket was waiting for him. He paid the tab, and when the big greasy man mentioned that there was a dried-apple pie included, he added a dollar.

He slogged through the awful storm alone, seeing no living thing till he made the hotel and went in, bringing a pint or so of rainwater with him and dripping it all the way to his room. The old squaw turned up from nowhere and he stopped her with a word in her own tongue. Setting the basket down, he rummaged till he found the big covered crock of hot buffalo stew. He handed it to her. "Eat hearty," he said.

"This is for me?" She took off the lid and brought her thousand-wrinkled face down close to the steam that arose. "You," she said in Navaho, "you are one

45

kind warrior. No one has ever gone through a storm to bring me such food. You should have been born Indian."

"I sometimes think so myself," he murmured, embarrassed at the tears in her eyes.

5

Bathed, shaved, and spruced up in less time than he'd ever taken before under similar circumstances—after such a frigid soaking outside, he'd ordinarily have wanted to loll in the big tin tub till the water turned cool—he slung on a clean shirt and pants and hustled back to the room. Brandy was lying in bed under two soogans waiting for him; she'd dragged the tiny bureau over next to the bed and set out all the food on it, with an opened bottle of bourbon. He stripped again and climbed in beside her, and they dined royally on son-of-a-bitch stew, cooked for many hours so that they couldn't distinguish one ingredient from another, though they both knew it contained practically all the innards of a calf, as well as tomatoes and spuds and God knew what else. They washed it down with still-hot coffee and gulps of bourbon for spice. After polishing the hot food off, they ate all the rice pudding and a big slab of apple pie apiece, saving the canned peaches for later. Then Slocum built them a brace of cigarettes and they set the bottle between them and leaned back and felt the food swelling them out and renewing them as they smoked and sipped at the bourbon.

Brandy groaned. "If we're going to have us a fuck any time in the near future, John, I'd better be on top. I'm so stuffed they could set me up in a museum."

"Bulging at the seams myself." He lifted her near breast and fingered it till the nipple came out hard and

46

eager. "I can wait a little," he said lazily. "I'm not quite as horny as I was twenty-four hours ago."

"I am," she told him.

"Happy to hear it. But let's be patient. That was one roaring hell of a lot of food to digest." He leaned over and perversely cut himself another slim wedge of the pie. "I never could resist a chesty woman or an apple pie. And I've had more woman than pie since I met you."

"Don't excuse yourself. Give me a small hunk of it too. We're crazy," she said. "We're crammed to the eyeballs and want to gorge down more."

"Well, it's almighty fine pie."

"Anything going on outdoors?" she asked lazily.

"Not much. I found out where you got the 'Kid' Slocum, and I had to kill a skunk, and met the sheriff and his fiancée, but nothing else worth mentioning. Except it's raining."

She rared round on him. "Explain all that, you bastard!" she yelled, poking him in the chest with a rigid forefinger.

"Well, you wouldn't believe how hard and cold that rain's coming down—"

"The rest, blast your big balls."

So he told her everything that had happened, leaving out most of the description of the Schmidt girl except that she was a schoolmarm and did McGunn's cleaning for him when his handyman was away. When he'd finished, they stared at each other. "And the 'Kid Slocum' last night, Brandy," he said evenly, "was no accident. You'd seen that flier, hadn't you? So you figured all that time that you were making love with a murdering thief."

"What you do outside a bedroom doesn't make a damn to me."

He swore. "You *still* believe I'm Kid Slocum?"

"I recognized you from the picture and description

47

before I ever heard your name. Look, Johnny," she said, taking his hand, laying it on her breast, "it really doesn't matter. I know there's another side to you that you don't show me—probably more than one—but what counts is how we are together. I don't care who you shot or what you robbed."

"Well, jumping Jesus, *I* care! And I care what you think you know about me! Damn and blast the burro-load of lies you got in your skull, Brandy. They ain't true! I never been called 'Kid' and that's that! When whoever-he-is was committing that atrocity in Tomb-stone, I was on my way from Tucson to Retch!"

"If you say so, John." She removed his hand. "But that sheriff is a babe in arms."

"Ah, hell," said Slocum, "you made me spill my tobacco." He plucked as much of it as he could off the soogan, swept away the rest onto the floor, and took her in his arms.

In the dusk of the curtained room, her long oval face brimmed with passion, and the lids shut down on the bright blue eyes as she worked him to a flaming hot erection and guided it into her muff, already her breath-ing quick and shallow in her lust. For a while Slocum forgot everything else but her fantastic body. He fucked her hard and fast and slow and gentle until she'd come twice and was losing her mind and screeching thinly and wildly; then he speeded up and brought her to a howling third as he climaxed himself and felt her filling up and running over with a gush of semen, her back arched up like a tight-drawn bow, her pelvis smashed hard against his, and making noises now like a wolf in the rut. Slocum wasn't aware that he'd made any ruckus himself this time—she'd created enough uproar for both of them. But it had been a hell of a good lay, he thought, withdrawing against the tight pleading of her arms around his back, slumping sideways to lie spent and happy. She was purely wonderful.

48

6

It was snowing when they woke, together, as, Slocum thought, they seemed to do so many things—bejesus, but they made a pair!—and it was nearly midnight. They lit the lamp, ate the rest of the apple pie, opened the big can of peaches with Slocum's clasp knife, and wolfed down the contents. They smoked and sat close together, feeling the thickening cold that crept in through unstopped chinks in the outside wall. Neither said anything for a long time.

Slocum watched her face, satisfied and sleepy and affectionate; he remembered how he'd thought she looked virginal last night in her spanking-white, crinkly starched cotton nightgown. She didn't look that way any more. It had been a trick of his imagination: foul-mouthed road kid changing into dazzling belle, that'd unhinge anyone's judgment. But it must have been quite a while since her blood-cherry had been busted. She was an expert. And loved it, thank God!

He turned to his minx again. And just as his hands started to slip under the blankets, he froze absolutely still for a split second and then whipped around and drew his Colt from the holster dangling on the wall. Brandy started to sit up; he could feel her move behind him and he gestured violently with his elbow to stop her. Then he was out of bed and catfooting toward the door, which he'd left unlocked many hours ago.

He saw the latch rising gently out of its notch. He'd

heard it start up—if the rain had still been pelting down, he'd never have caught the faint sound.

He was standing beside the door, naked as a plucked and singed prairie chicken, when it came easing in, a foot, another. Then the thick barrel of a Sharps Big Fifty poked in.

Slocum could smell the stink of the massive hunter before he saw him, a rancid mixture of never-washed flesh, old caked buffalo blood and guts, rotten teeth, poisonous whiskey, moldy buff hide, piss and musty denim. Slocum pounced down with his left hand and caught the steel tube, and, with a tremendous jerk, wrenched the man into the room. His thumb was on the hammer of his stripped single-action, and if the Sharps had been aimed anywhere near Brandy, Slocum would have blasted the great hulk in the guts. But it was angled at the corner of the room, so his reflexes held back. It was almost the death of him.

With a raging wordless bawl, the hunter swung his heavy rifle stock-foremost at Slocum's gun hand. In the instant of time before it connected, Slocum cursed himself for not noticing that the bastard was left-handed, so that the rifle was between him and the hunter, instead of on the outside where it should have been. Then the short, thick log of carved wood smashed into Slocum's hand and wrist and the Colt went flying.

They wrestled together, their hands on the rifle, their faces grimacing at each other a foot apart. Slocum was at a hell of a disadvantage: first, he was naked, which was both physically and mentally perilous—a man without clothes is vulnerable and knows it; second, his right hand wasn't worth a spit in the river. It was numbing and aching from the whack, while the hunter was bulkier than he was and had two powerful hands as wicked as a pair of steel-trap jaws. Slocum stepped back fast, conscious of his genitals just plain offering themselves to be kicked, and he held the Sharps at arms' length. The men waltzed round together, doing a ridiculous and deadly fandango, and Slocum half-saw Brandy coming up out of the blankets and reaching for her hanging holster.

"*No*, Brandy!" he shouted. "He's mine!"

She paused with her Army .44 in her hand, nude to the waist. Then she deliberately threw the soogan off so that she lay there half-sitting, resting on her left elbow, everything she owned showing in the flame of the big coal-oil lamp. The gun was ready, but she held her fire.

Slocum was whipped around, almost losing his footing, and the big ugly face grinned in its beard. The hair on that face was so thick and tangled and matted with filth that the only way Slocum could tell it was grinning was by the way the cheeks bunched up beside the flat, red ball of a nose. Then the buffalo hunter saw Brandy over his opponent's shoulder, and his scrunched-up eyes popped and somewhere in the beard his mouth dropped open and a yellow tooth glistened wetly.

"Holy old Lucifer!" said the giant. And he made the mistake of his life. He stopped tugging and wrenching at the Sharps for a quick breath.

It was all Slocum needed. He gave the rifle a yank, all the brawny force of his own iron body in the pull, and snapped it free of the vast dirty hands and flung it across the room. Then he backed up another two steps and wriggled his fingers to get the dulled nerves working again.

"Let me take him!" yelled Brandy.

"He's *mine*," said Slocum savagely. "Nobody bushwhacks me twice and brags on it." He circled the hunter, feeling the blood pump and sizzle joyously in his veins. Now he was between the enemy and the bed, where he wanted to be. Naked or not, he was ready to brawl on even terms. The wild intoxication

51

of battle seethed up through his chest, and he said, "Jesus, man, you smell like a garbage heap in a Siwash camp!"

"I'll have your nuts for breakfast!" said the hunter, coming slowly toward him, one hand fumbling open his old flinthide coat. He brought out a Bowie knife, a real gullet-tickler with a blade more than a foot long and a three-inch curved tip honed to razor keenness on both edges. He held it low and crouched, easing along toward Slocum like death ready to engulf a shaved rabbit.

"Lemme gun him!" wailed Brandy, frantic.

"No!"

Waiting until they were almost within reach of each other, Slocum stepped sideways, feinted with a left that had no chance of connecting, and lashed up with his bare foot. He caught the low-held fist just at the joint between hand and arm; the knife went up, still gripped in the massive paw. Slocum balanced himself swiftly and his body shot off the floor feet first, every ounce of power that he could bring to bear in the flying double-kick. He took the hunter in the lower belly and doubled him backwards and rammed him to the floor, falling off sidelong and taking the force of the drop on his spread fingers.

He contracted himself as quick as a sidewinder and was on his feet again while the hunter, not much hurt but for the moment sprawling all over the heap of Slocum's gear, strove to get a hold on the floor and come up too. Slocum took one step and slashed out a vicious drive with one granite-callused heel; it caught the hunter's jaw precisely on the point and snapped his head back. There was a dreadful grating snap of sound, and the brute collapsed in a welter of war-bag and blanket roll and clothing, so limp that they didn't need to hear the death-rattle that followed.

"See?" said Slocum, wheezing, bending down and hauling the body away from his equipment.

"I see. Heavens above," said Brandy, the cuss-word of her childhood coming to her lips automatically, "I thought you'd lost your mind when you wouldn't let me shoot him."

"I been saved once too often this week," he growled, regarding the late buffalo-killer with disgust. "Figured to handle it myself. A man has to water his pride now and then or it wilts on him."

"A naked man against a Sharps and a Bowie knife. Your pride is a shade the other side of loco, John. Where in tunket did you ever learn that kick? I never saw anything like it outside a circus."

"French sergeant taught it to me at Fort Hades," he said, grinning.

"How do you do it?"

"With the whole damn body. Seems they fight with their feet a lot in France. Comes in handy when you haven't got so much as a diaper on you."

"Speaking of which," said the girl, snuggling back under the covers again, "the door's open, and you're barefoot all over. I don't want some woman coming past and stealing you 'cause you're so pretty."

Slocum banged it shut. Standing on one leg, he massaged his foot gingerly. "Stubbed my toes on his wrist. I reckon I got to drag the whore's-git outside somewhere." He hauled on his clean pants, those that went with his Sunday faradiddle, opened the door again, got a grip on the stiff's coat collar and hauled him out and down the hallway. Two doors away he met the old squaw, who was carrying an antique Texas Paterson .40 muzzle-loader, a pistol such as Slocum hadn't seen since he was a kid.

"Spring Fawn see man go in your room, run to bring help," she said, hefting the cap-and-ball weapon. "Slocum need no help. Good."

"Thanks anyway, Spring Fawn. Where can I throw this carrion?"

"I show." She led him to the back entrance and

pointed to where the snow was banking up against the wall. "Drop in that, he—he—" she searched for the word, then lapsed into Navaho. "He will vanish until the thaw. How did Slocum kill him? I heard no shot."

"With my foot," said Slocum in the same language, and pulled the late butcher over and slung him onto the piling snow. He made an ugly blotch on its purity. Slocum thought of something, recalling how Brandy had salvaged the sheath of Barker's throwing knife. The Bowie lying back in their room was as good a blade as he'd ever seen. Mumbling, "Ought to get something for ridding the plains of this lout," he threw back the putrid coat and unhooked the belt, pulled the big brass-tipped leather sheath free and examined it. It was fairly new and maybe the man's stench hadn't permeated the leather yet.

The snow was cold on his bare feet and the icy wind on his naked chest reminded him that he wasn't dressed for hanging around out here. "If Spring Fawn can bear to touch this stinking carcass, there will be money in the pockets, I think," he said. "It would be foolish to let it rot here through the winter."

"I have been in wickiups out on the prairie that smelled as gamy as he. I will search. I will bring the white-eyes' money to Slocum."

"You will keep the money," said Slocum, his teeth beginning to chatter. "It is a very small payment for what this man and his kind have done to your people."

"They are destroying the buffalo," she said with dignity. "They are worse to the Indian than the horse soldiers, the traders, the cowmen and the people who build these towns. Spring Fawn will keep the money, and is once more in debt to her friend Slocum."

"There is no debt between friends," said Slocum formally, and carried the scabbard back to his room. When his smeller had unchilled, he sniffed it and coughed.

"Well, that's the first spark of common sense you've shown in practical matters," said Brandy, who was sitting up drinking cold coffee. "You can't tote a Bowie in an ordinary sheath; it'll chew its way clean through and stab you." She held up the huge Bowie knife. "Black walnut grip and the back of the blade brass-clad. It's a real fighting piece. Don't imagine you'd give it to me?"

"Nope. It's a keepsake. God Almighty, it's cold out!" He took off his pants and got into bed. He put his feet on the girl's ass and she shrieked with shock. "That snow's cold," he said. He took her in a firm embrace and she kissed him hungrily. Then there was a thump as she dropped the enormous knife on the floor. Neither of them made any sexual moves, but lay there hugging and nuzzling each other's faces and throats, and Slocum said, "Damn, if I don't feel great! You want to try our luck at the Palace?"

"Through that blizzard?"

"Not thick enough to be a blizzard yet. Come on, it's only halfway to the restaurant. Couple of hundred yards!"

"I won't get back into my outfit till it's been washed."

"Me neither. We'll go fancy. You carry any female duds besides the nightgown?"

"Yes, wrapped in my blanket roll. You think I ought to let this town know I'm a woman?"

Deliberately avoiding the sight of Brandy dressing across the room—not from politeness, Lord knew, but because he wanted to be surprised, and felt sure that he *would* be—he then arranged his saddlebags, blanket roll, and war-bag with his carbine and Bowie knife tucked in among them in such a way that he'd be able to tell if they were disturbed while he was gone. He checked the inside pocket of his fancy soft doeskin jacket, which he'd had tailored especially one time when he'd been in the chips, and felt the long even roll

55

of double eagles stacked through its length: must be better than a thousand dollars there, and the pocket's construction didn't betray the fact that he was carrying it. The little man who'd designed it for him had been a stitching wizard. He put on the jacket and said, "You about ready, honey?"

"Almost. You can look now."

Good God but she *was* a lovely sight! The gown must have come from New York, New Orleans, or maybe even Europe. It was scarlet and silver and as low-cut in the bodice as possible, with the heavy skirt just missing the floor by half an inch and a long slash embroidered with silver lace extending halfway up her thigh, but hanging closed so that nothing of her showed through it. It was a queen's dress, and with her upright carriage and her full bosom she lived up to it. The silken velvet stuck to her tits as though it were pasted there, and its neckline—a funny sort of word for something that missed her neck by six inches or better—was so obviously molded to her unique build that Slocum knew it had been made for her alone. She looked as if one deep breath would pop out her sizeable nipples. The material was so heavy that they didn't show through it, but he knew where they were, as well as the location of her navel in the skintight expanse between curve of breasts and mons veneris.

"You look like the fucking Queen of France," he said gallantly. "You have anything to wear against the snow?"

"A poncho is all, but it'll do."

He helped her into it, her head emerging from the dull gray and black wool and the edges of the blanket-like garment reaching to her knees. "What I want to know is, how could you toe a man in the nuts so's to cripple him enough to capture him, if you were wearing that dress and whatever little bits of custom-made moccasins you got on your feet?"

56

She lifted the full skirt, which hung in thick heavy folds, and showed him her regular boots. "If I wore ladies' gear on my feet, it would peel off when I got 'em wet, like tonight—and the hem would sweep the floor or the street and get filthy—and I'd be practically defenseless." She balanced on one foot and showed him the other boot. "That toe isn't just thick leather, Johnny; it's backed up with a steel cup. Get a nudge from that in your privates and you know you've been branded."

"Or split wide open," said Slocum. "I swear you can't ever be more than a short spit from a weapon."

"I had a rough childhood," she said, snorting through her nose with amusement. As she lowered her leg, the silver-laced slash in the skirt parted to show him a glimpse of a pearl-handled derringer carried on her calf in a fancy garter holster. He shook his head, speechless.

He slapped on his black town Stetson and they left, locking the door behind them. Slocum paused at the desk. "I had a visitor a while back," he said to the clerk, who looked permanently drowsy, "a buffalo hunter. Did he come past you?"

"He did. Asked which was your room."

"You may have heard the reception he got."

"No, I didn't hear anything. Got a bum right ear."

"Well, just lemme say that if you direct anybody else to my room, short of the sheriff, my friend Bill McGunn," said Slocum evenly, "you will live to be very sorry about it. Savvy?"

Outside, the snow still sifted down in satiny silence, gradually building up on the ice-slicked town and the desert beyond. Brandy lifted her skirts with one hand and gripped Slocum's biceps with the other. They struck out into the white curtain eastward, walking cautiously, their bootheels clunking on the hidden glaze. They passed the Christmas Variety brothel—

57

the name seemed more appropriate to Slocum than when he'd first heard it—and the hide-and-pole shanties. Nothing moved but the man and woman and the falling snow. It was bleak and raw in their noses, on their hands and faces; Slocum felt an urge to squint, not against the snow, but from the cuttingly cold air itself. But there was no wind.

He mentioned this. Brandy said, "There'll be one. The norther that started this is only resting. In a day or so it'll pick up and blow this part of the Territory right into Mexico."

7

He could see why they'd called it the Palace of Mirrors. There were no windows, and on each of the four long walls there was centered an enormous polished silvery mirror. After the first look, he began to notice others, set apparently at random here and there, some flat to the walls and some at angles in the corners. It wasn't any high-toned place that would have graced Kansas City, say, or Frisco: there they'd have slathered the place with mirrors till you couldn't have seen a patch of plaster or a board anywhere. But for Retch it was phenomenal. Slocum wondered how on God's wild earth they'd ever freighted those big plates of glass into this off-the-path hellhole. And how much it had cost them to do it.

He and Brandy stood in the foyer, where a huge open closet behind a counter was presided over by a pretty redheaded girl, who was older than her paint looked, and two medium-sized, genuine hard-looking men in black suits and white boiled shirts. This was as far as Slocum had ever penetrated till now, for he'd been stopped politely by the pair of guards and had it suavely suggested to him that he smelled a trifle high to be going into the gambling hall. He'd explained just as civilly that he realized this, that he wasn't utterly without social knowledge of such things, and that he understood he could buy a case of good bourbon here. One of the guards had brought it to him and only charged a third more than the going rate for it. That was to be expected here, and Slocum had paid and got out before he could stink up the place with vulgar sweat.

Now he carefully pulled the poncho off Brandy's head, so that she wouldn't have to lift her arms, and handed it and his Stetson to the girl behind the counter, who shook the melting snow off them and hung them on pegs behind her in the open cupboard. Cupboard, hell, he'd *lived* in smaller rooms than that!

"Your gun, sir," said the harder of the two men in black.

"My gun?" Slocum said blankly.

"All weapons must be checked here. It will be waiting for you when you leave."

"You saying that I got to go in and gamble without a sidearm?"

"It's the rule, sir." The fellow allowed a suggestion of a smile to crawl across his flat, scarred face. "Don't worry, you'll be quite safe. There has never been a gunfight in the Palace."

"That ain't handing me any pledge that there won't be!"

"Look there," said the other, pointing discreetly. Slocum looked. He saw a man sitting on a high stool that towered over the activity, near the farthest corner of the huge room. He was one of the most exquisitely dressed men Slocum had ever seen. He must have been six feet two or three and weighed no more than one-seventy. He wore a modishly cut gray suit with a matching vest. The lights flashed from radiant points that must have been large diamonds in each French

59

cuff. As he turned his head in a ceaseless overlooking of the room, Slocum saw his eyes kindle and scintillate like the diamonds. Slocum had a yen to see that man up close. He never remembered coming across any-one who resembled him, yet there was a familiarity to him that baffled the drifter. Who in hell—

The sleek bear-greased thatch of gray hair almost matched the suit—that was sure no accident—and the flowing stallion-tail mustachios were of the same glacial hue. His watch chain and a large signet ring on his left hand were of silver. His skin was as white as Brandy's breasts. There was really no color to the man at all, save that of hardened steel. Across his lap rested a double-barreled shotgun, not the usual Rem-ington 10-gauge but a beautiful creation of silver-plated, scroll-engraved metal and a stock covered with dove-tinted mother-of-pearl, something Slocum had never seen on any weapon larger than a handgun; he would have laid odds that it had been crafted in England by one of the great gunsmiths.

Why was this man so familiar? wondered Slocum, staring across at the tall figure sitting erect and stiff as an Apache arrow on the high stool.

"That is Mr. Maynard Savage," murmured the scar-faced guard in his ear.

"The owner," said Slocum, and discovered with sur-prise that he'd voiced it in a whisper.

"Yes sir. He's why you and your lady will be com-pletely safe and sound while you're in the Palace."

"I see what you mean," said Slocum, eyeing the lean figure and the terrible, elegant shotgun.

The door guard searched Slocum deftly. "You un-derstand that this is a formality demanded of all our patrons," he said.

"Just so long as you're not thinking of searching the lady."

"I'd lose my job if I even suggested it," said the

tough, smiling broadly at the thought. "Such an obvious lady of quality is above suspicion."

Slocum imagined him confronted with Brandy in her rambling-cowhand outfit and almost choked. "Thanks," he said, and tipped the guard a couple of big Mexican 'dobe dollars, because it seemed the thing to do in all this opulence.

"Thank you, sir, that's not necessary," said the man, and slipped them into his own vest pocket. "May I recommend a malt whiskey for the gentleman, as a change from bourbon?"

Holy hell, Slocum thought, he recognized me all along! No wonder he searched an Earthquake vagabond, however neatly dressed!

"Sure," he said. "I'll try anything once."

Slocum and Brandy walked through the crowded room side by side. He seated her at the poker table and took the chair opposite the dealer and beside her. The deal was made from a mechanical device that held a deck of house cards, with a square opening in the top so that the players could see the card drawn; it was pretty good assurance of an honest deal, though it could be rigged by a pro. Slocum resolved to watch the dealer carefully.

The hand in progress ended. A stocky man with a short beard flipped his cards into the center of the table, swore he'd never touch another one again, and stomped out. A tall man with drooping mustachios like those of Maynard Savage, but shiny black, came across the room to take his place. His skin was deep bronze, his slick mop of hair matched the long tails that sprouted from his upper lip, and he was a little taller and a little broader than Slocum himself. His eyes were the pale Anglo-Saxon sky-blue of the typical gunman. His clothing was a gambler's—brocade vest, fancy frock coat with velvet collar, brilliantly white shirt, expensive black pants tucked into calfskin boots, the works—but his bearing and self-contained silence said *fighter* to Slocum. This was the fellow who'd come in behind them. Slocum leaned forward and asked, "You wore a thick white coat, didn't you?"

The man nodded. "You wondering what it is?" Slocum inclined his head. "Albino buffalo. Keep a man warm even in what's ready to come down out there," he said.

"Never seen one, but heard of 'em. Plenty Indians would raise your scalp for it," said Slocum. "They're supposed to be sacred."

"I have a chunk of trouble now and then with Cheyenne or Blackfoot, yes." He thrust out a huge hand. "Name of Charles Tucker."

"John Slocum." They shook. Slocum tried hard to recollect the correct form of introduction for females above the rank of whore. "Miss Brandywine, Mr. Tucker," he got out. "The other gents are unknown to me at present."

Tucker inclined his big frame from the waist. "A great pleasure, Miss Brandywine. May I say you brighten up the casino even more than the score of Rochester brass harp lamps hanging overhead."

"Thank you," said Brandy, and actually blushed, the pink glow edging down over her bosom. The sensible part of Slocum's brains was glad that no weapons were allowed in the Palace. He sat on his irresponsible temper until it cooled.

"Just hit town, you three?" asked the dealer casually. Slocum and Tucker turned and stared at the man. He had just shattered the major propriety of the West: never ask personal questions of any kind. The dealer realized this and shook his hand with palm forward and fingers outspread. "Not prying, gents! I only wanted to say that if you have, you'd better plan on staying for a while. The Indians are coming in from their camps, have been all day long. They say this will be the goddamnedest storm we've had in the space of an old chief's memory."

The two big men relaxed, and Slocum noted that he'd certainly been right about Tucker's profession: permanently on the tetchy side, not picking quarrels but ready to horn the brush at meddlesome questions. Only an amateur or a drunk would rile this big galoot a-purpose.

"Been thinking the same thing myself," Slocum said to the dealer. He didn't answer the query about arrival time, nor did Tucker. "Thick snow on thick ice makes for a lot of frozen corpses and broken bones."

The dealer, whose name was John Henry, began to introduce the three other players. He was interrupted by a deep, protracted fit of ropy coughing. A lunger, obviously, come West to try and drag a few more years of life from the climate. And he'd ended up in Retch! Poor bastard, thought Slocum. What a hole to crawl into: a plush, well-heated, glittery sort of hole, of course, the Palace of Mirrors, but sunk in the middle of a dung heap.

Everyone said "Howdy." The others seemed to be your average substantial citizens, and one of the names, Jim Kinkaid, clicked. He'd backed McGunn for sheriff. Slocum gave him a sideways look. He wouldn't have trusted the fellow with his poke or his baby sister, in spite of the expensive, sober, businessman's get-up. Probably because he'd picked a clean-cut, innocent young dude to be the star-toter of this hell's pit. There had to be a reason for that, and it couldn't be reasonable or aboveboard.

The same went for the father of that pretty little untouched filly, too. Slocum had a hankering to meet the celebrated Mr. Schmidt. There was something going on in Retch that wasn't square. Besides all the hardcases and reptiles that hung out in the Earthquake, that was.

63

The dealer said huskily, "Game's stud, m'lady and gentlemen. The deal doesn't travel."

"You're on the payroll, then?" Tucker asked.

"Yes. Naturally that gives the house a slight edge. But the play is fair, and you have a lot better odds than if you'd chosen roulette. Mr. Maynard Savage runs a totally honest house, as you may have heard. No rigged wheels, stacked decks, or loaded dice."

"I'll vouch for that," Jim Kinkaid boomed. "I've been playing here three years, and by thunder, I'm still just about even."

"Ante up," said the dealer, and when they'd bought chips and done so, he dealt one down and one up for each player. A waiter brought Slocum a fat quart of Scotch and a tray of four glasses; he poured one for Brandy and himself, then one as a gesture for Tucker. The others had been there a while and had their own drinks. "Next bottle's on me, then," said Tucker, nodding thanks. He parted his lank mustachios with the back of a forefinger and inserted the glass between them. Goddamn, they were as coarse and long as a mustang's mane. Slocum wondered whether he could grow such a set. They were long enough to braid, like the hair of a Jicarilla Apache. Tucker sipped, savored, and grinned. "You have a good palate, Slocum."

"New brand of bug juice to me, Tucker. Recommended by the bouncer." He took a long gulp. "Not bad at all," he agreed. "Tastes like some sort of smoke's in it."

"Peat smoke," said Tucker.

The first bottle emptied fast, and Tucker ordered another. He was losing, not badly, and dropped out fairly early in each hand. His luck wasn't running. Brandy kept pretty well even. Slocum took one pot out of three on the average, and after an hour had a sizeable array of chip stacks in front of him. This was better than the Earthquake. It was that silver dollar in the road that had done it, though he wouldn't tell Brandy!

Another townie dropped out and a stranger sat down.

"I ain't had a hand I could play since Pony McTaver left," groused Kinkaid. "Here's a new man, John. Let's have a new deck too."

John Henry opened the pack and shuffled rapidly and professionally. Then he shoved the cards to Slocum. "If you'd just cut them several times," he said. Slocum did, one-handed. The dealer eyed him. "You wouldn't care for a good job dealing here?" he asked.

"Nope. Doing fine as is."

"The offer will hold any time you change your mind."

"Thanks, but I'm dusting Retch off my heels as soon as the ground's clear," said Slocum shortly.

"Sorry to hear that, Mr. Slocum," said the dealer. "You're a formidable opponent."

"I'd think you'd like to see the last of him, then," said Kinkaid, who had a loose mouth.

The lunger stared at him. His eyes were like chips of slate. "There's no pleasure in poker if you're up against a pack of yacks who don't know their ass from the queen of spades," he murmured. Then he looked at Brandy and opened his mouth to apologize.

"Fucking right," said Brandy. The dealer grinned and unbent. His smile said plainly that with that word she'd proved herself a lady of sensitivity, making it unnecessary for him to apologize. Slocum took a drink to hide his own expression. Brandy was an enigma to everyone here but him, which tickled his funny bone. He stood up and shucked his doeskin jacket, draping it carefully over the plush-seated oak captain's chair in which he sat. The room was actually hot. It was hard to realize what hell the weather was playing just a few yards away.

He glanced up; the celebrated Maynard Savage had not moved from his high stool. His eyes ran unceasingly over the crowd, and now Slocum noticed that his finger was curled around the front trigger of the double-barrel. God Almighty, he thought, but nobody stood a chance of raising hell in here!

Then, before Slocum could sit down again, the silver-gray man shot him a look like a needle of chilled steel and beckoned him over. Slocum excused himself from the next hand and walked past the roulette table, where the wheel whirred and the little ivory ball clicked rhythmically, past the faro table with its green felt playing board and its cue box where the red and white counters slid and snicked as the drawn cards were counted, seeing himself in multiple images in the facing lengths of mirror as he moved like a stalking panther among the sitting wolves and pikas. There was a little three-step ladder beside the stool. Since Savage showed no intention of coming down to talk, Slocum, feeling foolish, mounted the ladder to stand almost level with him.

A little reluctant to stare at the ice-tinted big augur of the Palace right off, Slocum glanced around him. Now he saw the reason for the tipped, tilted mirrors on posts and in corners: from this vantage point you could see every inch of the room, even those seats on the other side of the square pillars and stove. It would take some habituation, but eventually a man would know exactly where to look to see whatever he cared to inspect.

"Howdy, Mr. Savage," he said, and brought his gaze to the boss. He'd been right—the dealer with TB had eyes of stone, and this coldly flamboyant man had eyes of metal, and yet they were nearly the same color. Weird. "You wanted to speak to me, sir?" he asked. Good manners came natural in the presence of Savage, yes, and even respect.

"You're John Slocum."

"I am."

"I know about you. No trouble will visit you in my establishment." God, the voice was colder than the eyes, flat, expressionless, pitched low but carrying like a ranting actor's.

"I wasn't worried."

"I'm sure of that. I hear the sheriff knows you're in town."

"Met him a while back."

"He didn't want to lock you up?"

"He took my word I'd be in town. There's a mistake, see," said Slocum. "I didn't rob that bank."

The steadfast regard didn't waver. "I believe you." Savage shifted the greener on his lap half an inch. "I believe you were a major in the Confederate Army?"

How in brimstone tophet—"I was."

"No mystery. I was a colonel. Our paths crossed once, before Shiloh. I never forget a face. Yours has grown up and toughened, but you're still Major Slocum. Play here as often and as long as you like, Major Slocum. In fact, if you wish I'll take you on my payroll and you can live here. John offered you a position as dealer. He speaks for me."

Slocum gaped, and shut his mouth, feeling like a bumpkin letting his amazement show that way. "Could I ask how you know that, sir?"

"I read lips. I'm a little deaf," said the lean gray man. "The cannon; I spent too much time standing beside them. I can hear you well, Major, but at thirty paces I couldn't. So I read lip movements."

"I'm not a major any longer, Mr. Savage. Fact is, I was even a top sergeant for a time with the blue-bellies."

The eyes misted over like a crystal closely breathed on. "We come down, Slocum," he said. "We all come down in the world. Perhaps we should both have died in the war in our glory."

67

"I'm glad I didn't. Would have missed plenty of fun."

Maynard Savage focused on him again. "Not a bad attitude. Major, there are a hundred men gunning for you in Retch. Some for your poke, which is very large in the sight of such pus and slop as inhabit this quagmire. Some for the reward, the news of which is penetrating as more bounty hunters stumble in from the storm."

"More!" Slocum had never even *met* more than three or four bounty men in his life before.

"They congregate in town every now and then, whenever there's a really widespread manhunt. The one for you—I should say for the man who's thought to be you—has brought more than usual. Two thousand dollars reward! Why, I remember when Jesse James had less than that on his head, and he was known coast to coast even then."

"Why do you suppose they slathered such an amount on this Kid Slocum?"

"He killed two well-liked men, and got away with the payrolls of the Lucky Cuss and Tough Nut Mines. That would amount to one roaring hell of a lot of money."

"I hadn't heard any details," said Slocum. "I appreciate your bothering to tell me, Colonel."

"Way I heard it," said the gray man, his eyes reconnoitering the great warm room that twinkled with polished brass and glittering mirrors, shined mahogany and precious jewels, "the Kid had been lounging around Tombstone for two, three days, drinking in the Alhambra and bragging so loudly that eventually they threw him out." He gave a twitch of the long mustachios that probably originated in a tight smile. "One reason I calculate he wasn't you. You hold your liquor and you don't loudmouth it all over about how tough you are. I, ah, hear things from the Earthquake, you see. Then after the robbery, this short-trigger big-yap rode around a couple of times in a circle in front of the bank, shouting 'I'm John Slocum and I'll blow the ass off anybody that follows me!' " Savage looked at him once more. "Not your style, Major. Not your style at all. But tell that subtlety to a bounty hunter, or a posse or even a judge. No, you've either been neatly set up to die someone else's death for him, or a pair of John Slocums are drifting around the Territory."

"I'll be dogboned," said Slocum vacantly. "Thanks, Colonel. Calculate I'll watch the dark corners closer than ordinary for a while. Sheriff McGunn wired Tombstone for more details—"

"He never got through. The wires evidently thickened with so much ice that they're down in God knows how many places. Retch is isolated; probably Tombstone, Globe, maybe Tucson too."

"Hell's bells and panther tracks!" Slocum exploded. "Bounty men piling up here like crap in a privy, a bad-medicine pueblo glutted with slimy hardcases looking for a poke of easy money, reward posters out on me and no telegraph, and the worst weather in years! Makes a man think his luck's fixed to play out, Colonel Savage."

The gray man slitted his eyes, speculating. "How many times have you been in that frame of mind since the War Between the States, sir?"

Slocum laughed. "Maybe forty, fifty. But the odds are kind of higher than customary."

"Then why don't you take up residence at the Palace of Mirrors? I can start you at a poker table tonight. You'd be a fine asset to me, John—as valuable as that other John who's dealing for you now."

"The lunger," said Slocum. "He's a damn good player."

"He's the most dangerous man I've ever known."

"What?" Slocum was startled. "That poor devil hacking up his chest's insides drop by drop?"

"You don't know who he is, then." Savage waited, smiling more broadly now under the great mustachios. "Think. John—"

"Good Jesus! Not John Henry Hol—"

"Exactly."

Slocum considered. "You know, Colonel, he's maybe the one man in the West I would absolutely not go up against?"

"Showing your good sense. *I* wouldn't either. He's resting in Retch while certain matters cool down elsewhere. You're welcome to do the same."

Slocum looked down toward his table. Brandy stood out in her bright red velvet gown like one of those sensual paintings found in every other casino in the Territory. "I'd take you up on that kind offer, Mr. Savage, except for one item," he said slowly. "Comes a time when a man with any sense looks for a burrow and crawls into it, when the wolfpack is just too damn numerous and slavering. But I happen to be sharing a room with a purely fantastic woman, and for good enough reasons I'll turn my back on whiskey and cards and money, but not on a frisky lusty girl or a friend. I'll keep playing here, but I can't accept your proposal of work. Many thanks, though."

"As you please, Major." The steel eyes lanced downward at Slocum's table. "You refer, of course, to Miss Brandywine. I can't say I blame you. It's a rule that no woman lives under this roof, or I'd extend the offer to her. The lady with the hay hook," Savage said, with utter obscurity. "Well, good luck, Major Slocum. Remember that you're a walking bankroll, have annexed the finest-looking female in a hundred miles or more, and are known to be a top gunfighter; this town is loaded with bandidos, idiots, and cat-eyes whose primary target will certainly be you. I can't think of anything else you could have in the balance against you unless you happened to freeze and break off your trigger finger in the snowstorm. Take care. Remember too that I've said you're safe in the Palace, and my word is good."

Slocum stared at him. "There are five people I trust in Retch," he said slowly. "You, the lunger, the sheriff and his young lady, and Miss Brandywine. I've spent a sizeable slice of my life with a damn sight fewer people than that to count on."

"It's not a bad number of friends," said Maynard Savage. "Unfortunately you're entirely wrong about one of them. So be on your guard. I still believe and hope that we may work together one day. Good evening, Major Slocum."

"Good evening, Colonel Savage." Slocum stepped carefully down the three-rung ladder and went back to the poker game. Who in the goddamn hell had the silver and gray man meant to warn him about? Not John, the dealer. Nor Savage himself. Goddamn!

Don't trust anybody and you'll live to gum your gruel on some sunny front porch some day, Johnny Slocum. Or, better, trust everybody, but keep your hand near your six-gun and cut the cards.

"What did the great man want with you?" asked Kinkaid nastily as he sat down.

Slocum stared at him steadily for a long moment, enough to make the fellow fidget. Then he said, "He warned me to watch the aces up your sleeve, not to get too close to you because you got a breath that curls up lizards, and not to take any paper money off you because you print it yourself. He also said I shouldn't have anything to do with your wife on account of the chance of contracting a horrible disease, and not to turn my back on you less'n I was wearing a steel vest. Some other items he mentioned, but you'll have to ask him about them because they're too repulsive and you might get the notion I was insulting you."

In the dead silence that descended on their table, the

71

whirr of the roulette wheel and the little clunk of a keno pellet dropping out of the mahogany goose came plain to their ears. Then, as Kinkaid started to rise, his face purple, the dealer said softly, "You asked for that. Sit down and play your cards." Kinkaid swallowed hard and relapsed into his seat.

Slocum signaled for another bottle of whiskey. "Deal me in next round," he said comfortably.

8

When he decided to quit for the night, Slocum was more than four thousand dollars to the good and Brandy was down a few hundred. Kinkaid had long since gone bust and trudged out, scowling at the big drifter evilly.

"Going to the hotel? I'll walk along if you don't mind. Retch isn't a place for a solitary stroll," said Tucker in the foyer.

"I thought you'd left," said Slocum, instincts bristling.

"I was playing chuck-a-luck. It was a mistake." Tucker grinned ruefully, shrugging into his bulky white buffalo coat and slapping on a huge, broad-brimmed John B. "I'll stick to poker from now on."

"Don't you have a gun?"

"In the pockets," said Tucker. That was an advantage to the enormous buff and bearskin coats, as Slocum had found out a long time ago: you could carry your revolvers in the deep pockets, and in a tetchy situation you could keep your hands firmly around them. It saved about two precious seconds that would otherwise have been lost in brushing back the heavy skirts and slapping leather.

Pockets, he'd said. So Tucker carried a brace of guns too.

He'd been right, thought Slocum. Tucker was a professional. Whether he was also a bounty hunter remained to be seen. But he'd have to go some to get the drop on John Slocum, forewarned as thoroughly as he was.

Slocum nestled his hand over the butt of his thumb-buster and draped the doeskin jacket flap over them to keep off the falling snow. One of the guards opened the door for them. The white flakes had grown thicker and were coming at a faster clip. Three abreast they started into the storm, heading west down the street, even at near-nothing visibility taking the center of the road. There was a curious glow all around them, as though the snow were palely luminous.

"Yahoo," said Tucker sardonically. "Nice day for a picnic."

Brandy slipped her arm under Slocum's left biceps and gave it a squeeze. "Yeah," she said, "I think so."

If it had been possible to attain an erection in this bleak squall, Slocum figured he would have done it.

After a while Tucker asked, "Where are we?"

"About to the whorehouse."

"Hotel soon?"

"Next." Slocum loosened Brandy's grip and dropped back slightly. But the other big, lank man, muffled in his white shag, trudged right along without glancing at him, breath frosting out in a heavy cloud. "Here we are," said Slocum.

Tucker, gently brushing flakes of melting snow from his long drooping lip-hair, went to the stairs. "I'm on the second floor. See you two tonight, I guess?"

"Probably." Slocum watched him disappear. "Big son of a bitch," he said to Brandy. "You reckon *he* might be Kid Slocum?"

"Oh, for Christ sake, Johnny! How would he grow a mustache like that in a week?"

"Yeah, I forgot. I just naturally suspect anybody

73

over six foot now," said Slocum, rattled. "Not many men my size in town. I suppose the Kid is over the border by this time, anyway."

"Sure," said Brandy, holding her voluminous skirts up and heading down the passage. "Sure he is."

"Blast you, girl, you still think it's me, don't you? What have I done to make you decide I'm insane?"

She turned to look at him. Holy murder, that bust of hers seemed to leap out at him even when she was only breathing hard! "What do you mean by that?"

"The flier, it says Kid Slocum's 'perhaps insane.' I strike you as a demented lunatic?"

"No, but you never can tell about maniacs," she said, her smile taking out the stinger even as she touched him with it. "They go along as placid as an old Mex smoking wild tobacco, and before you can blink they're all over you."

"I intend to be all over you as soon as we get these duds hung up, so unlock that door and get tense, honey," Slocum told her, handing over the key. She opened the door and they went in. "I'll show you whose thinker is tied up in knots."

"So long as your cock's straight," she said demurely, locking them in. "Unbutton me, Johnny, my arms are all worn out from holding up cards."

A few minutes later, he was sliding in beside her. He was on her and in her and pumping away without preamble or caress as if he had three minutes' limit before he'd get tossed out. Almost at once she started yowling and bucking and slamming her groin against his, like to grind all their pelvic bones to dust before she was through. She started on a series of protracted, overlapping, rapid-fire orgasms that shook him with their incredible power. He came and kept doggedly on and never lost his erection. He came again and stayed where he was, with no idea of what condition his prong was in, with almost no feeling down there but a strange unending excitement. By the powers if after a while he didn't finish off for a third time and damn near die of it. The lamplit room spun around him and he thought Hell, maybe this is what it *does* feel like to go crazy. Then he was banged out altogether and couldn't have moved a muscle if he'd died for it.

And Brandy let out a scream that cracked in the middle into a piercing screech, and collapsed under him as if all her bones had turned to tallow.

Some time later she gurgled and sucked in a loud breath and let it out, a thin stream like smoke misting up from her lungs, hot and moist fog lifting in the cold still air of the room. Then she said, wheezing and struggling to regain her wind, "Oh, John, Johnny, that was real bicycling. You curried me out good. I been reefed and raked and gigged better'n I ever was before. Honest! You really were throwing the steel there, Johnny baby. Why the hell didn't you think to take off your gut-lancers?"

"Ma'am, I never wore spurs to bed even when I was alone," Slocum said. "Fact is, I ain't even got my boots on."

There was a discreet tap on the door. They both sat up. "If that's another buffalo hunter," growled Slocum angrily, "I won't even face him, I'll shoot through the panels. Who is it?" he yelled.

"Spring Fawn."

"And just who's Spring Fawn?" demanded Brandy suspiciously.

"The hotel squaw." He got out and pulled on his striped pants again and unlocked the door. "What is it, daughter?"

"Forgive me for cutting short your pleasure—"

"You didn't. I know you have an urgent reason to waken me. What is it?"

"The sheriff wishes to see you at his office." She was rattled, alternating between her own tongue and English, mixing languages in the same sentence. "Wants very much talk with you. He send Foot in Grave to bring you."

"He sent who?"

"My brother, Foot in Grave. He work for the law," she said proudly. "Foot in Grave always good man, never drink or fight except when he get hold of whole bottle of whiskey at once. He is deputy."

"The sheriff told me about him," said Slocum. "Glad he got back safe from his hunting. I'll be ready in a minute." He closed the door and groaned. "That means I have to get back into those damn filthy clothes! What in Halifax and points south does McGunn want with me at this ungodly hour?"

"Maybe to put you in a cell," said Brandy. "I'll go too. If that's it, we can shoot our way out."

"I can shoot my way out of some dumb little mix-up without help, thanks. Will you look at that!" he exclaimed. Beside his war-bag, where he hadn't even noticed them before, were his traveling clothes, washed and dried and flattened into a neat stack with his elk-skin jacket topped by his old flop-brimmed Stetson, now miraculously stiffened and looking scarcely more than eight or ten years used. "Now she shouldn't have done that," said Slocum. "That was one hell of a lot of work in this weather. Wonder how she did it so fast?"

"She's in love with you, honey."

"Spring Fawn is at least eighty, and I'll bet she's a sight more," Slocum told her.

"A heap you know about women if you think she couldn't fall for your cock at a hundred and twelve!"

Slocum all but blushed. "Brandy! That's obscene."

"It certainly isn't. It's feminine." The girl slid out of bed, followed her misting breath across the room, and fingered the clothes. "You'll have to give her a couple of dollars, Johnny, at least. This was *work*."

"No, I don't think she'd want to be paid. Because

76

we're friends." He didn't mention the huge hot meal he'd brought the squaw, or the pickings he'd left her on the buff hunter. "Sure is a relief not to crawl inside that stink again," Slocum said, sliding on his clean long-handles, "but I'd a sight rather stay in bed. I'll bring us back something to munch on." He noticed the big Hopi wicker basket by the door and put the empty coffee bottles into it.

Brandy was back in bed; she'd slid into her white nightdress and slung all three soogans atop her. "Make it hot," she said. "I didn't know I was hungry till you mentioned it, and now I'm one cold big hollow gut."

"I'll get home quick's I can." He strapped on one cartridge belt with his second-best pistol in the holster, looped up his elkskin over it, thrust his filed-down .45 into his pocket, put one of the three remaining quarts of Double Stamp into the basket—"In case I get lost in the snow," he said—and Stetsoned his head tight and low.

He took the basket and went out and slammed the door. Spring Fawn waited patiently in the hall beside an old, skinny Navaho wrapped in a soaked blanket. Slocum could never tell the age of an Indian, but if Spring Fawn was eighty or so, her brother must be pushing a hundred.

He bowed formally to her. "Thank you for what you did, daughter," he said in her language.

"It was less than nothing. Slocum is a man who should wear clean clothing. This is my brother, Foot in Grave."

Slocum stuck out his hand and the old man took it. He had fingers like the jaws of a well-oiled bear trap. His voice was a lost whisper in a storm. "I am sorrowful that I must bring you to McGunn."

"A man does what he must do. We'll stop first at the—the—ah, hell," Slocum said in English, "the restaurant."

"Yes." Foot in Grave didn't waste words. He walked away down the corridor. Slocum kissed the squaw on the cheek and followed him. They butted out the door into the snow.

"You know what the sheriff wants with—"

"No talk," said the deputy in English. "Walk." He strode into the white wall and vanished. Slocum hurried to catch up. They headed east in a thickness of quiet, not even hearing their own careful footsteps. Slocum found that he could see farther than he'd believed—possibly the snow had thinned, or the sun risen higher—perhaps eight or ten feet if he squinted. He could distinguish the long fancy sign of the Palace of Mirrors as they passed under it, though he couldn't have read the printing on it. But the buff-hide shanties were set farther back, and he couldn't discern them at all.

At his side, Foot in Grave never looked left or right, but plowed straight on. Then he stopped dead. "Restaurant," he stated.

"Come on in," Slocum urged.

"No."

"We can drink some hot coffee."

"No." Foot in Grave stood like the wooden sign of some dreary, run-down tobacco shop that couldn't afford a carved brave with feathers and tomahawk and some fresh paint. The snow swirled around him. Slocum reluctantly fumbled his way to the left and found the door of the greasy-belly's place. He left the basket and bottles, with the same order as yesterday's. He pocketed his quart of whiskey, and left, noticing that the hole in the roof had been plugged with a cork.

Foot in Grave opened the door of the office and stamped in, Slocum right behind. They stood there shedding snowflakes and puddling up the floor, and the Indian said, "Slocum," and went to squat down beside the desk.

78

Bill McGunn was behind the battered, three-drawered table, and Jim Kinkaid in his businessman's suit was warming his ass near the stove and looking mean. There was another man, whom Slocum didn't know, in a sheepskin coat. Slocum took off his hat and unsnowed the crown and brim.

"Must be goddamn important. Oh," he said, "Miss Amelia isn't here?"

"No, no," said the sheriff. "Not on a day like this. Slocum, these men think you ought to be in a cell."

Slocum leaned back slightly and grew a little taller and his eyes went darker than before. His hand slid into his pocket and rested comfortably on the butt of the stripped thumb-buster. "Do tell," he said mildly. "Well, why don't they try and stick me in one?"

"That would be my job if I agreed with them."

"You couldn't do it, Bill. I've seen enough jail cells I didn't belong in, I got no hankering to see any more." He stared down Kinkaid, who turned around irritably as if to warm his front half. "*Him* I know," said Slocum, "but who's the other one?"

"Mr. Chris Adams, who owns one of the silver mines in the mountains."

Slocum would have trusted Adams almost as far as he'd have put his faith in Kinkaid, which was nearly as far as he could have thrown a paper collar against a high wind. Adams had a receding forehead and a chin to match weasellike eyes and a little shitty grin. Slocum felt it did seem a shame that he ran a mine, because that prevented him from foreclosing the mortgages of widows and orphans, which nature had surely designed him for. He was nursing a Winchester.

"The better element of the town," Slocum murmured, feeling on the peck. "I'd appreciate it if Mr. Adams pointed that Winchester in somebody else's direction."

"And if I don't?" Adams said.

79

"Then I'll have to make the pocket of this jacket into an open-toed holster," said Slocum, shoving up his .45 so that it stuck out the elkskin, "and I'd hate to do that in this weather. Just lean it against the wall, Adams, old coot. Nobody's gonna bushwhack you in here." The man did as he was told. "You were telling me about cells, Bill."

"I've told these gentlemen, and Mr. Schmidt, that I'm trusting you not to leave town. They think I shouldn't. My deputy's going to ride to Tombstone— the telegraph lines are down—and see what he can gather in the way of details. He'll see if he can get any further description from the men who knew Kid Slocum there—maybe, something that will show he's not you."

"Wait a fucking minute," shouted Slocum, taking his hand out of his pocket and pointing a finger at Mc-Gunn's young face. "Your deputy is going to ride to Tombstone? Foot in Grave here's your deputy, ain't he?"

"That's right."

Slocum turned on the old man. "You can't ride there in this snow, man! He can't make you do such a fool thing!"

"Me no ride," said the ancient stoically. "Walk. Lead horse. Old horse."

"I didn't order him to," McGunn yelled at Slocum, getting up from his swivel chair. "It's his own idea. I ordered him *not* to go, but nobody can argue him out of it."

"Foot in Grave deputy," said the bundle of rags and dark copper skin, his eyes closed. "Foot in Grave take oath to do job. Job is find out truth. Foot in Grave do it. Snow makes no never mind to Injun."

Slocum looked at him steadily. "Why would you lead a horse there, friend?"

A sly smile like his sister's grew on the wrinkled face. "*Old* horse, ready to die. Think, Slocum."

Slocum thought. "How long would it take you to walk all that way?" he asked.

The Navaho unfolded himself carefully and went to open the door. He peered out at the snow as if he hadn't seen it before, speculating. Then he came back and sat down on the floor again. "One day, one night, one day."

"What's he need an old horse for?" asked McGunn.

"To keep him warm during the worst of the night," said Slocum. "Otherwise he wouldn't stand a shake. Comes the coldest time, he stops, cut the horse's throat, slits open its body and shoves as deep as he can go into the hot, steamy recesses of the carcass. By the time the horse cools down, the man's warm enough to tackle the trail again."

Kinkaid gawked. "You mean he'd get into a dead horse? In among the guts and blood and—" The idea made him go pale and sick-looking. "What sort of disgusting barbarian would do a thing like that?"

"A sensible man who wanted to live through the night," said Slocum reasonably. He looked down at Foot in Grave, studying the human rack of bones intently. Then he said in Navaho, "What is your real name, friend?"

"Kiwanwatewa."

"Kiwanwatewa need not do this thing. It is bad, dangerous." He put out his hand to Kiwanwatewa, who took it and hauled himself upright. "You have food?"

"Jerky. Plenty." The Indian looked at the quart of bourbon that Slocum held out to him. "Aiyee! That help." He had lapsed into English again. The sealed bottle vanished under his sopping blanket, and Lord knew where he put it, because he looked as skinny as ever.

"You have a gun?" asked the sheriff, resigned now.

"No need gun. Gun freeze," said Foot in Grave

scornfully. He pulled a knife that could have sliced off Goliath's head. "In case meet hungry wolf," he said, and made it disappear again. "Need money."

"How much?"

"Month's wages."

McGunn took ten silver dollars from a desk drawer and handed it over.

"You want to borrow my hat?" Slocum asked him.

"Injun still have hair," said Kiwanwatewa, and made the gesture across his chest that meant "peace"; Slocum returned it. The old man opened the door and went into the storm.

"Judas H. Priest!" said McGunn. "Might as well order a bat to sleep standing up as tell him not to go! *I* know he's heading out to his finish, and I don't know why, but I can hardly lock him in a cell till he comes to his senses. Whatever his reason, it's sufficient for him."

Slocum sloughed it off. "You want any more from me, Bill?"

"To put you safe in that jail back there," muttered Kinkaid.

"Nobody cages me. I don't suffocate in no lockup box."

"Obviously," said Kinkaid. "Maybe what we need is a sheriff."

"You sure's hell do. You got a decent boy who don't know up from sideways, but he was your choice, and it's your own dumb fault if he's smart enough to recognize an honest man and take his word," said Slocum.

Kinkaid changed the subject hurriedly. "You savvy that red elocution so well—what does a man need with money on the prairie in a snowstorm?"

"He didn't say, but I'd guess it's for another old horse to come back with—on account of the need for it at night, that makes poor old Adams turn green around his gills—that'll run him maybe four, five dollars in Tombstone. Then he'll buy a bottle or two of

82

red-eye. Then he may have to set up drinks or slip a small bribe out for information. I guess he'll shoot the rest on riotous living and girls and the like."

"Girls?" said McGunn, taking him seriously for a moment.

Then the door whammed open and a man with a tall Texas hat roared in along with a flurry of snow. He unhooked his coat to the warmth and Slocum checked out a bone-handled .44 on his hip, tied down and butt foremost for a cross draw. He didn't recognize the bozo.

"Say, where the hell you been hiding this jail?" he hollered, his voice accustomed to vast distances. "Swear to God I been two hours back and forth hunting it!" He shook himself and wetted down the dirt floor a little more. "I come to say there's a bad-wanted man in town, and I'm claiming the reward."

"Oh? Where is he?" asked the sheriff.

"In town, I told you!"

"How can I give you a reward if you haven't got him here?"

"Well, hell, I gotta be the first to tell you he's in Retch!" howled the Texan wrathfully. "There's maybe forty men blundering around in that blizzard and nobody can find their fly if they gotta piss, it's so thick! First one to spot him for you deserves the cash, don't he?"

Slocum moved casually over to the stove and edged Kinkaid away from the front of it, as if to warm his rear end. The Texan hadn't even looked at him yet. Slocum took his thumber out of his pocket and stuck it in his waistband, handylike.

"You get a reward when you deliver a wanted man here to me," said McGunn quietly.

"Ah, well, hell—"

"Who is the owlhoot?" asked Slocum.

"Goes by name of Kid Slocum."

"What's he look like?"

83

The Texan looked over at him. "Tall gink, dark hair, mean face. I seen his picture. Dead or alive, two thousand on him. Hey," he said, batting his eyes to get the melting flakes off the lashes, "he looks like you!"

"This is John Slocum," said Adams nastily. "Didn't catch your name."

"For the tombstone," said Slocum, "in case."

"Jesus God!" said the Texan, and went for his gun.

Slocum skinned out his Colt. He eared back the hammer and as the gun drew up level with the man's belly, let her go out from under the thumb's web. The slug smacked into flesh and gut and bone and the Texan's .44 exploded uselessly as he flew backwards and crashed against the door. His face went blank and slowly, slowly he slid down the door until his big spurs hit the floor and skidded him quickly to a sitting pose. Smoke swirled around the little room; echoes went on and on, at least in three sets of ears, for Slocum didn't notice them. He took two jumps to the man's side and knelt and said urgently, "What's your name?"

"Yavapai Joe," husked the man, and died.

"Enough to put on a wood cross, I suppose." Slocum stood up, sticking his gun in the pocket again. "Anybody think I drew first?"

"Nope," said Adams. For the first time he had a respectful face on. "I never saw such a draw. My Lord! Look there. His bullet hit the wall almost *behind* him!"

"That's the big trouble with a cross draw," said Slocum, buttoning his jacket. "You gotta pull your piece and turn it around. He was as slow as a frog swimming through molasses. Never ought to of gone for me."

"There'll be others like him," said Kinkaid. "Now will you let us put you in a cell? For your safety, at least?"

"No." Slocum settled his hat. "You can find me again, Bill, but don't do it unless there's a real reason."

"Right," said McGunn. "Another corpse. And I don't believe the undertaker ever picked up the first one."

"First one?" said Adams, but nobody answered him.

Slocum rolled the late Texan aside with his foot and went out and closed the door.

He wanted a drink bad. Before he picked up his grub and returned to Brandy, he needed a drink. He wanted to get away from the malevolence of "decent" men like Adams and Kinkaid, and even from the pleasurable, thought-distracting sex of his woman, and put his mind to a few questions that needed answers. He stumbled his way over some drifts and found himself in front of the Christmas Variety crib. What a Boot Hill of a town this was! Not even a decent dance hall, just one grimy whorehouse staffed by painted cats as ugly as the men who dug out the veins of silver in the ugly mountains.

Slocum went past the crib and his hotel and stopped in front of the first saloon: a grim, ill-shaped wooden wart partly disguised by the snow. He stared up at the sign. Crude lettering announced to the world that this was The Bull's Pizzle—Whiskey and Ammunition. On the board was an extremely poor drawing in black paint of a bull, or something that the artist had meant to be a bull; it looked like a randy hippopotamus with spreading horns and an erection that extended out between his front legs and ended just under his chin. Slocum remembered The Bull's Head in Abilene, on Texas Street, which had sported just such an obscene eyesore; Bill Hickok had taken his shotgun down and waited with that slit-eyed glare of his until the owners had had the critter emasculated with paint to such an extent that wags had taken to calling it The Steer's Head. Apparently nobody in Retch had complained to McGunn about this gross pollution of their town.

He could make out the drawing plainly, so the snow

was a little thinner than it had been half an hour ago. Maybe it was blowing itself out.

Maybe pigs had wings, too.

Slocum shoved through the door, opening his coat to expose the holstered gun and settling the other properly in his pocket for a hideout, thumbing back his John B. The place was crowded, a big raw room of a drinking den with a bar made of a gigantic plank spiked into sawhorses. The atmosphere might not have been considered much of an improvement over the jail's—a big iron stove in the center of the room glowed dull scarlet, and its heat sent out waves of warmed air loaded with mean whiskey and stale beer, with sweat and stogie smoke and nine-times-breathed vomit fumes. But, it was a reek that Slocum was used to and didn't mind. Nobody had ever been locked up here to piss his pants with dread of the hangman or the lynch mob. Men came and went as they liked. If some had died here (and they surely had), it hadn't been from lack of the freedom to walk out if they'd wished.

Slocum parked himself at the near corner of the bar, one foot comfortably on the edge of a big spittoon in lieu of a brass rail, his back to the wall. He settled himself to be aware of both the door and the rest of the room, and relaxed and sighed his relief. Not a respectable citizen in the place.

"Whiskey," said Slocum. "Not your goddamn bar slop, but the best you got."

"I got some rye," said the fat barman, who was breathing wetly into a glass and polishing it with a rag that Slocum wouldn't have used to rub down a mule.

"Leave the bottle," said Slocum happily.

9

There was one lamp hanging over the middle of the room—not far from the stove—and black-gray wisps

86

of smoke from the burning kerosene, which was generally called "coal oil," drifted toward the rafters and beams of the roof; the lamp had a round wick, so it threw a good deal of light. Slocum flicked his eyes at each of the drinkers in turn, all the way down to the single table with five chairs in the back where the older fellows sat, those with legs that wabbled after a few drinks. He recognized some faces from the Earthquake and the restaurant, but none from the Palace of Mirrors.

He was instantly aware that the word on Kid Slocum was universally out. Not a pair of eyes could hold steady under his gaze. There was here and there some furtive loosening of coats and jackets in the vicinity of holsters, but no open moves yet. Mainly the movements seemed to be for self-protection, not aggression. But there was one hell of a stack of coin on his head. Slocum cleared his throat and spat. The rye wasn't bad for frontier booze. He said loudly, "All right, I'm John Slocum. I ain't Kid Slocum. The sheriff knows that and he's letting me run free, so if anyone's considering turning me in, heels first or otherwise, forget it. I ain't on the peck for anybody here." He let his eyes focus wide so that nothing escaped them. "You-all know Yavapai Joe?"

One ranny, who looked like a top hand gone to seed, said, "I worked with him once in Texas."

"What kind of feller is he?"

"A bastard. Got a loud mouth."

"And a slow draw," said Slocum. "I had to hang up his hide for good just now. Happened in the jail, and the sheriff didn't make a big fuss. Which ought to convince anybody that that wanted flier ain't being taken serious by anybody but a lot of dismal yacks that believe there's money on my head. So let's all just drink peaceable and forget about trying for a bounty that wouldn't be paid, right?"

87

Several men said, "Right," and some more nodded. The barman said hesitantly, "Could I shake your hand? Yavapai Joe shot up my place last year and put a hole into Nellie."

"Who's Nellie?"

The fat man pointed at a nude portrait behind the bar. It had been done by an artist about two cuts above the one who'd drawn The Bull's Pizzle sign, evidently in crayon. "Shot her in the belly button, see?"

Joe had indeed. The slug-hole had been repaired by a piece of paper glued over it, which gave the reclining lady the appearance of having been born with a large, square white navel. "A man that'd do that," said Slocum judiciously, "would kick his best friend, if he had one."

The barman grinned. "Shake," he said again.

Slocum had known some who'd been gunned down that way. He drew his thumb-buster and held it in his left hand and reached over the bar with his right. The fat man was strong as an ox. Slocum gripped back hard and nearly made his knuckles pop. "Man of taste like yourself," said the bar-dog, who evidently admired his nude beyond the dictates of sense, "he's always welcome here." His eyes swiveled. "Anybody starts anything with this gentleman got me to deal with too," he said loudly.

Slocum took back his hand and pocketed his gun. He drank another glass of rye, watching from his right eye, but nobody took the challenge.

Well, maybe he could think things out here.

First there was that cryptic remark of Maynard Savage's: *You're entirely wrong about one of them— so be on your guard.* He'd been referring to the five people Slocum claimed to trust: Maynard himself, the dealer with TB, Bill McGunn, Amelia, and Brandy.

It didn't even occur to Slocum to doubt Maynard's word. What he talked about, he knew. If ever Slocum had met a man who impressed him that way, it was the gray Savage.

Brandy. There were a powerful number of unanswered questions about Brandy. Slocum purely hated to think ill of her, but by God when it came down to pawing dirt, all he knew was that she was tough as a deal board, fast as quicksilver on a steep slope when she handled her shotgun, and a hell of a romp in bed.

What had Savage said about her? Some odd phrase: the lady with the hay hook. That was it. Whatever the hell *that* meant. Slocum shook his head and poured out a little more rye on top of what he'd already put in the glass, absentminded-like.

What did she do? Man's work. But a man can do anything from breaking broncs to tending store, from rustling to preaching the gospel. *What* man's work? It had toughened her palms and given her the burnt-gold face of the long rider. Her clothes for the trail were as rough as a prospector's. And there was that damned shotgun, cut short to pulverize anything she aimed at. And her other weapons—good gracious God Almighty, Brandy couldn't be a hired gun? She'd make some star pistolero! He chuckled at the thought of the opposition when she'd throw back that coat and they caught sight of those tits of hers, just before they got their eyes closed forever.

There weren't any hired female slingers, surely? Belle Starr didn't count; she ran a robbers' roost west of Fort Smith in the Indian Territory, and was the brains behind a gang of rustlers and moonshiners, but Slocum had never heard tell of her killing anybody.

The only answer that made sense—and a damn poor kind of sense, but what other explanation could there be?—was that Brandy was a member of a floating outfit, who rode the country in winter branding late calves and mavericks for some big rancher. Then she'd never have to take off that furry, smelly bearskin. Slocum chewed on this notion a while. She'd be restricted to less than half a year's pay.

Ah, *hell!*

Maybe she was a high-priced fancy woman. She had the frame and the talent and the temperament for that. Yet, why the men's clothes, the masquerade as a boy, the appalling firearm? What would such a woman be doing in Retch, anyhow?

"Mother of Moses!" said John Slocum loudly. It had all clicked together.

Then the door whumped open and a man came in with a load of snow. He shook it off and bellied up to the bar beside Slocum. The albino buff coat identified Charles Tucker even at the perimeter of Slocum's dazed vision.

"Howdy, John. Have a drink?" He shoved his forefinger against the roots of his stallion-tail mustachios and carefully sleeked them down to get rid of the melted snow in them. He tilted back his hat. "You all right?" he asked.

"What? Yeah. Have a drink, Tucker." Slocum shoved over the bottle of rye and the barman set out another glass.

"You look like an elk stomped on your groin."

"Just about. You hear of the Kid Slocum bullshit?"

"All over. Is that what's itching you?"

"Hell, no. It's what I'm changing the subject to," Slocum said. "What in hell is a hay hook, Tucker?"

Tucker stared as if his companion had confessed to a blazing desire to rape the hot stove. At last he said slowly, "I've been in places where they put that name to a scythe. Why?"

"Scythe. The old man with the scythe. Death." Slocum laughed bitterly. "Death warned me about Death last night, Tucker."

"John, how much—how long have you been—well, painting your tonsils?"

Slocum looked at him and laughed again. "I'm not

90

on a high lonesome. I just put a lot of thoughts together."

"How'd they pan out?"

"Damn little color, except black. Have a drink."

"Look, John, I came in and offered you a drink, and this is the second time you've offered me one back without answering me, and I'm damned if I let you get roostered when nine-tenths of the town is laying for you." Tucker let his pale blue eyes roam the drinking room. "There's some slavering greedy jackals and coyotes right in here, working themselves up to be wolves. Best we back out and go someplace less populated."

"Hell, I like it here and the bottle's half-full." He poured both glasses to the brim.

"I've drunk a lot of your whiskey already," said Tucker, unfastening his huge white coat to the radiating heat. He had a brace of well-worn old Colt .44s in holsters tight to the flank.

"And I drunk yours last night too. Thought you favored carrying those in your pockets."

"That's another pair."

"Oh," said Slocum. What a fellow would do with four revolvers he couldn't imagine. Tucker had changed his gambler's clothes for Levi's and a wool shirt. He looked even bigger than he had last night. Both men were standing stiff upright and about half a step away from the bar, anticipating trouble without actually thinking much about it. Little things like that kept a man alive in the Territory. "I heard tell," said Slocum, "that a whole freight-car load of bounty hunters were showing up just about the time this storm turned into snow. You figure that Kid Slocum is headed this way?"

"What I heard," said Tucker briefly. He drank half the booze and set the glass down and then Slocum drank. As they talked, they kept up this alternation, again more from instinct than out of expressed thought. One of them was ready at any time, both hands free.

There was an unnatural quiet in the room; the wood popped and crackled in the stove and a few old bow-legged geezers straddling chairs at the far end yarned away in low tones.

"Could I ask where you heard it?"

"Here and there."

"Sheriff hasn't got wind of it yet, but I think Maynard Savage has. What the hell," said Slocum angrily, "if he come southwise from Tombstone, there's half a dozen places he coulda lit a shuck for besides Retch! My guess would be Agua Prieta, over the border, if the dumb anvilhead has the sense of a louse. But Jesus, *I* came down from Globe to Tucson to here, and if anybody was on *my* trail they'd have the whole fucking country from the Papagos west to New Mexico east to hunt through, not even taking in Sonora and Chihuahua! I don't calculate Kid Slocum told anybody where he was headed any more'n I did."

"You really aren't Kid Slocum?" asked Tucker diffidently.

It was John's turn to drink. He did so, and poured out the last of the rye. "Shit and tarnation! No! You hear my brains rattle when I shake my head?"

Tucker grinned. "All right, I believe you, and I'll side with you because you're outnumbered so bad you make Samson with his jackass jawbone look like a man pestered by flies. But we sure make a hell of a big double target standing here."

"The bardog likes me. I admired his girl's picture."

"And he's as much target as you and me put together."

"If the place makes you itch so, why don't you cut out?"

"Figure you can use an extra gun."

"Or four. Yeah. Well, I didn't ask for it, but it's my fight—by God," said Slocum, struck by the idea, "if that ain't the story of my life, nothing is—so I'll stand for it, but you needn't."

"I have a partiality to long odds," said Tucker.

"Well, in my position I suppose I gotta admire that." Slocum drained his glass. "Down the bar. Gent in the John B. that used to be white."

"Watch him. I got my eye on a nasty specimen in a red neckerchief and an old Confederate frock coat at a table. Can't see his hands, but his eyes are fixed to do something silly any minute."

The urge to collect the bounty hit both of the loungers at the same instant. Slocum whammed out his thumb-buster and took the dirty-white-hatted skunk just three inches below the brim with a slug that turned his face into a mess, while Tucker filled both his hands and put lead through his man, one and then a second with scarcely a blink between them. He was one of the very few men whom Slocum had seen who actually could shoot both left and right with only a quick sucked-in breath between the triggering. The standing enemy sprawled back and dropped a big hog-leg with a clatter before he hit the plank floor himself; the other catapulted backward and got his corpse all tangled with a couple of chairs, knocking the men who'd been sitting in them catawampus.

"More a-coming," said Slocum, carefully thumbing off a shot into the middle of a knot of jaspers who were all pawing for their weapons. A tall lean gink with no teeth and one eye reached around and hauled up a rifle. Slocum maimed him with a bullet that cut through his forearm and into his elbow. The barman was bringing up a shotgun. Slocum yelled at him, "No! Get down!" and the fat man dropped: it must have occurred to him, as it had to Slocum, that he owned the place and couldn't up and run away when the fight was done. Through the racket, Slocum could hear him grumbling down there behind the openwork bar, swearing blue and bloody words in a steady stream.

Damn, if there'd only been a side to this thing that a man could duck behind! It was nothing but sawhorses and the huge plank. Slocum, crouching, got the crosspieces of a sawhorse in front of him and fired between them and took a cowhand in the gut just as the fellow's slug whined past his ear. Tucker was off to the left, standing straight up and firing left and right and left and scoring every time, from the sound of it—the howls and curses and yelps and *thunks* of lead ripping solid flesh and bone. He looked like a man on a shooting range, knocking bottles off a fence.

The great advantage they had was that there were too many disorganized shooters after them now. The Bull's Pizzle was jammed and everybody got in somebody else's way. A couple of slugs rang off the iron stove and sang around among them, scaring hell out of those who weren't too tanked up to care. A man shooting at you is a mean danger but a ricochet is blind and somehow more horrible. There were men down and dead too, and they made hellish stumbling blocks. A couple of men who looked like low-grade war-hands tilted the round table up on edge and had themselves a better fort than Slocum. They began firing around it and Slocum felt a sharp punch in the ribs under his left arm. He waited a second till one of the bastards stuck his head out, and shot him along the side of the face, giving him something to think about; the pistol flew from the man's grip as he screeched and clawed at the wound. Slocum knew he was out of cartridges. Kneeling there on one knee, sore as a boil at the fate that had brought him to a bar without thick mahogany sidepieces, he pulled his elkskin back as he dropped the thumb-buster into the pocket, and stroked out his other .45.

Tucker exchanged his pair for the second couple—also Colt .44s—from his buffalo coat. He held one out, arm's length and steady, and carefully put a shot into the tipped table. A body pitched out from behind it and fell on its face.

A scruffy gent in an antique beaver, who was likely

94

a tinhorn with an itch for prize money, made the fatal error of aiming a rickety .36-caliber five-shooter at Slocum from very close. Slocum snapped a shot at the idiot across his own body, being squatted at an angle to him, and the shabby one folded in half and collapsed, giving a cold-faced shark behind him a clear view of Slocum.

Slocum went flat and rolled between the sawhorses under the bar. He steadied himself at once with his left arm on the floor and shot up into the shark's throat. The gullet exploded with a crimson gush. That left Slocum three bullets, and no time in the near future to reload. "Goddamn!" he roared, rolling back out from under the gigantic plank and coming to his feet. "Time to haul freight, Tucker!"

The man in the albino coat coolly killed two men charging up the room toward them. "I'll cover you."

Slocum, wounded but without pain, pounced the few yards at a crouch, hearing Tucker's guns crashing behind him. "Come on!" he yelled. Tucker backed up till he stood at the door, a great pale target in his unique coat against the blackened boards. Slocum had fished out a double eagle from his shirt pocket; he flung it at the bar-dog, hitting him on the ear. "That's for the bottle," he roared, "and the lamp!" Then he raised his .45 and put a slug into the fat bright glass belly of the hanging oil lamp.

It exploded like a kerosene grenade, spouting and hurling blazing oil in a fireworks display that Slocum under other circumstances would have paid to see. The big blobs of flame fell among the struggling, raging gang of men, and Tucker coldly chose two who were still aiming through the splatter of boiling hot liquid and shot them dead, one in the heart and one in the forehead. Then he and Slocum were backing out side by side, nearly jamming the doorway. A stray bullet or two whistled past them or thunked into the planks, but mostly the squalid crew were dancing and flapping their

95

arms and yipping with sharp pain as the burning coal oil dripped down their necks, set their hats afire, or seared the backs of their hands.

"Want to wait here and pick 'em off?" Tucker asked, reloading like a fast machine.

"We killed enough. We can disappear in the snow before one of 'em makes the door," said Slocum curtly. He walked away toward the western end of town, milking cartridges from his belt and filling his own cylinders. "You're good," he said. "You're damn good, Tucker. Handy as hell to have you around with that quartet of lead pushers." They were out of sight of The Bull's Pizzle already—in fact, out of sight of everything but snow. Slocum chuckled. "I hope that oil didn't get onto poor Nellie."

"Who in God's name is Nellie? The bartender?"

"No! The lady with the square white belly button, hanging behind the bar. That's why the fat boy wanted to join up with us with his shotgun. I admired her pretty fierce, and he appreciated that."

"You're a strange one, Slocum."

"Want to make certain my horse is being took care of proper," said Slocum, as they approached the livery barn. He was deliberately as ungrammatical as he could get, to confuse the other man further. They plowed to the double doors and went in.

It was cold as an old whore's heart in the place. The stableman hunkered forlorn beside a small pot of a stove. "Gents," he said, looking up.

"Can't you warm up this goddamn barn a little?" said Slocum angrily.

"How?"

Well, it was a reasonable question. Short of setting it afire, there wasn't any way. Slocum went to his horse's stall. There were two blankets over the black gelding and the light harness that held them in place wasn't too tight for comfort; the special oats he'd

96

bought were in the trough, and the straw was pretty clean. Slocum looked into the stalls on either side. Those horses were all right too. They'd all be chilly, but they wouldn't freeze. The man had done everything he could for them. Even, Slocum noted, to cracking up the scum of ice on the drinking water and throwing out the bigger pieces of it. He went back to the stove.

"Sorry, friend. You're doing a good job."

"Best I can. Only wish I had the stove outen the Palace o' Mirrors."

"Maybe Slocum can get it for you," Tucker said. "He's a friend of Mr. Savage."

The rheumy eyes flicked upward. "Kid Slocum?"

"No. John Slocum."

Something passed between them that he couldn't have put a name to: something that had to do with a mutual admiration for horses, a desire to see them comfortable against the time when they'd be asked to work their asses off and possibly to die in service, and an unspoken, maybe not even understood trust in another man who felt the same way. "Right. But if anyone asks, which they may, I ain't seen you and I don't have no horse of yours."

"If they gun me down by mistake," said Slocum on impulse, "the gelding's yours. He's a good nag, a long horse."

"Knowed that from handling him. Don't worry about him."

"I won't," said Slocum, and instead of tipping the man, thrust out his hand and shook hard. "He's got enough oats there for another week, I judge."

"Yep. I'm feeding him other truck too, you know. Can't stick just to oats, ain't good for 'em."

"Right." Slocum pictured the old man's expression if Slocum were gunned down and in a week or so the oats were low enough in their heavy burlap sack to disclose the golden fifty-dollar pieces, better than eight

97

thousand dollars' worth. Slocum's playing money and his winnings from last night were at the hotel, but his loot from the long spell in the Earthquake was hidden right here in the livery barn.

Maybe the old fellow would buy the biggest stove west of the Mississippi!

"Where to now?" said Tucker, having checked his own horse.

"I got to pick up some food at the grease castle, and then go get some sleep."

As they left the stable and walked down the street, a man came out of the storm, looming right before them. He recognized them, screeched, and disappeared backwards like a ghost.

"Must have been somebody from that saloon we just smoked," said Tucker, and chuckled. "Can you locate the hotel for me, pard?"

"Sure." Slocum went on a ways and said, "Ought to be about here." He'd missed it by only a few feet, they found as they veered left. With a word they parted.

He came into the restaurant, eyeing the mob, and with his Colt in his hand for everybody to see, announced, "There's about twenty knotheads at The Bull's Pizzle with sawdust in their beards this minute. Anybody twitches, I'll be happy to boost their ranks. Got that?"

As he walked to the counter, someone called out, "No man never gunned down twenty men in one fight!"

"That's a fact, but how many friends you figure I got waiting outside that door?" Slocum snarled, and paid for his basket and picked it up.

No one budged. The cook said, "Sheriff'd like to see you if you can spare the time."

In the front office of the jail were McGunn and his intended, the green-eyed ash-blond jolly-looking little Amelia Schmidt, all swaddled up in six or eight shawls and coats and a bustle and a long sacque of serge with green stripes and a thick strip of wet black feathers down the front. Her round face was still as pretty to Slocum as a Cupid in a painting.

"Miss Amelia, ma'am," he said politely. "Bill, there's a satchelful of fresh relics at The Bull's—at The Bull Saloon. But I'll bet you a porcupine-quill vest that none of 'em ever get reported to you. Just see by this time tomorrow if I'm right."

"Why?"

"It'll prove something I've told you already, and I'm like to tell you again, is why. You wanted to see me?" He glanced around; Yavapai Joe's carcass had been removed, probably to lie beside yesterday's frozen remains outside the door. Kinkaid and Adams were likewise gone. "What's the problem this time, son?"

"My father wants you to take dinner with us to-night," said Amelia in her lovely rippling-brook voice.

"Why?" said Slocum blankly.

"If Mr. Schmidt intended to arrest you, he'd have me there, wouldn't he?" McGunn demanded.

Slocum gave him a long look. "Oh, I suppose," he said at last. "Thank you, Miss Amelia. I'll be happy to come. How do I get there?"

"It's the second house over the low ridge, west of the telegraph office. My father's had stakes driven along the road and a rope strung between them from the office to our house."

"What time?"

"Eight."

10

Brandy was awake as Slocum entered the room. She watched him shake the snow off in the hallway and step inside and bolt the door. She said, "You've had three visitors."

"Anybody you know?"

"Three yacks. I had the clerk pile them out back on top of the buffalo skinner."

"Oh," said Slocum, shedding his outer clothes, hanging the elkskin on two wall hooks to dry and his pants on another. He slung his holstered gun on top of his gear and put the thumb-buster into its hanging case beside the bed. "So the lady with the hay hook did the honors in my absence."

"What in hell's that mean?"

"I figured out who you are, honey. I mean what you are. Took me so long, I reckon, because you're such a great partner on the feathers. Did they come one at a time or all together?"

"Two and then one. The clerk said he didn't tell them, that they just walked by him. I suppose the news about where you're staying is all over the place now too."

"Yeah," he said, shucking down wearily, "I guess it would be. At least they're not liable to shoot through the window; there's a snowbank halfway up the glass."

"So what am I?" she asked, sitting up with the blankets under her chin. Her wide eyes had gone all hard turquoise.

"You never did lie to me about it," he said, walking back and forth checking on things, naked as a little Mexican dog. "But you sure gave me taffy about a sight of stuff."

"Like what?" She sounded as offended as a virgin who'd just experienced her first ass-pinch.

"You know better'n I do." He slid into bed, sighing involuntarily. "I think I'm too tired to prong you," he said, shaking his head in surprise.

"You said I gave you taffy about a lot of things!"

"Right." He groaned at the pleasure of snuggling down till his head dented the pillow. "Say, love, there's a basket full of food over there. Why don't you dish it out? Eat a bite before we go to sleep." He closed his eyes and began to hum; the tune was "The Devil's Dream," a grand old fiddle stomp.

"God blast you to Halifax and spit your soul on a fishhook, John Slocum—"

"All right!" He snapped his eyes open, dark and bloodshot. He gave her a look that would have cut a diamond in half. "You know 'em as well as me, but here goes! You caught that amateur curly wolf, Knots Barker, fair and square, but you wouldn't take him to the sheriff to collect the bounty—"

"It was only $25, you red-assed baboon!"

"Still, it was money, and you had him memorized, all his weapons and everything. But you wanted to stick close to me because you'd been trailing me a long time. So you let him go, gave up $25 for $2,000. I remember exactly what you said. 'Not worth the pester to walk all that way.' Two, three hundred yards!

"And when you were still playing boy, you made sure you had a weapon at hand, in case that flier on me was right and I *was* crazy; you even carried the throwing knife to the bathroom and back, were wearing it when you made your grand entrance. And you'd made sure before that that I liked girls, probably figured I wouldn't go loco with one as handsome as you —but if I had, there was your .44 by your head.

"Then you were really dejected after we made love the first time, and handed me that slurp about female animals being mournful after rutting," he went on, gathering steam. "Hogslop! You were sad because all of a sudden you didn't want to take me in! To blow my backbone in half because you wouldn't dare try it with me alive—that gnawed on you considerable, didn't it! It still does now and then."

"How the fucking dadblame hell would you know?" she screamed at him.

"Because I feel the same way about you! I wouldn't

101

want to harm the littlest fleck of a freckle on your ass! But *I* don't have to, and if you still intend to claim the reward on Kid Slocum, *you* do. You have to take my life, after we gave each other our lives time and again! And in spite of what's between us, you *do* mean to count coup on me, and stick that two thousand in your Levi's, and it's tearing you to flinders!"

"Shit!" she howled, throwing off the soogans and bounding out of bed so she could do a kind of enraged war dance. "Shit-shit-shit! Who told you any such goddamn lies?"

"I figured it, with an assistance from Maynard Savage, who called you the lady with the hay hook. Go on back, though, or I'll forget some of it. I asked what you did for a living and you said, 'Man's work,' and wouldn't explain. That narrows it way down." He barked a laugh. "I tried to make you out a four-up driver, a mustanger, a hand in a floating outfit—anything that'd account for your weathered parts as opposed to your satiny stretches. Anything that would let you go disguised as a boy. But nothing washed."

"I'm just an ordinary hand, free-lancing—"

"No, that hound won't hunt, Brandy. Girl like you in a bunkhouse all year round, she'd have to do things, have things done to her, that you'd never stand for. You're a lady, for God's sake."

She scratched her ribs through the white gown. "A lady?"

"In the way I'm meaning it, you're goddamn right! But if you were a professional mantracker, a bounty hunter, you could live and travel alone, and them you dealt with would know you by rep and keep their hands to themselves, or have their blood let out and the daylight let in."

"A bounty hunter?" she exclaimed, and cinched in the middle of her nightgown with both hands so that the slim waist looked even more slender than before

102

under the jut of the beautiful bosom. "Oh, this is insane," she said, getting back into bed. "Make me a cigarette."

"In a minute. Now God alone knows how you ever came to the trade, but that's what you do, and unless you have an explanation for all those things I just said that's any better, then I *know* you're after my scalp. And it gravels me because underneath you blazing well *know* that I ain't Kid Slocum, but you've had it in your head so long that I am, you won't let loose of it! You really have yourself convinced, an otherwise smart little cuss like you, that I am an insane murderer of helpless bank tellers and a big-time robber."

"No I don't," she said sullenly.

"And you intend to blow my brains out and tote my hide, or maybe just my head cut off and pickled in whiskey, to Tombstone for that reward."

"Only when I'm sure beyond any doubt," she muttered, not looking at him.

"Listen," he said reasonably, reaching for a hand which she pulled out of reach, "I was going to light out for Tombstone because I got to hating this burg so bad I could taste it in my tonsils. Then I met you, and I stayed. When I heard about the Kid Slocum shit, I still had time to get out ahead of the worst of the norther and make it to Agua Prieta in Mexico, which is a damn sight nicer place to be snowed in; but there was you, so I stuck. The sheriff is a tenderfoot from the ears down, but he's no moron, and he's letting me roam on my own word that I'll stay in Retch. Before I knew how you earn your money, I knew from your own mouth that you figured I was Kid Slocum. But, I thought I could change your mind when we'd got to know each other really well."

"Where's all this heading for?"

"I'm still staying put, even though the town's ninety-nine percent after my life. Two reasons: I gave my

103

word to McGunn, and I want some more days and nights with you, Brandy. What you do for a living ain't my affair, so long as you don't decide to hang my hair on your belt alongside however many others you've gunned down. No," he said, thinking, "three reasons: out there in that white hell somewhere there's an old man trying to get to Tombstone and prove I'm innocent."

"Who?"

"Spring Fawn's brother. He's about a hundred and six and he's out there with an old horse to sleep in overnight, a bottle of my bourbon, and enough good will to shame Santy Claus. He means to find out everything about Kid Slocum that ain't on that poster. He'll listen and ask questions and come back when he's proved it wasn't me did the robbing and killing. So I can't hardly crawl away like a common cur with a yellow stripe before he gets back, can I?" He grabbed at her hand, caught it this time, and squeezed hard. "Can't you promise, honey, to wait that long? If an old Indian, a perfect stranger to me, is risking his life for the facts, can't you just wait?"

"Johnny," she said, abruptly soft and husky, "Johnny dear, do you believe I'd just have gunned you down without warning? Do you know me so little?"

"There's an important side to you I didn't know at all till today, Brandy."

"That's so. I'll be fair. You're right. But I promise you'll have warning when—I mean if—I come after you."

"I'll accept that word," said Slocum. "And now I'll make us some smokes, and we'll have a meal." He slid out of bed and went over to fish the makings out of his shirt.

She yipped. "You were shot!" she said.

"What?" he said, startled. Then he remembered. "Jesus to Betsy, I clean forgot it! It hasn't hurt since

104

it happened." He lifted his left arm and craned his neck down. On his naked side a gray-black lump of lead thrust out, a trickle of dried blood lining down from it.

"If that don't beat all," said Slocum. "Twenty-two, looks like. Probably fired from a derringer the full length of The Bull's Pizzle; either that or the cartridge was stale and didn't have much power. I felt a sharp little thud and knew I was hit, and by thunder if I didn't go and let it slip my mind."

"Come here and let me take it out," she said, sitting up in bed and looking as desirable as she had before he'd known she was a killer by trade.

"No trouble." He took it between his fingers and jerked it loose. The hole began to bleed again. "Like pulling a cork from a bottle that's close to empty. Smarts a little now, but it's nothing." He checked on his elkskin jacket, then got tobacco and papers from his shirt. "I had my coat open and it missed that, but my shirt caught a hole. I'll be switched," he said mildly.

"Come here!"

"Coming." He sat down on the edge of the bed and she took one of the two quarts of Double Stamp, opened it, and carefully poured some into the wound. "I ought to bandage it."

"It ain't hardly more'n a dent," Slocum said. He laughed. "I bet there was fourteen pounds of lead whistling around that saloon, and all I got was a bitty old tooth-filling of a slug."

She put a bandage on it in spite of his protests, saying she hated blood on her blankets. Then she set out the food as they'd done before, while he built a couple of cigarettes. The damn whiskey stung his scratch, and he swallowed three or four ounces to dull the pain. They ate without talking, both of them ravenous; then she said, hesitant, "You want to make love, Johnny?"

"I'm not half as tired as I was," he said, and rolled her sideways and began to stroke her gently all over.

"Oh *Jesus* will you please *aiyee!* put it in?" she begged him, and then let out the first of a series of caterwauls that would have shamed a bitch wolf in heat.

He slipped his ramrod up her wide-open crotch and began to piston back and forth with tremendous strokes. If she'd yowled before, she really bayed the moon like a full pack now. Slocum hadn't exactly been saving himself for this during the past couple of days, and it took him some time. He was tired but it didn't matter. She climaxed again and again, until finally he felt himself rushing toward his own finish and rammed his elbows into the tick and seemed to enter her with everything he had clear back to his ass. The world spun around him as he drowned in her and went out of his head very satisfactorily. Luxuriating, as he came out of the whirl, he felt his final spurtings go up that all-but-insatiable flue and grinned to himself as he felt her body sag.

This was one bounty hunter who wasn't going to wake up and blow out his brains in the next few hours.

He pulled out and forced himself to struggle out of bed and crack the basin ice to bathe his privates in cold, cold water. When he came back the girl was as sound asleep as some old gristle-heel after a three-day toot. He climbed in, rolled a smoke, enjoyed it, loosened his .45 in the holster next to his head, took a last big bite of raisin pie, hauled the blankets to his nose and fell into oblivion.

When he finally woke up, Brandy lay motionless in the exact position he'd seen her in—when had it been? —a little after noon.

He dressed, took her derringer, and wrote her a note on an old envelope from his war-bag. *Been invited to meet the gentry of Retch. Back early. Get prettied up to play some poker, sweetheart. Sincerely, Jeb Stuart.* He stuck this on the door with her throwing knife, went out and locked the place up, slid the key back under the door, and took off, whistling.

The rope was there as promised. Slocum edged along beside it until he came to its end. He couldn't see anything whatever. He inched forward and kicked against a board: the step of a house. He went up onto a porch that he couldn't see, groped till he found the door frame, and knocked. The marrow in his bones was frostbit.

A great blaze of light opened before him, in which a man stood waiting. "Mr. Slocum?"

"That's me."

"Come in, man, come in." The door shut behind him. He found that the explosion of light had only seemed brilliant; the parlor was actually lit only by a good fire and two white-shaded Rayo brass lamps. The antimacassars and doilies lent a feminine touch to a pleasant, typical frontier-town home of the upper class. The furniture was imported from back East, massive and dark, and there were family gewgaws in little open-face cabinets. The warmth was a panacea for all Slocum's ills, thrown out by a roaring fire of fragrant apple wood (also certainly imported at much expense, but worth it); the wood's scent was laced with the bitter smoke of good cigars, the tang of old bourbon, and the light flowery traces of Amelia's perfume. Slocum hadn't been inside a house like this for years. He politely scraped and shook the load of snow onto a thick cotton rug that was spread before the door for that purpose, stomped his boots and wiped them, and slapped his hat clean before stepping on the curlicued woven carpet.

"Nice of you to have me," he said, sticking out his hand and adding "sir" out of all-but-forgotten Southern politeness.

"Very good of you to come through this dreadful night for a stranger," said Henry Schmidt, shaking his hand firmly. Although he had the big voice of a wrestler with two pounds of gravel in his throat, he was actually a slight man, brown and dry-looking, clean-

shaven and barbered and pomaded neatly. His haber-
dashery was solemn; his shirt was of the boiled variety.
A gold-nugget stickpin glowed in his tie and a sizeable
diamond glittered from one finger. "You'll need a
drink. I believe you know Jim Kinkaid and Chris
Adams?"

There sat Mr. Cholera and Mr. Smallpox themselves in overstuffed chairs by the fire. They nodded.
Slocum nodded. Henry Schmidt beamed, as though
he'd brought about the reunion of old school chums.
He poured out, thank God, a real man-sized glass of
bourbon from a cut-glass decanter and handed it to
Slocum. Slocum said thanks and here's to happy days,
and drank half of it in one long swallow. Slowly his
bones began to warm up toward the zero mark.

He took a seat at the far end of the sofa and lit a
thin dark "long nine" cigar handed him by his host. He
took a draft and complimented Schmidt on his taste.

"I have a barrel of them, sent me from the Connec-
ticut Valley. Less than a thousand left, I suppose," said
Schmidt, perching next to him. "We came from that
part of New England, you know, Amelia and I, several
years ago. Her mother is gone," he said, hushed, looking into his crystal bourbon glass as if it held a drink of
the River Styx. Then, brightening, "They tell me there
was quite a Colt serenade this morning in The Bull's,
ah, The Bull Tavern."

"Kind of a quick little dust-up, yes. A lot of people
seem to think I'm a badly wanted character called Kid
Slocum."

"Sheriff McGunn says you're not."

"That's true. He's got good sense. In some directions," Slocum added deliberately. Nobody picked up
on it. "His old deputy is out in this convulsion of nature on his way to Tombstone to clear up the charge."

"That redskin's dead by now," said Adams sourly.
"No man could live in that storm."

"Don't kill him off before they bring in the carcass," said Slocum mildly. "He wouldn't have started out if he hadn't been fair-to-middling sure he could make it."

Amelia came in from the kitchen looking heavenly in a blue balmoral skirt and a basque waist protected by an enormous apron of white linen. Her blond hair was freshly bunned and impeccably sleek and shining. Her eyes twinkled at Slocum, who smiled at her and leaped to his feet.

"I believe you have met Mr. Slocum, my dear?"

"I've had that pleasure."

"In rougher surroundings, I'm afraid," said Slocum, and wondered whether, now that he'd gone back in time to the precise and fantastic convolutions of his boyhood speech, he could manage to get away from them and sound human. "You look marvelous, Miss Amelia. Don't tell me you've been doing the cooking?"

"No, supervising. I hope you like filet of buffalo?" she asked, sounding as if she really cared about his taste. "Garnished with mushrooms? We still had a few fine ones in the cellar."

"My favorite dish," said Slocum.

"Have we time for another whiskey for our guest, Amelia?"

"Oh, plenty."

Schmidt refilled Slocum's glass, even higher this time. Slocum drew on his long nine and sat down, as the girl took a straight-backed chair near the sofa.

After he'd taken some swallows, Slocum lifted his glass and noted that it had been brimmed a third time. Schmidt must be under the impression that he could either loosen Slocum's tongue or muddle his wits for what was plainly to come later, which evidently had to do with Maynard Savage. Slocum drank off the tumbler without pause. He'd never taken on a talking load or been liquored into being a sucker in his life, but Schmidt couldn't know that. The three glasses had just

109

taken the chill out of his frame. He thanked his host gravely for a fourth.

At the dinner table, Slocum listened carefully to his host's voice, inflections, and opinions, and came to the tentative conclusion that Schmidt was of the same breed as his two friends: a pious, swallow-tailed, shad-bellied galoot who talked a lot of high-flown twaddle while studying all the time how to steal a thousand acres of grassland and enough hot tar to pave it.

He looked across at Amelia and with his eyes undressed her to the waist for the twentieth time. She'd removed her white apron and the hundred-buttoned blue-and-white basque waist fitted her natural form just this side of immodesty, at least to the frankly carnal eye of John Slocum. Her roly-poly Germanic breasts were even more evident than they'd been in the checkered gingham in which he'd first seen her. He speculated on the probable color and size of her nipples. It made the meal pass pleasurably.

Amelia stood up. "I'll leave you men to your cigars and brandy," she said quietly, looking at Slocum. "And say good night, too; it's been a long day. I do hope we'll see you again, Mr. Slocum."

"Thank you, ma'am; I'll certainly be in and out of the sheriff's office," he replied, grinning and bowing to her. He watched her from the corner of his eye as she swept out. Her room was on the southern side of the house, opening off the dining room, which meant from the arrangement of doors that Henry Schmidt slept on the north side, two rooms away. He made a mental note of it.

They went into the parlor to have brandy in big round glass shells. The booze was 3-Star Hennessey. Slocum preferred whiskey, but forced himself to drink half a pint or so for politeness. The three somber worthies stared at him silently. Finally, Schmidt said, "We want you to do a job for us."

110

Slocum, who'd been afraid that he'd have to haze the talk around to the subject over a long spell, finished his brandy and set down the glass with relief. "Shoot," he said, building a smoke.

Schmidt leaned forward, his lean dry face tightened up over the cheekbones, and in a low, gritty tone said, "We want you to kill a man."

"I'm not a hired gun."

"This is a civic thing we're asking, for the good of the community. It's a necessary act. You're very fast with your weapons but we see you as an honest man—" *oh,* thought Slocum cynically, *sure you do—* "and we believe you'll understand why we're asking you after you've heard the whole matter."

"How about your sheriff?"

"He couldn't do it," said Adams with scorn. "He couldn't outdraw a horned toad with arthritis."

"Then why in hell did you put him in office?"

"That's beside the point. We think you're the only man in Retch who could manage this job properly," said Schmidt. He got up and closed the door to the other room.

"We want you to kill Savage," said Jim Kinkaid.

11

Slocum reached the whiskey decanter and sloshed a ten-minute supply into his brandy snifter. He swished it around and guzzled some. Then he crossed his legs to bring his Peacemaker within easy reach. "Oh?" he said, and waited.

"To explain that, I'll have to tell you about this town," said Schmidt, pouring himself some more brandy and making much play with cutting and lighting a cigar.

"I got the time."

111

Schmidt coughed, with a sound like rattling pebbles in a sluiceway, and launched into his yarn. The silver mines in the nearby mountains had been discovered perhaps ten years before; they'd been worked, but not as expertly and profitably as those in the Tombstone hills. First Adams and Kinkaid, then later Schmidt when he came out from New England with his young daughter, had begun buying up the claims. Some they got cheaply, some cost them dear when word leaked out that they were buying. But about three years ago they'd realized that all the silver claims known hereabouts at last belonged to the three of them. They went into a loose partnership, each of them holding about a third of the producing territory. They'd imported men to work the mines—experienced fellows, rough and tough but hard toilers—and they'd paid well. They'd formally founded Retch, which up till then had been nothing but a saloon and the Earthquake gambling room.

Good people had come: Bud Chimneyworth the undertaker, Clabe Jones who ran the general store, Old Man Rascoe who'd built the gigantic livery barn single-handed and had a wonderful touch with horses, Cicero Welch the outfitter, Red Bass the telegrapher, and a few others. Unfortunately they'd never had a regular preacher, not even a circuit rider. There weren't enough kids to warrant a school, so Amelia taught the young-uns. George De Moss who had the little billiard parlor was a fine fellow too.

Slocum had played cards with George De Moss in the Earthquake, and privately considered that he'd slit his grandma's weasand for a mangy raccoon pelt and a bottle of cold piss. But he only nodded.

"Alas!" said Schmidt, rolling up his dry-looking eyes to an incomprehensible Heaven, "at the same time, that's three years ago give or take a month, Savage and his dreadful crew appeared from Kansas City—"

"On the run, most likely," said Adams.

112

"And the Palace of Mirrors was built. A plague spot."

Slocum had been trying to remember if he'd ever heard a man exclaim, "Alas!" But this brought him back to the tale. "Wait a minute," he said, "the Palace of Mirrors is the only safe, clean place in that whole town till you cross the ridge and get out here. Why in everlasting torment do you label it a plague spot?"

Well, Schmidt went on, it was a focus for half of the badmen in the Territory. They drifted in, got their orders from Savage, went out again on raiding parties—

"You mean paint up like Indians?" Slocum was bewildered.

"No, they raid distant farms, towns, banks and so on, then hightail it back here and they're safe. Savage protects them. Gunmen on the run. Highwaymen who work the passes and trails from Old Mexico. Cattle and horse thieves. They all hide here when things grow hot for them. Then there are the nightriders who raid across the border into Sonora and Chihuahua for beef. Retch has become a haven for outlaws, or at least for the chosen ones who pay tribute to Maynard Savage. We'd do anything to clean it up, but—"

"Why don't you import a marshal, somebody like Tilghman or even Hickok?"

Schmidt smiled thinly. "One man against all these wolves?"

"That was a pretty good description of Abilene once, and Dodge City and Kansas City—only took one good man with a marshal's badge to tame each one."

"There are hundreds, *hundreds,* sir, of unsavory characters under the thumb of Savage."

"So you think I could blow him away and everything would be dandy?" Slocum demanded. "None of those hundreds of faithful and loyal retainers would lift a paw against me? I wouldn't be ripped into dog-

113

meat? Nobody would take over and run the town the same way it's being run now?"

"Savage has the brains. None of the others do. We could—"

"You could crap in your vest pocket. Nothing would happen except maybe they'd all run wild and level your homes, steal what you own, rape your women, roast you over slow fires, and sow the ground hereabouts with salt. If what you say is true, Savage is the only reason you don't need a genuine lawdog here. He'd stand between you, his front, his camouflage, and all those slimy ruffians."

Schmidt winked. "You leave that to us. We have plans. But Savage must be gotten out of the way first. An official lawman couldn't do it; Savage covers his track well. But if a gunman such as yourself—"

He let the sentence hang in the air between them. Slocum said coolly, "I am not a gunman. I carry a gun, as almost anyone over nine years old does, and I can use it. I don't hire it out. I don't assassinate, which is what this deal would amount to if I meant to escape with my life. I shoot a man if he's shooting at me. If you think you'd be better off with Maynard Savage dead, you'd best hire a squad of top-pay gunnies— gunnies, gents, as opposed to plain honest gunfighters; and even they'd have a bitch of a time trying to get at the quarry. Or else send the information you've just passed to me on to Washington, and maybe you can get a troop, or even a squadron, from the regular Army to ride down here and clean out the hive of murderous ragtag and bobtail that calls itself Retch." He stopped himself as he saw their expressions toughening. He wanted all the information he could suck from them. So he quit being honest and, going all wily on them, purred, "However, it might be that we won't have to rile up the U.S. Government. Tell me what else these scum do."

114

It had been almost too late in coming; suspicion lingered in the squinted eyes, and Slocum cussed himself for a jackass that brayed too quick and too righteous. But then Schmidt appeared to relax, and sipped his liquor and puffed his cigar and grinned narrowly.

"We've offended you by appearing to consider you a badman. I assure you, Mr. Slocum, no badman would ever be invited to my table no matter how much I required his services. We need a *good* man, one with skills that you have and we don't. I offered you the job clumsily because I hadn't thought it out sufficiently —you see, when I heard of you from Bill McGunn, I looked on you as an answer to a prayer, and it never occurred to me what a delicate matter it would be to, ah, to broach."

"Never meant to jump down your throat like I did," said Slocum, off-hand and careless as he could manage. "It's just being taken for a loose gun with a vacant head behind it that riled me. You go ahead, sir."

Adams still eyed him suspiciously. Kinkaid huffed and puffed in irritation, looking malevolent. But, Schmidt was too anxious to enlist him, and plunged on.

"One of their chief targets is Skeleton Canyon. Their other main choice for the site of robbery and murder is Box Canyon. Do you know it?"

"I've seen plenty of box canyons, been trapped in a couple, but I gather you're speaking of a particular one," said Slocum.

"Yes. That's what it's called, just Box Canyon. It lies southeast of here, not far, where New and Old Mexico corner in next to the Arizona Territory. It's a hellish place, so deep that neither man nor horse can escape via the sides, and it's on another of the regular routes between the two countries. Just a handful of men, half of them at each end, can bottle up and slaughter and loot a train of laden pack mules, a Spanish grandee's carriage, a string of good horses or even

115

a bunch of cattle that have already been stolen and are being spirited away by other, unrelated thieves." He babied his snifter in both hands, staring into the little amber pool at the bottom, as reverent as a parson mulling over a passage in Revelations.

Slocum could have puked right on his expensive carpet.

"Lord knows how many innocent victims lie in shallow graves in those two sinister valleys, Mr. Slocum—perhaps just beside the corpses of wicked, lawless men slain by their own kind."

With an effort, Slocum prevented himself from exclaiming, "Amen, brother!" What he did say was, "Terrible thing, Mr. Schmidt. It's hard to believe there's so much villainy all around us, as we sit here in this humble, honest home."

He had seldom laid it on so thick and sticky. But by Jesus if they didn't all three rise to the bait! Kinkaid nodded and Adams said, "You might wonder how honest men come to know so much about this matter?"

"It flitted across my mind."

"The fools talk of it openly. Jim and I have heard it discussed in the Palace of Mirrors as though it were as common as the weather."

Slocum glanced at Henry Schmidt, who said, "I don't gamble, never have, so I don't hear these things; but I don't consider cards or dice a sin, if you're thinking that!" He produced a rattling laugh. "My own vices are practiced in this room—old brandy and fine tobacco."

Slocum contributed his own imitation of laughter. "What a dull world it would be without a vice or two," he said, momentarily attempting to add up his own. "Well, gentlemen, you do have a problem, but I doubt you can solve it by eliminating Colonel Savage. You folks are his front, after all—his pride and joy. I haven't a doubt that he protects you and your families from the desperadoes who'd like to treat all of you

116

the same way they treat their trail victims. Then if word got to high places that Retch was a nesting ground for bandits and organized gangs, Savage could say, 'Why hell, that's ridiculous, look at all the fine people who live here! Ask them!' "

"Then you won't draw him into a fight and kill him for us?"

"You let me give it some thought," said Slocum heartily. "Like I say, it seems to me a bad idea; but I'll sleep on it. Maybe I can come up with a sounder notion."

Slocum stood up. He figured he'd heard enough, and wanted to chew it up and spit out the real shape of things. "Getting on toward time to wager a few chips, I reckon. I thank you for your hospitality and the offer, Mr. Schmidt. I'll be speaking with you sooner'n you can say 'skunk.' " He put on the doeskin jacket he'd hung beside the front door, made certain his Colt was covered against the snow, and donned the black John B. They crowded around him, urging him to think hard, not to jump to conclusions, and so forth. His hand was shaken, his back thumped. Then he was in the blizzard again.

He walked carefully on the ice, his left hand trailing along the rope until the light from inside disappeared and he heard the door shut; then he turned and walked with great cautious prowling steps to the stoop again, turned and felt his way along to the corner and looked, eyes slitted against the snow, for any glow from a window. He saw nothing but the driving snow and darkness—although this was the sheltered southern side, the wind was playing tricks and flinging its burden everywhere, like a dust devil spinning dead leaves. He walked toward the back of the house, guiding himself by frequent tappings on the wall.

Then he banged into something and fell forward, and felt a myriad of tiny stabs through his Sunday pants

117

and the left hand with which he caught himself.

"Goddamn cactus," he mumbled.

He backed off and tried to pull out a couple of jaggers that had stuck in his palm, and found that his fingers were rapidly going frigid on him. It must be even colder than it felt. He muttered "Shit!" and went on, skirting the vicious stuff, and saw an oblong of radiance ahead. He angled in to it and tapped on the frosted-up glass. After a minute he tapped louder. Then he saw, a little above his own eye level, a clear circle being smeared by her hand. The ghost of her face looked through at him, but she obviously couldn't make him out. He pushed his face right onto the pane and mouthed "Open up" without sound. The lower half of the window was raised, creaking and sticking, about a foot.

"It's John Slocum. Please let me in."

"Oh," she said, "wait a—"

"No, now! It's very important."

To her credit, she didn't argue, but lifted the wooden sash to its limit. He crawled in over the high sill and hit the floor as quietly as he could. "Sorry, but I have to hear what's being said out there," he whispered, not looking at her but picking the broken spines of cactus from his left hand. "I'm afraid it may be bad news for Bill McGunn."

That struck the right chord. "Wait," she said, and glided to her door and eased it open a mite. Slocum pulled the last pricker out and dumped the lot of them on her night table where she'd see them and not get stabbed herself. Then he looked up at her.

She beckoned to him urgently. She was wearing red flannel unmentionables under a long-skirted chemise; she'd been undressing when he rapped. By God, but she had sand, letting him in like that, taking his word that it was important! He was hardly more than a stranger to her. For a second he wondered whether she might be playing with him, luring him with the

118

sight of all that forbidden underwear—a nice girl would die, or believed she'd die, before appearing like that to a rough hardcase like Slocum—but then he realized that she was blushing ferociously, and didn't have any idea what to do with her hands. He averted his gaze and touched the brim of his hat, hoping she'd take that as it was meant: apology, thanks, and respect.

He came over and put his ear to the crack between door and jamb. She backed away.

Schmidt's gravel voice said, "He believed it. Why in hell shouldn't he? It's mainly the truth."

"I'm not sure," said Kinkaid. "He had a funny look on his ugly mug."

"I'll get you for that, you lizard-headed galoot," Slocum promised silently, his ears straining. The men were two rooms off, but no doors were closed between them and Slocum.

"He was being smart, you stupid bastard," growled Schmidt. "If he was a yack who'd walk into the Palace and simply try to shoot Savage off his stool, with that abominable shotgun waiting and all the staff too, he'd hardly be of any use to us. They'd take his gun away and make him talk. But he's too fly for that. He'll think of some way to—where in hell's that draft coming from?" He raised his voice. "Bella! Is the kitchen door open?"

Slocum eased his door shut. Muted, he heard the maid call that it wasn't. He oozed the door open again.

"What if he's smart enough to go to Tucson, say, and spill it all to the marshal there?" grumbled Kinkaid. "That would fuck up everything to hell and back, wouldn't it? What if—"

"What if your ass was your kneecap?" said Schmidt. *"What if* is no argument, you idiot. The man's a drifter, and badly wanted to boot. *What if* peels no potatoes. He's not going anywhere. If he turns the offer down, we have him killed. That's all."

Kinkaid laughed with no mirth. "Having him killed.

119

Sure. Easy as throwing down on Wyatt Earp. Easy as eliminating Savage."

"Oh, shut up. Don't we have the law on our side?"

"What law? That Eastern glass of milk who thinks he's a sheriff?"

"We could deputize half the town if we needed to. Slocum is no threat, and he may be just the man we've waited for. Give him a day or so to think about it."

"You never offered him any money."

"I didn't need to. He knows there'd be plenty. If he lived to collect it." Schmidt laughed in his turn, hoarse and harsh.

Amelia pressed against Slocum's arm and he felt her body shuddering. He put an arm around her shoulders and patted her as one would comfort a scared pup. "Don't worry, honey," he whispered, "it'll be all right."

"Are you sure?"

"Certain sure I'm sure. Count on me." He glanced down at her, saw nothing but big round breasts just outgrowing the baby-fat stage into real woman tits, and jerked his head up too hastily. "Promise you I'll see it right," he husked out of the side of his mouth.

"Besides," Schmidt was saying, and Slocum heard the clink of crystal on crystal as he poured a drink, "money won't be the main consideration. The Southern fool has some damned outdated code of honor that'll demand he take action against all that awful immorality. He's—"

Slocum shut the door. That was Amelia's father speaking, exposing his real character to the girl who had no one in the world but Henry Schmidt and Bill McGunn. Slocum had heard enough. There was no sense in tormenting the kid further.

He faced her. Her long luscious hair had been let down and brushed till it shone; the gold flecks swam in the big green eyes that were trying valiantly not to weep. "I don't understand," she said quietly.

120

"I think I do. You let me think on it and I'll talk with you and Bill in a day or two. Now I'd better heist it."

"Father never comes in here without knocking and waiting till I open the door. You're safe. Please wait just a few minutes."

He opened his mouth to ask why and shut it without making a sound.

"Turn your back," she said.

He did so, and found himself looking into a mirror that showed her beginning to lift the chemise over her head. John Slocum did something he'd never have thought he'd do in a million years. He shut his eyes. The slithery sounds of the material moving on her body filled the room, driving him clean crazy. Then there came the slightly scratchier noises of flannel on skin —the red drawers coming off.

It was automatic. Slocum flicked his eyes open and shut. As fast as the movement was, which was about the same length of time it took him to draw his six-gun and fire, he was left with a photograph on his brain—clear and sharp as a Mathew Brady portrait but in delicate, lovely pastel colors—of the beautiful girl standing stark-naked behind him. Slocum stood there turned to solid granite. Maybe he heard her putting on her nightgown and maybe he only imagined it.

"You can turn around now," she said. Then there was the sound of her catching her breath, and afterwards, incredibly, the light silver laughter that was so like rippling water. "And open your eyes," she said. "I forgot the mirror. You *are* a gentleman."

Slocum hoped to God that he wasn't blushing. He felt scarlet all over. He turned around. She was not the staggering sexual creature that Brandy was in a starched white nightdress, but she made him want to tear all the buttons off his fly, with his teeth if necessary, and fling himself at her. He made a gallant effort and

121

took her by the shoulders and said, his voice pitched low: "You're a lot of woman, Miss Amelia, and I thank the powers you belong to a nice boy because otherwise I'd kiss you good-night so hard that I'd bust all our molars!"

"What a nice thing to say, Mr. Slocum," she said, with a demure glance downward. "Thank you."

"Thank you for trusting me so far. Miss Amelia ma'am, I'd plumb die for you if it was needful. Now I'll get along before I bring you trouble."

She looked up into his hard face, into the dark unfathomable eyes, and said, "I only wanted you not to remember me in those awful red unmentionables!"

"I won't. I never noticed them at all," he lied. "But I'll remember you like this." He cleared his throat. "I wouldn't mention it to Bill."

"But why not? There's nothing wrong with it. I'm completely covered." She put her hands half-consciously over the centers of her breasts. "It's just like a dress, really."

"Some fellows don't like the idea of another man seeing their girls ready for bed."

"How silly!"

"Well, no ma'am," said Slocum, starting toward the thick-frosted window. "No offense, but I'm having a heck of a time just not kissing you, and, ah, and—well," he ended lamely, "I hadn't ought to see you that way."

"Mr. Slocum, that's the nicest compliment I've had in ages. I think you could kiss me good-night with propriety," she said, catching his damp sleeve. She looked like that old sugar-and-spice, everything-nice rhyme, more than any girl he'd seen in a buzzard's lifetime; and she wasn't deliberately enticing him, he felt positive. She'd had a terrible shock hearing her daddy talk that fashion, and she needed comforting. He took her in his arms gently.

122

"It'll be all right," he told her earnestly, trying not to touch any more of her than necessary. It was she who snuggled up tight to him, and, *por los santos,* he thought, if she stayed there for more than a minute she was bound to feel something mighty hard and on the prod go ramming against her belly, something he knew she'd never felt before.

"Oh, Mr. Slocum," she whispered, still very proper with his name even though she was just about buttering herself all over him like he'd been a slice of toast instead of an all-too-human man, "this isn't as bad a shock as you may think. I've suspected something wrong for months. Maybe years. I don't eavesdrop, but I can't help hearing things occasionally when those two men come here. They're involved in something criminal—them and my father, as deep as anything. I never heard them slander poor Bill like that before, though, and they plan to kill you!" She somehow got even closer to him. Cold, almost icy sweat came out on his face as he fought for self-control that he doubted he had.

"I thought over what you said in the office, about Retch being a hideaway for some low gang of cutthroats. It isn't such an outlandish idea as I first believed. I couldn't talk it over with Bill, he's so old-fashioned! Crime isn't a proper concern for young ladies! But now I'll have to tell him what I've heard."

"Just leave out the nightgown and me being in your room," said Slocum, his voice throttled. "Bill wouldn't understand."

"I guess you're right." She pulled his head down. "Kiss me good-night now."

"Honest," he began, feeling like a jingle-brained village idiot, "I really don't—"

"All I have left is you and Bill," she said, her voice rising, "and I need you! I want you to *know* I'm your friend!"

With that she kissed him. After about fifteen seconds

he gave up and kissed her back, and wondered whether the front of his tight pants would stand the strain. He thought she'd back off a little when she felt the swelling staff shove into her soft and unprotected stomach at about navel height, but she only seemed to wiggle closer.

Then she started to moan throatily. It was time to get out, unless he changed his mind and decided to take her cherry away from her in that big bed with the white sheets and fat feather tick.

Slocum disengaged his mouth. "I know you're my friend, Miss Amelia," he assured her, trying to back away but feeling her lower body follow his as if they'd been pasted together. "You don't have to convince me any farther. And I'll stand by you in your hour of peril. And now I got to *go*."

He slid up the sash and went over the sill, landing on ice and going to one knee with both hands spread out to break his fall. The snow wasn't piled here. He heard the window begin to close and then an almost silent, whispery kind of *swish* . . . a rattler striking silently, a butcher knife whipping round to split a skull—that sort of barely heard sibilation, signaling danger by no more than the noise of air being cloven nearby. Slocum reversed his movement, starting to go flat instead of standing up, and something very hard took him alongside the temple and blotted out all his senses, plunging him into a black silence that could well have been death.

Except that, far down in his being, in his mind or at the center of his animal instincts where something glowed and would go on glowing until he was truly dead, he was aware of a fact that had been staring him in the face for minutes without his noticing it.

He must be getting old. There had only been *two* voices in the parlor, and Chris Adams wasn't the strong silent type who'd not stick in his oar. At some time after Slocum had reversed his path and walked around to the side of the house, Adams must have come out and tracked him.

There was then only nothing.

12

He had no conception of the length of the hiatus; a man who's been knocked out never really does. But he felt his consciousness come floundering up from the depths of the void and thought groggily, *Damn, I went to Hell like they all said I would,* because it was so hot he could fairly hear his flesh bubbling below the hide. He struggled to bring his eyes open and to start up the works of his mind. The first thing he realized was that it wasn't hot, it was infernally cold. The next thing was that he heard someone wheezing nearby, and felt a hand on his shoulder trying to roll him over on his back.

No telling who that would be. He let his eyes stay half-open, and his mouth hang slack, and he focused on an imaginary point about three yards beyond him. Even in his condition—which was either dying or getting better, he couldn't tell which—his iron control of himself when in danger held true. His face was flaccid and the eyes stayed converged on that distant point as he was finally heaved onto the flat of his back. There was an inky shadow hanging over him but he wouldn't allow himself to see it, save as a blur. He had to look dead. If it was a friend, McGunn or Brandy maybe, then they'd have to stand a momentary shock. It was a flaming lot more likely that it was an enemy.

A lucifer rasped across sandpaper, and a yellow-white glow burst out above his face. He didn't know what his pupils were doing—contracting or staying the same—but he knew that nothing else was moving by a hair's breath. He was holding his breath now, so

125

that no wisp of steam would fog out to prove his torpid but unquenched existence. Time stood still.

"That did it for you, you lecherous son of a whore," murmured the bass voice of the weasely Mr. Adams. The match was blown out and cracked between finger and thumb and tossed away. The shadow stood up. Slocum let his eyes change their focus and saw the outline, against the whirling snow, of the man and the long straight stick protruding from below his arm that would be the barrel of his Winchester rifle.

So that's what the bushwhacking bastard hit me with. Lucky I was born with a cobblestone for a skull. A rifle barrel against the temple ought by rights to crack through the bone.

Hellish headache it gave me, though. I'll pay that back, Adams, old coot, you see if I don't.

He saw the figure disappear, heard the light stamp of boots on ice receding to the front of the house. Slocum heaved himself into a sitting position, ignoring the way his head split right apart at the motion. He made sure he still had both his weapons, and managed to stand up. He felt sick as a poisoned wolf. He leaned far over, resting his hands against the cold timbers of the house, and threw up.

The temptation was to just stay there until the pain went away, but if he did they'd find one froze-solid drifter in the morning. Worse, they might be on their way out here now to pick up the carcass and fling it away from the place into a snowbank. Slocum felt for his hat, which turned up missing; he saw it out on the edge of the piling snow and retrieved it. He walked as fast as he could to the west, keeping in the lee of the building, and came to the corner and turned. He found the rope, stepped over it and went staggering down the walk toward the road, the damnable snow whipping into his eyes and open mouth.

Then he heard the door open behind him. He spun

126

round and drew his Colt, a flood of joy drowning the agony in his head. He'd take all three of the rotten scalawags now and be done with them. The light from inside went out as the door closed. Then one of them opened the side of a dark lantern and the beam came out right at Slocum. He leveled his piece and just touched the hammer with his thumb. But the pallid ray turned, swept around toward the side where he'd been lying, and moved across the porch, the black vague figures huddling around it as it passed. They hadn't even seen him. Too dark, of course, and the snow too thick. Slocum swiveled, skidded, balanced and went on, guiding himself with a raw and glacial hand on the rope. He picked up speed as his progress cleared his brains, went down the rise, then left his rope and veered right, marching through drifts of varying depths, trying to imagine himself an Indian going on infallible instinct. It worked to the extent that he did get across the broad street and eventually rammed spang into a hide-and-pole shanty. He groped back a way, got what he thought were the right bearings, and came to the restaurant. Drawing an ice-cold Peacemaker with a hand that was nearly as chilled as the metal, he walked in.

The fat cook stared at him as he weaved to the counter and sat down. "You been gunned, son?"

"Buffaloed with a Winchester. I'm alive. Gimme two cups of coffee and a plate of whatever's hottest from the stove."

They were there almost before he'd got out the words.

After he'd eaten, he ran his eye over the other customers, contemptuously holstered his gun, and strode outside.

This storm was never going to quit. It was going to snow until the whole continent was covered three feet deep. A man ought to be in New Orleans right now if he had a lick of horse sense. Slocum withdrew as far as possible into the too-light jacket and aimed himself for the hotel.

"Any more visitors?" he asked the clerk.

"No sir, except Mr. Tucker came back to see what was keeping you. He talked to the young—young lady," the fellow said, stammering over which word to use for Brandy. "Then he went back to the Palace of Mirrors."

Slocum flipped him a cartwheel. "Keep up the good work," he said, and went down to the room and rapped, identified himself and was let in.

"Jeb Stuart, I presume?"

"Yes ma'am."

"Well—" she began, and saw his face and shrieked. "What happened?"

"I got throwed and branded when I wasn't looking." He kissed her. "How long you been gaudied up and tapping your foot, sweetheart?"

"About an hour. That looks *terrible*."

"Yeah, for a while I felt poorer than skimmed milk, but it's better now. Can you clean it up without me taking off all this gear? I want to get down to the tables."

She inspected him, tipping his head gently.

"Buffaloed," she said at last. "Your face is sloshed with blood but somehow you managed to keep it off your precious clothes. Sit down, I'll fix it. What was it, a Buntline Special?"

"Nope, rifle. In the dark."

"Kill him?"

"Not yet," said Slocum levelly.

"If you'd taken me wherever the goddamn hell you went, it wouldn't have happened."

"You weren't invited, Brandy. And I had to go because there were things to find out." He pictured her waiting outside the window for him while he was genteelly fighting off Amelia Schmidt, and almost choked. "Which I found out," he said.

"Anything about Kid Slocum?"

"No, but about this louse-crawling town."

She was washing his temple with a towel dunked in cold water. It hurt. He built a smoke and lit it. "You gonna tell me what?" she asked irritably.

"When I've cyphered it all out, sure. Meantime I can tell you that there's one man I can trust with my life for dead certain, and that's Colonel Savage."

"Why?"

"Because they tried to hire me to kill him."

"Who's they?"

"A trio of wharf rats dressed up in puppydogs' skins. Schmidt and Adams and Kinkaid."

"And who are *they?*"

"Mainstays of the community and gopher-gnawed pillars of the high society of Retch. They put McGunn in office. And now they want me—or wanted me— to do his job for him, only underhanded and illegal. I said I'd think on it, but then one of 'em, Adams, followed me and swiped me with his Winchester barrel and left me for dead. So I guess they didn't believe I'd be true blue and keep my mouth shut."

"You want a bandage on that," Brandy asked as he stood up, "or do you just want to bleed quietly into your collar all night?"

He sat down again. "Go ahead." As she wrapped a long strip of linen from his war-bag around his head over the pad of bandage, he told her rapidly what he'd found out about Retch and what he'd deduced from it.

"What the hell are silver-mine owners doing in a gang of thieves?" she asked, stepping back and looking critically at him.

"I got a theory. Have to talk to somebody about it. I don't yet know who."

"Like what?"

129

"Like maybe there aren't any silver mines. Maybe there's only other folks' livestock and money and goods. But I don't know that, I got to check on it. I wonder if Maynard Savage knows the story? If he does, that's enough reason to hire assassins to sic onto him."

"You sure seem to be poking your long nose into something that's none of your business, Slocum."

"I been forced to. They're after me now, too. Besides the Kid Slocum crap, there's this. I bet there won't be twenty men in Retch, come morning, that won't be after me."

"You want to stay alive till that Indian comes back, if he does."

"You starting to believe I'm *not* the Kid?"

"I wish I knew," she told him. "I wish I knew for sure."

"And I wish I could prove it to you. At least you'll wait; some of those dumb waddies won't."

"What you need is a good lay to take your mind off all this," Brandy stated flatly, and began to unfrog the back of her dress.

"Whoa! Think a minute, you beautiful single-minded little cuss! It even hurts me to *shout*," Slocum said, touching his wrapped skull. "If you swell up this pecker of mine and get it slamming away, what do you figure will happen to my head? Have a little mercy!"

"Don't you want me any more?"

"I was hit hard enough to break an andiron in two. You got no conception how it feels? It only happened half an hour ago!"

She put her hands softly on his lean hard cheeks. "Oh, Johnny, I'm sorry. I'm a selfish bitch. I—was only lonesome for you. And you weren't here when I woke up and I felt deserted. And you haven't kissed me since you came back. So I thought there was—"

"Somebody else?" he asked, amazed. She nodded. "How could a man need two women if you were one of

130

'em?" he demanded, his conscience giving out a faint twinge as he repudiated his lust for Amelia. "I don't hardly recollect coming through the door, let alone not kissing you. Here," he said, and took her face and smudged the lip paint all over both of them. "Evening, Brandy. I missed you."

She held him tightly. "I missed you. I'm sorry." She kissed him again, and buttoned her dress.

There was something wrong with her; there was more to that little scene than met the eye or the ear. Slocum couldn't get a fix on the flaw, but it was there. Some faint false note. Something rotten in Arizona Territory besides Retch.

She cleaned his face of the scarlet smears with the cold and bloody towel. He gave her her derringer and they went to the Palace of Mirrors.

Inside they were escorted to a poker table. Slocum ordered a bottle of Double Stamp, two glasses, the best cigar in the house, and then he murmured in the servant's ear that he wished to speak with Mr. Savage. The man in silver-and-gray livery nodded. A gaming rack on wheels slid to the table and Slocum gave this member of the staff $2000; his big octagonal slugs were dropped into the slots that gleamed with gold and silver, and a couple of stacks of chips were set at his right hand. The Wilton carpet felt lush beneath his feet, the glowing mahogany and porcelain and crystal soothed his eyes, the aromatic pecan wood blazing in the fireplace tickled his nose pleasantly, the dice rattled in the chuck-a-luck boxes and the roulette wheel clicked merrily. A man was a plain dolt to go anywhere else, for any reason, outside of this hall.

He said to Brandy, "Retch may have more ugly to it than most towns, but this casino beats creation."

John Henry, the tubercular dealer, was playing at this table tonight, as well as big Tucker in his velvet-collared frock coat. Slocum said hello to them in turn,

131

and they gravely saluted him with their glasses. They were a study—different and much alike. Tucker would have made two of the lunger.

Tucker was as dark as the dealer was fair . . . their eyes were identical, blue and hard and utterly expressionless. Each wore the so-called "killer" mustachios, the drooping longhorn style—Tucker's coarse and long and jet black, the other's neatly tended and sandy blond. Slocum was exceedingly glad that if it came to a showdown fight, these two men wouldn't be ranked against him. He'd faced plenty of cat-eyed delicate-triggered pistoleros, sharks on high pay, star gunnies with reputations, and unknown kids who'd practiced behind the barn for a thousand hours and were ready to build their own reps on anything that wore artillery— but none faster and deadlier than Tucker, and certainly none as famous and terrible as the thin fellow with the caved-in chest across the poker table.

He wondered if Brandy knew who had just dealt her a busted flush.

After two hands, he looked up at Savage and saw him beckon briefly with the hand that wasn't lying on the shotgun across his lap. He went over and up the ladder.

"News?" The ice-cold metal eyes flicked at him. "Decided to accept the invitation, Major?"

"I may, sir. I probably will have to. News—yes. I was almost hired to kill you."

His meaning was grasped instantly. A smile barely lifted the gray stallion-tails on Maynard Savage's lip. "So you weren't for sale. Naturally. Tell me."

Slocum did, as fully and quickly as he could: what he'd been told, what he'd overheard, what he surmised. When he'd finished, Savage said, "They'll slaughter you like a shoat, Major, if you go out there to them. You've already been wounded. How bad is that head?"

"I feel like I been sent for and can't go," said Slocum.

132

"Yes, you look it. Stay here. But you can't bring your woman.'"

"It's your house. But I know what she is, and she knows I know. She's waiting till the facts are all in."

"Man, don't trust her word for that! If she even suspects that you're going to be out of her sight, she'll blow out your light without a qualm."

"We've been close. I don't think—"

"I do. Take my word, Major. That woman is hell on wheels. I've heard federal marshals call her the deadliest bounty hunter in the West."

"Funny I never heard of her before."

"None of us can hear about *everything*. There are at least a dozen other scalp collectors in town. Professionals, I mean. But none as dangerous to you as she is. Let her go home alone."

"No," said Slocum, stubbornly. "I can't do that. I've got to talk to the so-called sheriff before I fort up here, and I owe Brandy the courtesy of telling her why I'm coming. I intend to do a chore or two to clean up this lousy burg somewhat before I make tracks for wherever I'm going next."

"Why? What business is Retch of yours?" The question wasn't impertinent, but a sign of genuine curiosity.

Slocum struggled with some pretty vague feelings. It sure wasn't because he was a do-gooding long-nose. He wasn't horrified at the existence of a nest of hell-hounds in this glorious desert country—the scenery matched the inhabitants, and the hideous hills and raw sandy stretches deserved their human dwellers. Finally he said, "Thunderation! Because it makes me mad, and that's enough reason! One o' those slime puddles said last night, after he thought I was gone, that I operated on 'some damn-fool outdated Southern code of honor.' I maybe *do*. It sounds like a lick shy of insanity, but I've been shot, buffaloed, insulted and made a fool of, and I don't plan to overlook it!"

133

"So, beyond taking care of the three who made their quarrel with you, which is only what any real man *would* do, you plan to go on and clean up the town. You're an idealist."

"Me?" said Slocum, amazed.

Savage resumed his reconnaissance of the hall. "Anything I can do for you?" he asked, almost indifferently.

"Who could I ask about those silver mines? Somebody who wouldn't lie to me."

"I wouldn't lie to you, Major. There are no producing silver mines. Some years ago a prospector found color, if that's the term, and sank a shaft and then another, but the yield was perhaps one ounce to the ton—poor even for gold, I believe. So there's just enough puny fact behind the story for Schmidt and his cronies to pretend to be silver-mine owners. The 'mines' are a smoke screen for both masters and servants: that is, Schmidt and about eight others at the top of the heap, and a couple of hundred outlaws beneath them."

"Which explains why I felt from the first night that something was rotten in Retch."

"Of course. The miners, hill rats, and most of the others are actually crooks, ambuscaders and road agents who are only brave when they're part of a mob."

"I wondered why the hell they could all afford to come into town ahead of the winter," Slocum exploded. "What miner winters in town?"

"Exactly. No trail herds in bad weather, and fewer travelers. The outlaws have a very good situation here. They're allowed to keep most of their loot—they think —and they're protected and ruled by iron fists, which is what they need and probably want. They're the sort who're good only for bushwhacking and back-shooting. There's no real guts in them unless they can swarm over the victims like starving rats in a pack. Someone else has to do their thinking for them. They gladly commit

134

their filthy crimes for a share, a hole to hide in, and a strong kingpin to guide and command them. Mind you," said Savage, looking at him, "everyone's not here in disguise. The buffalo hunters come in to drink and gamble with men they think are miners; I'm almost positive of that. Some of the cow hands drift by and take Retch at its face value, rough low men but not born criminals. It's hard to tell the difference here. That's why I can't estimate the foe accurately."

"I see. Colonel, when you built the Palace, did you know what Retch was?"

Savage glared at him under the heavy steel-gray brows. "As one officer to another—I did, damn your eyes, sir! But I have never been a part of Retch. Schmidt and his ilk hated me from the start because I siphoned off a great deal of their crew's cash, but they couldn't do anything about it. An element of the outlaws like to dress up and pretend to be respectable, and I offer them the only chance in town. Swiped cash is fast cash, goes the adage; they lose it here, then they exist on Schmidt's bounty till they can pay it off with high interest by another job. There are two hundred miles or more of frontier between the States and Mexico that are covered sporadically by these predators. When the blizzard's over and some trails are cut through the snow, they'll be out again, like a skulk of foxes—say rather a clan of ghouls."

"I never meant to imply that you were in with them, Colonel," said Slocum, chin high and eyes dark and glowing.

Savage slapped him on the shoulder. It was the first physical contact between them, and it eased Slocum's mind, for he'd been thinking maybe he'd gone too far. "Don't mind my bristling, Major! I tell myself that money carries no taint, even out of the gutter, but sometimes I'm not positive it's true. I came here when I heard there was big money around—very soon after

135

Retch as such was founded. I thought it was silver money. I knew before I'd finished building that it wasn't. But there was the devil's plenty, so I stayed. I still own my place in Kansas City—where I met your busty wench, by the way—and plan to go back there soon." He chuckled, a noise sliced from an iceberg. "Sooner than I expected, I reckon. But when I can fish up diamonds and emeralds out of dung, Major, I do it. I have three daughters in Maryland. I intend that they shall be astoundingly wealthy when I die."

"I'm a mite surprised that Schmidt hasn't turned his jackals loose on you."

"I have a well-chosen staff of twenty men. Any of them is equal to ten of his. Also he forbids any trouble whatever in the town, on pain of agonizing death. I choose those words carefully, Major Slocum."

"How could such a monster sire a girl like Amelia?" John wondered aloud.

Maynard Savage laughed again. "It's my opinion that his late wife was unfaithful to him! She is a miracle in the desert, the young Amelia. Naturally Schmidt never intends Bill McGunn to have her—and naturally you mean to do something about *that,* too."

"I surely to God do."

"A Daniel come to judgment, and the sword of the Lord and of Gideon to Retch! I'll be damned, Major, if you aren't the most refreshing jackass I've met since the War! You almost make me believe you'll do what you want to do here. Some power watches over fools, madmen, and plumed knights. But for both our sakes, laddie-buck," said Savage quietly, "let me give you two men to side you. No sense in playing lone hero, is there?"

"I move around better alone. Thanks anyway. And Tucker sort of keeps an eye on me without being asked."

"I question his reasons."

"Why, sir?"

"Damned if I know. But John Henry doesn't cotton to him, and—have you thought that his purpose might be the same as Brandy's?"

"I have peered at that possibility," said Slocum. "It doesn't keep me awake nights all sweaty and chill."

"It wouldn't. Jesus! Watch yourself, and come back here as soon as you can. I'd like to take you to Kansas City with me."

"I travel a solitary trail, Colonel, but many thanks."

"Yes, you would. Well, well! Travel it as cautiously as your principles allow, Major." Savage turned slightly on his high stool, and Slocum understood that the interview was finished.

He went down the ladder and to the game, where he proceeded to lose some $1800 during the course of the night.

He hoped that his luck had not run out at last.

13

The man with the flat scarred face was waiting just inside the big front door for him. He stepped forward and held out a long double-barreled shotgun. "From Mr. Savage," he murmured. "He says, don't be a stiff-necked bullheaded hard-bitted runaway bucker, but accept this in the right spirit, and *hook 'em cow!*" He gave Slocum a box of shells too. "With all respect, sir, those were Mr. Savage's exact terms, not mine."

Slocum grinned at him. "Taken as such, and no offense. What handle do you go by?"

"Chicago Ed Sealey." They shook. "You're Major Slocum."

"Just John Slocum now."

"You'll be back?" There was a bare shade of meaning in the tone, which no one else could have caught.

"You bet your bottom Blue William on it," said Slocum. He and the ponchoed Brandy left the Palace, Tucker in his great white bulk of coat following at their heels. "I think it's thinning out some," said Slocum, glancing up from under the Stetson brim. "Looks like I can almost see the dawn." He hefted the shotgun under his arm; it felt comforting and he knew it was loaded, because Savage's people were thorough.

"What was all that mealymouthed shit?" asked the girl irritably.

"Merely a polite meeting of two gents. Why?"

"Oh, horse turds," she growled. "Steaming goddamn horse turds! Keep your secrets, then."

"No secret. Savage worries about me, Kid Slocum and all that."

"He's gonna wind up bringing you hot broth for breakfast."

"Good old bourbon, more like." They stomped down the street past the unseen hide shanties. Slocum distinguished a figure leaning against a post of the tin awning in front of the Christmas Variety whorehouse. "Spread out," he said, urgently; he sensed Brandy and Tucker step away from his side. With three of them now as possible targets, he challenged loudly. "Who goes there? Talk, or you're a dead hombre!"

The man stepped into the street, then spang into a big drift of snow, where he foundered and went to his knees. But Slocum saw his right arm thrown out, crooked and then straightening, and he leveled the shotgun and let go one barrel. The shadowy figure did a flip-flop onto his back and disappeared in the bank. Slocum went forward at a crouch, saw movement to his right in the alley beside the crib, turned and blasted the second charge into an indistinct knot of men waiting there. He sidestepped and broke the weapon, moved again and fumbled open the box of cartridges, loaded up with the roaring of six-shooters echoing like cannon fire and slugs whining nastily by his ears—Christ, what a bunch of amateurs, going for the head of a target in thick weather, instead of the belly—put two more gutfuls of buckshot into the thick of them, and slammed the greener under his left arm and drew his Colt. By then there was only one of the bushwhackers on his feet, a vague moving shape that froze for an instant and then went to his knees and scrunched down behind a couple of fresh corpses. Slocum aimed carefully and dropped him all the way.

In the stillness that followed the last echo, when he had begun to hear the faint moan and hiss of the storm once more, Slocum said, "You two still healthy?" Brandy and Tucker said they were. Slocum holstered the sixgun, loaded the borrowed greener, and went to check out the various remains. There were six, counting the first man in the street. Slocum didn't recognize any of them. Two were still alive, though one of those wouldn't be for long.

Brandy went around after him, checked faces, said there was a reward on one of them but it was about six bits and not worth the effort. Slocum assumed that this meant $25 or $50. Obviously, she still didn't want to let him out of her sight. As they slushed back to the street, Slocum heard two distinct cracks, as of steel on bone. Then Tucker joined them. Slocum looked at him inquiringly.

"Freezing's a slow death. No sense letting them tell whoever sent 'em that there were three of us."

Cold-blooded bastard, thought Slocum. Just the sort who made a good bountyman. Likely Savage was right about him.

And probably Brandy would have done the same thing, or given them their *coups de grâce* with her derringer, if she'd been alone. Or with just Tucker.

He wondered for the first time: how long had Tucker stayed with her last night, while he was over at Schmidt's?

139

Slocum was glad that he had the shotgun, and cradled it semicasually over his right arm, aimed in Tucker's direction. In case.

They reached the hotel. The snow was definitely thinning, because they could see to the second story. They went in, waking the clerk by slamming the door; he was evidently on 24-hour duty. Hell, maybe he was the owner. Slocum thought, *Maybe he's a Schmidt man too.*

Brandy closed and bolted the door behind him. In no time, she was shucked bare and under the soogans. "You up to it?" she asked.

"Head aches fierce," he said, "but let's try anyway." He shed down and wrapped up his good duds in the blanket roll carefully, stowing his black Stetson in the war-bag. She studied him critically while he did this.

"You plan to light out soon?"

"Just don't forecast any more poker at the Palace. My luck's played out."

"Oh for Jesus, Mary and Joseph! You and your goddamn witless superstitions!" she yelled. "What broke it off, you getting buffaloed or the storm slacking off?"

"Something did it," he grunted, edging in with her.

"Couldn't be that you were off your game because you had a half-open skull, I guess," she said caustically, touching the white bandage. "Oh, hell, no."

I wasn't off my game, I just didn't get cards, he thought. *Might be it was that damn Winchester did it —knocked the luck out of me—*

"I bet a person could have seen it flying away like a chunk kicked out of a fire! You moronic big *zorrilla*," she said, which meant *polecat,* "that's like saying it came on to snow because you laid a blue-eyed woman that carries a shotgun! Luck's like a force of nature, like the wind: it comes and it goes, it's there but you don't see it, only its effects—and nobody understands it any more'n they do the wind! You can't change it

140

by walking under a ladder or chucking your hat on a bed or crossing your fingers!"

"How can you be sure?"

"Oh, you're hopeless." She wrapped her long delicious body around him, her breasts smashed against his ribs, and kissed him hard.

Slocum had been keyed up for many hours, and had been in considerable pain until a quart or more of bourbon had kind of settled the twinges down. He'd had to gun down he didn't know how many men in two separate scrambles, five or six of them for breakfast at that. He'd been driven right to the ultimate brink by Amelia, whom he now lusted after even fiercer than before. He had the Kid Slocum affair and the Schmidt gang on the brain. But his limp old John Thomas, all shrunk up and shy from the cold, now began to distend and swell and throb and stretch out its head until he felt half of the blood in his frame rushing down there to his groin to help it along. It must have been trying, all by itself, for a new record. He groaned in his throat.

Brandy drew back her head, solicitous. "Does it hurt bad, Johnny dear?"

"Who the hell cares?" said Slocum, and parted her lower lips with a couple of fingers, found the place all slushy and fiery, and shoved his cock into it luxuriously, inch by inch by inch by. . . .

"Ooh," she breathed. "Johnny, you amaze me."

"I amaze me." He pumped experimentally. The vagina clamped him tightly all along its fantastic length. His penis grew thicker. It was completely impossible. He slid back and forth, slow, faster. His oversized tool was like a wet ramrod in a slippery bore. His head wound didn't pang at all. He was aware of having only one head, carried in and out on the end of a shaft of joy.

"Are you comfortable enough?" she whispered. She

141

wasn't quite ready to abandon herself to the usual round of loud and raptured gratification. She was actually concerned about his noggin-bump. Brandy was a strange amalgam of very good and very bad, thought Slocum in his last completely conscious moment; but then, ain't we all?

"Yee-oo-ow!" he hollered, throwing back his upper body and looking at the ceiling, weight for the moment all on the heels of his hands. "Let 'er buck. Front Street in Dodge City on the Arkansas by sundown, and beef at prime prices and the whiskey free!"

"Whooeeoop!" Brandy yowled. And they went at it, slam and bam and wham away without a thought between them, but more feelings than they could have put names to, more salacious lechery in that one bed than all the rest of the Territory could have produced, swift cock oozing to and fro in cunt till their juices soaked into the tick and they were like two wild wolf-dogs wallowing in a luscious sinkhole.

There sure wasn't counting of orgasms and deliberate stringing her out to exhaustion this morning, not by John Slocum. He was clean out of himself and absorbed into a universe of rigid bursting rise-up spiral-down-to-Hell sensations, doing all his living and thinking in the loins, just as though it were his first such experience. He never even gave Amelia a blink of recognition in his mind. He barely *had* any mind, only a collection of nerve endings at the base of his skull to inform him that he was having one convulsive uproarious unbridled hell of a grand fuck and was close onto flying to pieces like a raging locomotive whose boiler was set to explode.

After a while, Christ knew how long, it exploded all right, and they were both drowned in the steam and shattered to gobs of hot flesh and whizzing and scooting out over the landscape until they blanketed Arizona from Pastora Peak to the Gila Bend Mountains.

142

And then they were lying there, his enormous body cushioned on her slim frame with the tits that beat creation under his head. He sucked in a deep breath and tried to heave up and away and he plain *couldn't*. He was that finished. He told her so.

"Me too. Stay there, I'm not too smashed in yet." Her voice was clotted, and it broke like a boy's at every third word. "If . . . oh, Johnny, if you're *not* Kid Slocum, we ought to team up. We're so good together. It's a shame to break it up."

"If I'm not the Kid," he said heavily. "Oh gentle God, *if*. Brandy, why do so many take my word I ain't, but not you, who ought to know me best?" He slid sideways till he was beside her, and drew the blankets up to their chins. "And what if I was? Is a miserable $2000 better'n me to you?"

She said, "It's my trade. I can't make exceptions. It isn't personal at all. I'm a lawman."

"A lawman! You're a bounty hunter with a pocketful of reward handbills."

"Same thing. Except that I ordinarily only go for the high bounties. I'm just like a marshal without the tin badge."

"If you see it that way." He shrugged, drowsy and not wanting to argue after that wahoo frolic.

"Would you side me—or let me side you—if the Kid's someone else?"

"I figure I'm not a hoss can trot very far in double harness, honey. Let's grab some sleep."

She let out the longest sigh he'd ever heard; when it was finished, she'd fallen asleep. Slocum waited for about ten minutes, then poured himself out of bed and dressed in his trail outfit: the long-handles first and the elkskin jacket last, with his old Stetson, not so floppy in the brim after Spring Fawn's ministrations, perched across his bandage, two .45s in his pockets, the pair of gunbelts stuffed with cartridges, Bowie knife hung over

143

his groin handy-like, and a pair of thin leather gloves that he hadn't worn in a while hauled onto his mitts. The Spencer .52 carbine and Savage's shotgun he leaned beside the door. He put most of his money in his war-bag, tightened the buckskin straps of the big blanket roll, laid them both beside his saddlebags, did a couple of other things, and sat down in the chair. He watched Brandy sleeping for an indefinite time. Studying her face, he couldn't see any of the cold stone-hearted ruthlessness that must lie inside her. She was one beautiful woman. He gave a sigh himself. He went over, knelt, and kissed her on the mouth. Then he stood up and humped his blanket roll and saddlebags, slung the war-bag from one shoulder, and tucked the two long firearms into an armpit. He put his hand on the latch.

"Hold it right there," said Brandy behind him.

"I figured," said Slocum. "Well, I'm leaving."

"Not without me, Johnny."

"Yes ma'am, entirely and especially without you."

There was the click of a .44 being cocked, a bleak sound in the bleak room.

"You'd blow me through the back?"

"If I have to. Put that gear down and—"

Slocum opened the door without looking back. "I purely hope and believe you won't shoot me when I'm not looking."

"If I have to," she said again, her voice algid as a frozen water moccasin. "Nobody else is gonna take you, Johnny."

He stepped across the threshold. He heard the hammer crack down on an empty chamber, and Brandy cursed. "Neglected to tell you, sweetheart," he said, "I unloaded your gun before I kissed you." He walked into the hall, listening to her rage behind him. "I really reckoned you wouldn't use it. Sorry I was wrong. Thanks for a jim-dandy good time." He shut the door without looking at her, locked it, and toted the key to the front desk. "What's my bill?" he asked. "And hers." He paid it and shifted the shotgun to his right hand. "Take this key down to the lady in about three minutes," he said, listening to the thumps and shrill swearing from his room. If the clerk was in luck, Brandy wouldn't have thought to put any clothes on when he opened her door.

Slocum walked into a diminishing storm. Visibility was nearly a dozen feet now. He slogged eastward to the Palace, where he left his paraphernalia with Chicago Ed, keeping the shotgun but not the carbine. He transferred his thumb-buster to its holster and filled the empty pocket with greener shells. He said, "I'll be back," and canted across the street to the jail.

Bill McGunn was talking to Amelia Schmidt when he stomped in. They both stared at him, and he felt in the old stale air that a gush of words had been cut off at his entrance. He grinned stiffly. "My ears burning?"

"Likely. You're not thinking of blowing town?"

"I gave you a promise," said Slocum meagerly.

"Sorry, John. Amelia's been telling me—"

"What happened to your head?" said the girl in a stifled shriek. She was muffled to the nose, and couldn't have been there long, for snow still lay along her heavy-coated shoulders.

"Mr. Chris Adams happened to it."

"See?" said the girl triumphantly. She turned to Slocum, and the pinkness of her face that the wind had bestowed on her darkened slightly. Slocum kept his own mug expressionless. "I was telling Willie—I mean Bill—that after you left last night, I overheard a great deal of terrible information," she said, voice in a hurry. "Even worse than the things they talked about with you."

"Oh, you heard our conversation?" he said, half an eye on McGunn to watch reactions.

"Yes, I listened," she said, glancing at her fiancé defiantly, and proceeded to repeat all she'd said to him before, for Slocum's benefit.

Slocum nodded. "That's true. That's what was spoke of among us."

"But after you'd *gone*—" she told him, and ran through the talk that she and Slocum had heard from within her room as if he'd never been there. The girl followed orders nicely, he thought. Had a good streak of common sense. "And then," she finished, "I heard Chris come in, and they all growled so that I couldn't tell what they were saying, and left together, and came back in a few minutes cursing and slamming around, and the only thing I heard clearly was, 'Of course he wasn't dead, you—' well, Daddy said a word that I wouldn't use, but he must have meant you, Mr. Slocum."

"Call me John, it's easier. Bill, what your fine young lady says is fact. And only what I'd expected."

McGunn took it in for a silent minute. "You expected to discover that they're crooked?" he asked a little plaintively. "Why?"

"First off, I'd seen Kinkaid and Adams under circumstances where they acted pretty naturally compared with the smooth and mealymouthed chat that went on at supper. I knew they were both reptiles. And I'm sorry, Amelia, but I figured your pa'd be one too, being associated with them; and he turned out so. I honestly am sorry to say it."

"Yes but it's *true*." The green-gold eyes flashed; she had spunk. "He's worse than they are, because he's the leader!" Slocum guessed she'd got all her crying done in the night, and was dried out and growing used to the fact. "I don't know why they want Mr. Savage assassinated or a lot of other things—"

"I do," said Slocum.

"Talk, then," said McGunn shortly.

"I intend to, son. First off, Maynard Savage is a thorn in their sides and has been from the word go. He owns the biggest gold mine in town, and they can't take toll of him because he's got a nice little army. They figure if he's bucked out, they'll just take over the Palace and increase their share of the highwaymen's cash by a damn fat wad."

"How do you know?"

"Experience and horse sense. He's the only man in town they can't rule. And it galls them worse than cockleburs under their saddles. By the way, Bill, I've thrown in with Savage, and I'll be staying at the Palace till Foot in Grave gets back or the telegraph wires are up again. Savage is hard but he's honest, and he's on the side of the law. In fact," Slocum said, hating to tell the boy but bound to do it, "Maynard Savage is right now the only real law in Retch. Schmidt and company boss everyone else, but Savage stands beyond them and he's as straight as an Apache arrow."

"What about me?"

"Son, you're likely the nicest fellow in miles, and you mean well, and God knows if you can shoot but I expect that you practice at it; however, you ain't no sheriff and you never have been. You're no kind of lawdog at all."

Evidently recognizing the open sincerity, McGunn didn't take offense. "Explain that, John."

"I will. You're sitting in a seat that ought to be occupied by a pro gunslinger, a man who's maybe even been an outlaw himself, who prowls the middle of the street catfooted and cat-eyed, who can stop a mob in its tracks with just two hard words barked over the barrel of a shotgun. Do you kick in a door when you go into a saloon, in case an enemy's waiting behind it? Then do you keep your back to the wall while you're inside? Hell and damnation, you don't even go into saloons! You don't know you're supposed to! You're a green-

147

horn that nobody's ever tried to educate in Western ways, and that's why you're on Schmidt's payroll. You don't even realize that you aren't now, and never have been, a sheriff at all, like I said. If you *were* a lawdog, you'd be a town marshal!"

"Why?"

"Lemme ask you this first: have you ever ridden out beyond the border of dear old Retch town on official business?"

"No." McGunn looked very blank.

"Ever led a posse? Gone mantracking? Do you recognize an arroyo when you see it?"

McGunn slowly shook his head.

"Those are part of a sheriff's job. Were you elected or appointed?"

"I was told"—he was feeling his way in this jungle of wonderment—"told that I'd been elected."

"Had you been running for office?"

"No. I'd just come to town on my way West."

Slocum grunted. "I could have answered all that as easy as you. I knew it the first time I talked to you. Because, son, you were appointed by the mayor, or maybe they don't even call him the mayor, but the boss, of Retch, who told you as a kind of joke that you were sheriff of the town. Ain't no such thing. A man is elected sheriff of a county. He's appointed marshal of a town. When he's a sheriff, he rides from hell to breakfast on the trail of owlhoots, does all those things I mentioned, and he knows his territory, which can be awful big, by heart. Calling you a 'sheriff' was by way of being one of the meanest and most stupid practical jokes I ever come across. It told everybody who knew his big toe from his asshole that you were an early bouten—pilgrim—tenderfoot, new to the West and not liable to bother anybody on account of being ignorant. How long had you been in town when they 'elected' you?"

148

"About a week. Just meant to pass through, but I met Amelia."

"And sensibly stayed. Good for you. How many people do you know in Retch today?"

"The storekeepers, Henry Schmidt, Kinkaid and Adams, their wives, Amelia, the kids, Bob Cook." McGunn frowned. "About all, I suppose."

"Who's Bob Cook?"

"Chap runs the restaurant."

"Cook. I'll be doggoned," said Slocum mildly. "Never knew his name, but admire his handiwork. Cook's the cook and McGunn's the gunslinger. Except that he's an expert, and the nearest you come to being a law officer is your name. Is it real?"

"Sure it's real!"

"Keep your hair on, son. I don't mean to taunt you. You're ignorant of a lot, but you aren't stupid."

McGunn sagged back in his chair, looking abruptly defeated. "Why in tunket do you say I'm not stupid?"

"Because no stupid galoot could make Amelia here fall for him."

"That's so," said the girl. "Last night Daddy called you 'that Eastern glass of milk' and worse. I never knew it before, but he wouldn't have let us get married."

"How could he stop us?"

Slocum snorted. "Schmidt can do almost anything he wants to do in Retch, short of buying Maynard Savage. Or me. If you gave him six cents' worth of trouble, he'd have you killed," he snapped his fingers, "like that."

"That's illegal!"

Slocum brought them up to date on what he'd learned. They both grew a little paler in the face. "The whole town's a fake from top to bottom. There aren't any silver mines. Set you two aside, and some hunters and trappers and drifters, Savage and his boys, Cook, the fat bar critter at the Bull, and odd folks here and

149

there, this entire place is undiluted pestilence. Bill," he said, laying one enormous hand on the smaller man's shoulder, "don't blame yourself for the past, You were cut out to be a smart farmer but no more than a kidney plaster on a real lawdog. That's not your fault. A man's cut out for one thing in life and if he knows what it is, he ought to *be* it!"

McGunn looked up at him, sank into the swivel chair, and his handsome gray eyes filmed over. "John," he husked, "what the hell should I do? What can I do? Arrest her father?"

"You can't arrest three-quarters of Retch," said Slocum. "Speaking strictly, you can't arrest anybody at all. I'd just ride it out. They can't suspect anything about you, Bill, 'cause they cipher you out as pure dumb. Chances are they'll simply ignore both of you if you lie low."

"I can't do that," McGunn said stubbornly. "I can't be a part of something criminal and go along with it and abet it—"

"You won't be doing anything except sit on your butt for a few more days, dammit! Both of you act normal and lay low. Wait for—"

"For what?"

"Your deputy to get back or hell to break loose, whichever happens first. That's all. I'll be seeing you when it's time to do something. Trust me?"

McGunn stared. At last he grinned. "Absolutely."

"So do I," said the girl. She eyed Slocum and he had a swift remembrance of his manhood sticking straight up and shoving against her belly. He cradled the shotgun and stepped to the door, not meeting her gaze.

"Bill, you were a farmer and you were made into a straw sheriff, but what did you come West intending to do?"

McGunn said, "You mean, what do I want to be when I grow up?"

150

"You could put it that way."

"Anything but a farmer, at first. Now I'm not positive about it. I miss the land."

"Then you and Amelia talk it over every chance you get. I think you're a born farmer."

14

He didn't know how the eating was at the Palace of Mirrors, so he went back to Cook's greasery for a final feed. The place was more crammed than ever with dregs and flotsam and scum and there were plenty of rifles in evidence. He knew at once that he'd made a mistake. With Schmidt's outfit after him—officially now, most like—as well as the Kid Slocum bullshit, it was half-stewed bravado on his part to show his face in Retch, with nobody to side him, and indoors. Slocum hated bluster and swagger and stupidity, and here he was exhibiting all three to the highest pitch, without meaning to do it but out of negligence. He'd no business daydreaming about a plump virgin or concentrating on such secondary subjects as what McGunn ought to do and what should happen to the rascals of Retch. His prime concern was saving his own hide from Brandy and Schmidt and the devil and everybody, and clearing his name of the robbery charge and then getting the hell out of this town.

He was two steps into the room and had time to backtrack fast and disappear into the blizzard, but that was one act he couldn't manage, not even to save his life. That looked like cowardice. He did stop in his boot tracks, which gave the appearance of being jolted by the sight of the mob, which was another error; but he wouldn't retreat. So he glared around; at the near end of the counter he saw slim Chris Adams with his weasellike eyes glowing triumphant over the fleece col-

151

lar of his sheepskin coat, with a plate of buffalo balls in front of him. Slocum let his instincts take over. He sidelonged like a wakened 'winder on a hot rock, jerked Adams, who was flailing and yipping, back off the stool, hove him straight up over his head one-handed, and pitched him across three strides of room to a bunch of buff hunters, whom he trusted farther than most to be independent and even hostile to the Schmidt rabble. Of all the types that swarmed over the West, only the mountain men were more free and less fettered than the buffalo hunters.

"Know what you got there?" roared Slocum, sitting down at Adam's place, wiping the fork on his pants, and shoving a big fried testicle into his mouth. "You got a rat that gimme this—" tapping his bandaged skull—"when I wasn't looking. Then he left me in the snow while he went to get two more pricks to help him kill me before I woke up."

The play of the hunters turned serious. Adams shot upward as though tossed in a blanket, and fell among them; they let him hit the floor, and one or two booted him. "He's lying!" Adams cried out, terrified.

"I played poker with Slocum for a week," said one of the men loudly. It was the dead skinner's partner. "He's no liar. He's straight, Slocum is."

"True words," rumbled another. "I knowed John Slocum at Fort Hades on the Texican border. He don't crawfish and he don't forswear nor hatch windies." He was six feet four and built like the brutes he killed for a living.

Slocum ate at his normal pace, which was fairly fast, had a second cup of Arbuckle's, and told the cook quietly that he would not be around for a while but he'd see him before he left Retch. Bob Cook—a name that Slocum really couldn't get used to—said, "Don't let anybody come up behind you. There's been a slather of talk about you today."

"I feel certain o' that." He paid for the meal, including Adams' nuts. By then the buffalo hunters had tired of their brutal game of round-and-round, and had pitched Adams out into the street. Then several of them left. There was a kind of undercurrent in the place, a drone of low voices and an occasional surge here and there that brought more of the rank and file of Schmidt Inc. to the front of the restaurant. "Whatever you do, don't throw in with me," said Slocum, urgent but soft-spoken. He took up his shotgun and turned on the stool. He saw the partner of the man he'd killed, and beckoned him over. The hunter was grimier than ever, and stank like a honey-dipper. "Friend," said Slocum, "I'm afraid I had to polish off your pard."

"Shoot him?"

"Nope. Hand-to-hand."

"I'da give a gold eagle to see that. He was hard as flint."

"His neck wasn't. But I think your Big Fifty is still in my hotel room, and there's a female there with it who's plumb cultus, mean as they make 'em."

"Shit! I've had that old poison-stick fifteen years."

Slocum, against his better judgment, but beholden to do it, said, "I'll go back with you to retrieve it. She's laying for me, but I can't leave a man without his weapon."

They went into the hotel. The clerk laid eyes on Slocum and fidgeted. Slocum grinned. "What happened?"

"I unlocked the door and she hit me with something in the pit of the stomach. I think it was a chair. Then she walked over me and went to the outside door there and screamed something vulgar, and slammed it and came back and stepped over me again, and told me to get moving or she'd carve off my nose." The clerk blinked hard. "I thought she was serious, so I got out."

153

"She meant it. Was she dressed?"

"Not any more than a plucked jay. My God, that woman has big tits!" The clerk shut up, aware that he might have gone too far, but Slocum only nodded. "Then she left after a while, with her big bear coat and black Levi's on, and a shotgun hanging from her shoulder under the coat."

"How long ago?"

"Ten, fifteen minutes."

"Good. We're going to get this gentleman's rifle from the room."

"Sure. Go right ahead. Do you think she'll come back?"

"If she didn't have her tack with her, she will."

"Oh, dear," said the clerk.

"Right." Slocum led his companion down the hall, found the door locked, and opened it with the flat of a boot applied over the latch. He located the Sharps and handed it to the hunter. "She's loaded, but there wasn't a powder horn or anything with her."

"Powder horn? She ain't a muzzle-loader, she's a metal-ca'tridge gun, and my pard took just the one bullet, figuring he wouldn't need more." The Big Fifty swept slowly round to cover Slocum. "How come he never got that round off? You dry-gulch him?"

"Nope." Slocum described the fight. The Sharps moved away, was canted over the man's shoulder. "You believe me, then."

"Hell, yes. Phil said you don't make a habit of lying. Good enough for this old boy. Let's get out."

They walked into the hall. Slocum heard Brandy's voice lifted in a one-sided argument at the front desk. He beckoned, turned a corner, slid out the back, closed it silently when the other had come through like a ghost in his old moccasins, and headed for the street.

"Appears you don't hanker to see that big-titted woman again."

"You're right, I don't. She'd *make* me shoot her, and I'd have to do it so fast I couldn't count on just winging her."

"She 'n' you been running mates, or you just mounted her now and then?"

"Now and then," said Slocum. It certainly was no secret he was telling; all the hotel had heard them at their rutting. "Which way you headed?"

"Out. Had enough of this town."

"Can't say I feel different. But this storm—"

"It's nigh gone. Rather kick drifts than see walls." He turned away.

"Oh, Christ!" said Slocum, remembering. "Check your Sharps. I think I unloaded it."

The hunter looked. "Emptier'n a cowhand's head. I held a empty gun on you," he said accusingly.

"I didn't know it. I'd forgot."

The fellow came back and stared into Slocum's dark, fathomless eyes. "I credit that. Man can't recollect every damn thing he does. I got plenty of ammunition at the livery barn with my gear." He tugged out the big revolver from his belt. "I'll just hold this handy till I get there. This town ain't the kindliest spot in the Territory. So long, Slocum."

"Good luck."

Slocum trailed up the street, kicking loose snow and thinking wicked thoughts about Brandy, Retch, and Fate, till he reached the Palace of Mirrors. Chicago Ed Sealey let him in.

"Very sensible," said the scarface. "I'll have the girl show you your room. Your bags are there."

Bertha took him to a room out beyond the big empty gaming hall, where a narrow corridor ran the depth of the place with half a dozen doors on each side. He had a room to himself, smaller than the hotel's but a sight warmer.

"How many of us are there?" he asked.

155

"Altogether? Three girls, Mr. Savage, twenty men, and half a dozen servants."

Slocum went in, found that the door had a big bolt, and used it. He slept deep in nightmares from which he couldn't wake, and the day passed, the blizzard died, and the wind howled outside like a tortured spirit, empty now of snow but as cold as Henry Schmidt's heart.

15

Two days and two nights dragged their slow lengths through Retch while Slocum waited and champed at the imaginary Spanish spade bit in his mouth, feeling himself tied to an invisible hitching rail and unable to bust loose. The Palace of Mirrors was like a plush jail, with great food and fancy fittings and a tremendous cast-iron padlock on every door.

All the men wore their guns now, which made a lot of the customers stare and blink.

One of the guards told him that Brandy had shown up that evening, with her gown tugged so low and her breasts pushed so high that the rims of her nipples showed, but had been refused admittance because, she was told, no unescorted ladies were allowed in. Swearing like two bullwhackers, she'd left and come back shortly with Charlie Tucker in tow, and they'd both been blocked at the door and informed that the Palace was filled. The guard said that Tucker had been indignant and then abusive; and that Brandy by then "had a face like a ripe beet and was using words seldom heard outside of a two-bit panel-kip with wallet-snatchers behind every wall." A pair of leveled .44s and the menace of cold steel eyes above them had shut Tucker up, if not Brandy, and they'd been ordered not to return.

"Bounty hunters of a feather," grinned the guard, who was called Long Slim. He was an educated native of Nova Scotia and damn near seven feet tall.

"Right. Colonel Savage thought it might be so." Slocum went over to John Henry's table, a mite sad that someone else was making Brandy whimper and bawl and bay the moon already. He sat down and the cards slid out of the dealing box. He won $3000 that night, and felt higher and wider than he'd been feeling for a while. To hell with Miss Lady-with-the-hay-hook.

The third day of his sojourn in the Palace, he ambled to the front door to throw a few words with Bertha, whom he figured to bed soon, and discovered Chicago Ed in front of a mirror gumming down a false mustache. "Never knew anybody used those but Pinkerton men and play-actors," said Slocum.

Sealey rubbed some dirt on his face to cover his identifying scar. "I'm going out to scout. The chief thinks that they won't wait much longer. We can all feel things coming to a head."

"Me too. While you're out, would you try and see if the sheriff's Indian deputy got back from Tombstone?"

"Sure. But I mainly have to listen, not ask questions. My voice is too damnably well known." Ed smiled. Slocum wouldn't have recognized him. He wore tattered broadcloth under two yellow oilskin slickers, one over the other, and a cartridge belt with a holster and a Colt outside the whole shebang.

"You can trust the sheriff. He's in the know, and dead set against Schmidt's gang."

"So Mr. Savage says. If I can get into his office without being seen, I'll check."

Slocum jerked around at the sound of a fiddle. He'd never heard anything in the Palace but voices and the rattle and clink and snap of the gambling devices. He saw Maynard Savage sitting on his tall lookout perch, but instead of the gorgeous greener he held a violin, and he was making it talk as pretty and sweet and fast as any old-time kitter at a cowboy hoedown. The tune was an old favorite of Slocum's, "Cotton-Eyed Joe," played in double-quick time. He found that his right boot was tapping on the thick carpet. If Bertha'd been handy he'd have swung her around in a grand sweep.

Without pause, "Hell Among the Yearlings" followed. There was a gradual slowing, and suddenly old Savage was bowing "The Bonnie Blue Flag" and one of the black servants let out a rebel yell from down beside the hearth. Slocum answered it joyously, and half the men who lived in this great lush gambling hall were whooping and screeching and waving their arms high. Marse Robert himself might have walked in and felt at home. And Maynard Savage grinned ferociously, stood up on his stool so that he loomed higher than Satan on his throne, and fiddled away like mad while the Confederacy breathed again, and its blood, what was left anyway, coursed through veins that had nearly forgotten the pump and hotness of it beneath the skin. "Dixie," oh yes, chasing on the heels of "The Bonnie Blue Flag" as fast as ever a man could play it, and the ear-piercing yell, the Yell, that had almost been lost to them, it went a-rocketing back and forth amid the velvet and dark shining wood and polished mirrors. This time we'll take the bastards, *eeeee-yooow!* Aim for the big oval brass buckle and lift your sights a touch and splatter crimson all over that dark blue wool and you got you another Yank!

Slocum could fair whiff the acrid stink of the massed rifle firing and the cannon, scent the spilt blood and feel a certain big old gray cavalry horse under him again. Maynard Savage grinned and bent his head over his fiddle and threw the music down to them, his gray face all ruddy and glistening with sweat, and it was 1863 and the world was going to be all right.

And "Dixie" came to a last chorus and a sawing

final note that tore the throat out of Slocum with emotion that even a woman couldn't give him. Then there was silence and almost every man in the room realized that he'd been either yelling or singing right along. They fell dead quiet and looked at one another, a dozen or so of them old unreconstructed rebels and the rest foreigners or Yankees who'd been just as caught up in the song as the Johnnies, and three women gaping at them as if they'd all gone loco.

Four of the black servants, to judge by their enthusiasm, had fought for the South. The other two looked indulgent and even sympathetic. There wasn't a male in the place who wasn't excited.

Savage lowered his violin. He was ice again, sweating ice with a fire behind it. "Men, there's a fight coming. We've got a fortress here—I build all my houses, wherever they are, whatever they're for, to withstand sieges. That's why we've got no windows, two-foot-thick log walls, and a parapet around the flat roof above us, as most of you know." Slocum exclaimed profanely under his breath. The old boy was rich in surprises. "Lads," he went on, "it may be ten to one. They may come with dynamite or even crude mortars —I've heard they own several, which they use on wagon trains in ambushes.

"You're aware of the sort of critters we're facing. Cowards alone, wild dogs in a pack. You all know everything that I know about 'em, including what Major Slocum found out for us. I've heard they'll come by full moon. Likely tonight. Chicago Ed's scouting, and he may discover for sure. But I plan on tonight. It's a full moon and the town's been seething for days."

His hard eyes glowed as vivid as the diamonds in his shirt. "They want to kill me, and Slocum, and Long Slim who hasn't exactly been gentle with 'em, and probably more. They want to steal the Palace of Mirrors and run it themselves. They've stolen everything

159

within a radius of a hundred miles but this house, and now they want it. Will you let 'em do it?"

The expected roar went up. *No! No! Hell, no!*

"Now gather your heavy clothing, your rifles, and all the ammunition you can tote. Stack it on the steps that lead to the roof. Slim, you show Major Slocum where that is. I've already had the side door bolted and blocked. I want four men on the front door from this minute on. I want kegs of water up there, and I want the snow cleared entirely from the roof in the next two hours. Most of it's blown off already, but I won't have my men lying in puddles of slush."

He pulled out a linen handkerchief and mopped his face, then dropped his fiddle, which Long Slim caught. He sat down on the stool and the tall man handed up his shotgun. "If I'm killed, Major Slocum will take charge. He was a brother officer of mine in the late fracas."

"Mr. Savage?"

"Yes, Andy?"

"I've heard that Slo—that Major Slocum robbed a bank in Tombstone and shot down two tellers."

The eyes lanced across. "There is no truth in that rumor. It's a lie, as everything in Retch is a lie except among ourselves. You're all damn fine men, but Major Slocum is the best of you. However," said Maynard Savage, twinkling frostily, "I have no intention of dying, anyhow."

They cheered. "Dixie" still ran in their blood.

"In two hours, open the door to the usual business. Every man is to be double-armed, but keep the rifles on the stairs. You'll all take your cues from me. I believe that's all." He crossed one leg over the other and cradled his shotgun and hooded his gaze like a brooding hawk on a high tree.

What a letdown, thought Slocum, if nothing happens tonight! But the man was a born leader and this corps of hardcases would plainly follow him to Hell. He glanced around and caught the lunger's eye. John Henry grinned.

"I'll happily fight alongside you, Slocum," he rasped, "but don't ever try to give me orders."

"The most I'd hand you would be a mild suggestion."

They both laughed. Slocum knew that he'd spoken the truth. This was the one man he'd never willingly go up against.

He went back with Long Slim and was shown the steep, narrow steps to the roof behind a door just like all the others. On the other side of it leaned a huge beam, and cast-iron brackets were on the door and the wall beside it. Already some of the guards were stacking their rifles alongside their coats and hats and fine gray buckskin shooting gloves with big gauntlets against the cold. Slocum got his own trail stuff and his carbine, the extra .45 and all the ammunition from his room, and put them on the eighth step up.

Downstairs, an enormous sideboard which usually held little bite-sized fancy things for the gamblers to eat—a kind of high-toned free lunch—was laden with real food: antelope and buffalo steaks, kidneys, brains, tripe, roasted buff's balls, even boudins for those who'd learned to appreciate them, hot tongues, already sliced, the meat and the innards that would give a man strength for a long brawl. The girls—Bertha, Sadie, Chloe—were filling plates as fast as the delicacies were pointed out. Slocum got himself about two pounds of everything all heaped together, and ate hearty. Before he'd finished, Chicago Ed came in blowing with the cold, and bellied up to the sideboard.

"Chuckaway! I'll have a little of each, barring the boudins," he told Chloe, who seemed to be his girl. "Retch is fizzing and bubbling and got hell in its neck, but the word is they attack tomorrow."

Maynard Savage was there among them now. "I'm

going to push that appointment up to tonight," he said quietly.

"How, boss?" asked someone.

"With a lee-eetle shove," said Savage. "You'll see. Ed, any specific news?"

"I hear Schmidt hired that big bastard with the albino coat, Tucker, to play his right bower."

"Jesus!" said Slocum, aggrieved. "I thought Tucker was above that."

"Now you know better," said Savage. He sipped coffee laced with old brandy. "Watch yourself at the door tonight. If Tucker shows up, gun him instantly," he told Chicago Ed.

"Due respects and all to Sealey, Colonel," Slocum put in, "that could be more'n a one-man assignment. Tucker is fast and always on the peck." He took his last bite of tongue. "Goes double if the woman's with him."

"They probably won't come openly if the attack's set for tomorrow; if they do, there will be four men at the door all night anyway, so we won't fret."

"It's full moon," said Slocum, stubborn. "Men sometimes go just as loony as jackrabbits under a full moon."

"I'm counting on that," said Savage coldly. Slocum shut up.

Chicago Ed drew him aside. "I couldn't get word of that Injun deputy for you. The sheriff's office is locked tight, and Bob Cook, the only man I could ask, didn't know."

"Thanks for trying," said Slocum. Damn it all. He felt a cold, purposeful anger building in him. Where was McGunn? Had they gotten tired of him and bedded him down with a spade? He wasn't any use to them now, with everything out in the open, at least starting to come plain to most and sure to reach every ear in town before long. Slocum felt like going out to find the boy and Amelia. He sat on that impulse hard.

"Ed," said Maynard Savage, "pick your three best men to do sentry-go on the door tonight. You know what's going to happen. Your gear's on the second step from the bottom."

"Yes sir, thank you." He went off to wash his face and put on his uniform for the night's work. Slocum wandered to a poker table and sat down. The lunger joined him; he wore two revolvers in hard leather holsters, one tied down to his right leg and one a half-breed shoulder holster. Somehow he looked more comfortable than Slocum had ever seen him. Slocum mentioned it.

"Fight coming. Lets a man breathe, good for the chest." He sat down behind his dealing shoe, smiling thinly. "And God knows I feel naked without the guns. Even here. Where's your second? Savage said every man's to be double-armed."

Slocum pulled aside the left half of his doeskin jacket, to show the gigantic Bowie knife. "Figure that counts."

"Nice arm—the proper length. Nothing better in that line but a saber. I think you're a persuader man, though, from what I hear."

"I can use a knife a little," said Slocum.

The other laughed. "Not many men in this burg would face you if you were carrying so much as a rolled newspaper. I wonder when they let in the suckers? I'm not wearing my watch."

Slocum checked. "About two minutes." He hadn't realized the time was flying so briskly.

"Lot of fellers gonna be surprised when they walk in tonight," Slocum remarked.

"Not as surprised as when they walk out." John Henry leaned back, luxuriating, as though his lungs had miraculously healed. Slocum recollected that in Jacksboro he'd been told that the only time you'd never

163

see this man cough or double up was in action or on the verge of it. He speculated on the curious fact and concluded that it must have something to do with a ferocious, conscious controlling of the terrible disease.

The doors opened. The night had begun.

16

Midnight had passed, then one o'clock. Slocum was wound up so tight he thought his mainspring would snap. There was a full moon out there, but when in tophet was it due to set? They'd be sitting ducks when it went down. And Slocum, who ordinarily kept such elementary facts at his fingertips, couldn't think to save him how many hours of moonshine were left.

Then Savage shifted around on his stool, looked at Slocum out of those steel eyes, groomed his mustachios with one lean hand, and winked.

"A moment, gentlemen," said Maynard Savage, his voice ringing over the great room as it had once carried across a parade ground. "Please lay down your cards. Barney, stop that wheel."

A stillness came down like that before Shiloh. Seventy, perhaps eighty faces looked up at the two men.

"Most of you know what Retch is," said Savage calmly. "Others don't. For those of you that haven't heard, it's the devil's sanctuary; an outlaw shelter, a refuge for the incompetent scum and the off-scourings of the West who can't even steal horses or rustle cows on their own." A murmur rose, which he quelled with a gesture of the iridescent mother-of-pearl and silver scattergun. "Some of you may have guessed its secret without becoming part of it," said the cold voice. "This is not mining country nor ranching country. There are no farms in this vile landscape. Retch is certainly not a center of trade or commerce. Where, then, does all the money come from? Whence the inhabitants?

164

"Retch is owned and run by nine men. They rule an army of dregs—bandits, thieves, highwaymen, ambush specialists who never gunned down a man to his face unless two others were holding him. They run a primitive criminal organization that will commit any crime so long as there are enough of them and they can attack from the rear. That is what Retch is, gentlemen. It's a private army of low scoundrels who pay the political and economic faction for protection and for the gathering of information and the planning of their depredations, their plundering, murdering, ravaging raids on the country for many miles in every direction. The nine rascals who head them, led by one Henry Schmidt whom most of you know, have enough influence to keep this sinkhole a secret . . . though I believe the secret's been leaking, and will soon be out."

"Schmidt's my friend," a man called angrily.

"I know that, Cicero, but I consider you an honest fellow anyway." Savage shifted the greener by a hair. "If you aren't, you're free to go now, but I have more to say."

"I'll stick," said Cicero Welch. He ran the outfitting store. "I take it you can prove all this?"

"I can, but not tonight. It's my word for now, and that of my friends."

A cool-looking one-eyed man lifted his hand. "Ain't that Kid Slocum standing next to you? Mighty poor company for an honest man!"

"This is Major Slocum, but not 'Kid' Slocum. I believe you're a bounty hunter?"

"What if I am? I trailed that shark from Tombstone! I know who he is!"

"You are wrong," said Savage icily, "and you can check *that* with the sheriff or the federal marshal, who's on his way now." It had to be a bluff, but it worked. The one-eyed man subsided, and some others looked at one another with alarm. "The men at the top," Savage went on, "fence the looted property in other towns, where they have connections in places high enough to have kept away any serious investigators for three years. They are, if you don't know the term I used, receivers and sellers of stolen goods; wagon trains of blood-stained booty go out of Retch regularly in traveling weather. The killers get about a tenth of the spoils; Schmidt, Adams, Kinkaid, Jones, McTaver, George De Moss, Howard, O'Fenneran, and Matt Floyd take the rest. They pay off a sheriff or a marshal here and there, and for their own law they set up a pea-green Eastern kid who knows what's going on here about as thoroughly as a rock rabbit. I'm talking about Bill McGunn. He's not the law. There's no law in this town above or below Henry Schmidt."

"Where's all this palaver headed?" shouted a tipsy gent whose store clothes couldn't disguise his bronc-scratching profession.

"To this: Schmidt and Company want me dead, and they want this place for their own. I know too much about them, and I don't plan to knuckle under or keep my trap shut on the information when the federal government comes checking. So they're going to come and take us—the Palace and me. That's what they think, at least." His glare bored round the hall. "I don't mean to let myself or my property be taken by a dolled-up hunk of Yankee dogshit like old Henry Schmidt and his mange-bitten imitations of that bastard Quantrill who gave the South such a bad name. We're in for a little shooting scrape. There'll be some new faces in Hell for breakfast."

"*Some* fun!" hollered the bronc snapper lustily. "Can I throw in with you, mister?"

"Glad to have you." Savage smiled under his gray killer tails. "Anybody throws in with me and the Major here, they won't end up in Hell, because Confederate officers don't go there."

"Where do they go?" asked John Henry.

166

"Why, they're carried back to Old Virginny, man!"

It raised a scattered laugh and a couple of subdued hoots. Savage leaned forward. "A lot of you—most of you—already belong to the muster of rapscallions I've been talking about. But a few are there for reasons I understand, and if you throw in with me I'll treat you square and you'll gain back some lost pride." The place was dead quiet again. Slocum watched for movements, his hand resting easy on his Peacemaker.

Maynard Savage stood up and stepped to the top of his high stool. The shotgun poked forward. "That's all. Whoever wants to stay and side me, make up your mind now. The rest of you get out, and tell Schmidt what I've said. Tomorrow I'll be saying it again to a federal marshal and some Texas Rangers, because those gnat-brains you work for have sent crews as far as El Paso at least twice. *Now sit or git!*"

Most of them stood up, scowling, snarling, but making no furtive moves, for every Palace man had drawn his guns. Slowly, arguing among themselves, they moved toward the foyer.

"And no arms go with you," said Savage. At that there was an outraged cry. The guns of the guards came up, and Slocum's with them. The door was opened, and they began to file out.

Welch called, "Savage, you ain't offered me any proof of what you're saying! I can't accept this kind of thing about Henry and Chris—"

"Then leave, Cicero. No hard feelings. But don't come with the mob when they attack. You're no fighter."

"I'm going home to bed," said Welch.

Savage surveyed the emptied room. Nine or ten men had stayed.

He began climbing down to the floor. "Longest damn speech I ever made, Major. If it doesn't force the enemy to advance his plans, I'm a Dutchman."

167

Standing on the expensive rug, shorter than Slocum beside him but still dominating everything, he inhaled deeply. "You lads who stuck," he said, "I'll tell you now, there's $1000 in gold for every man who lives through the battle." Chicago Ed and Long Slim were heaving two huge thick planks into the brackets beside the front door. "I could have had four times your number, but I don't want a man who fights only for money."

Scarborough, a wide oaken chunk of a man, said, "How in blazes are we to fight? You have no windows, no gunports. Enough men on a log will batter in that door—"

"We have a fortified roof. It's not known to anyone but us, I think, because the Palace is higher than any other building in town. We'll all be up there shortly. Now go and collect your coats and hats, and any weapons that you fancy as well as your own. There's crates of ammunition waiting above, with two kegs of old bourbon and tin cups and—other things. When you're ready, we'll have a round of my best liquor and hit the roof and wait. But hear this, gentlemen," he said tightly. "Anybody who gets too drunk to shoot straight will be chucked off the edge without mercy."

The bronc buster, who was about twenty-five and already bowlegged as an old hairpin, grinned sheepishly and said, "I got me half a skinful right now, mister, but the cold air'll fix that in two-and-a-half shakes." He pointed at Slocum. "Wasn't you in Hidalgo a couple years back, and bust up the Red Star Saloon and get shanghaied for it?" Slocum nodded. "I seen that fight. You're a hardcase, you are. Cleaned that bastard's plow till his own wife couldn't tell him from a fresh-skinned ox."

"What of it?"

"That's the reason I throwed in with this outfit. I don't know the *presidente* here from a bucket o' guts,

168

but you, you'll do to ride the river with." He stuck out his hand. "Name of Blue Davies."

"John Slocum." They shook. "Glad to have you with us. That hogleg looks fair well used."

"I can hit a barn if you turn me in the right direction."

Savage smiled. "Major, I'd like to hear about that affair some day. Girls, drinks all around!"

Ten minutes later, after a toast to Savage and victory, they were ready. Slocum had gone and exchanged his pale doeskin jacket for the elkskin coat, which made a poorer target and was a lot thicker.

He wondered where Brandy and Amelia and McGunn and Tucker were now. And old Foot in Grave. There was a palpable air of anticipation in the Palace of Mirrors, not leavened with fear, but calm and nerveless, a kind of agreeable tension shared among these gristly fighters. Slocum thought, it's better'n waiting for the Yanks to come at you—maybe because you're older—but it's a little the same too. He counted noses. Colonel Savage, twenty-six of his men, ten newcomers who mostly looked capable, and himself: thirty-eight men and the three females. How many opponents, if they did come? A couple of hundred or more? Or would they rebel against Schmidt when it came to attacking a fortification like the Palace? From the looks on the mugs of those who'd left, they'd be back all right.

Chicago Ed and Ambrose, a man with skin the color of ebony wood and muscles like it, too, were left to watch the front door. Savage told them that if it was broached, they were to retreat to the roof. The girls would sit on the stairs with that door barred, and open it only to the password—"Aura Lee."

The men trooped up to the roof, collecting their gear as they went, cautioning one another to be quiet up there. Slocum heard the beam thunk into its brackets

169

behind them. Now they were either safe in a garrison or trapped like field mice in a box; it depended on the equipment, tactics, and valor of the enemy.

The roof was of planks laid across timber beams, with a parapet all around made of logs and somewhat over two feet in height; at the front left corner, the southeast one, a tall brick chimney reared up against the clear black windy sky. Savage gathered his men at the center of the square platform, and spoke softly. "Major Slocum, take command of the front; Long Slim, the back; John Henry, the western rampart; and Barney, the east. I'll be where I'm needed at the moment. We'll leave the trap door to the stairs open, so watch yourselves and don't fall into it. There are two water barrels in the corner beyond it, with dippers and a bucket in case of fire bombs."

"Fire bombs!" said someone fearfully.

"Possible, after they've been repulsed a time or two," said Savage, voice as bleak as the air about them. "I estimate the odds at not much more than five to one, and we have all the advantages but mobility. Every man will take a position in the lee of a wall, nobody to show himself until the shooting's started. With luck, they'll expect us all to be huddled downstairs, and come openly to the front door."

"How long will it hold?" That was the lunger, laconic, almost uninterested.

"I hope till the end of the hostilities. If it doesn't, you'll get further orders then. Two kegs of bourbon are broached vonder; you'll find tin cups there. Not too much drinking, though—save it for the wounded. We'll put them by the chimney, where it's warmest. Shoot to kill and fire at anyone you think you may hit: there's all the ammunition we need, and we have to thin out this rabble to an ineffectual force before we lose the moonlight. Remember you'll be shooting downgrade, and make allowances."

170

"Savage," said a huge shadow under a wide Mexican *sombrero*, "go teach your granny to suck eggs! You think you got childerns here?" It was a buffalo hunter, cuddling his Big Fifty.

"Sorry," said Savage, and Slocum saw his teeth flash in a grin. "We're not all professionals. If your rifle jams or gets too hot, drop it and take one of the extra Winchesters. They're stacked beside the ammunition crates between the chimney and the whiskey. The cartridge boxes are caliber-marked in large figures; you'll be able to see better after a few minutes in the dark. There's dynamite—two boxes—beside the trap." He gestured at the west end of the roof. "Each stick has a ten-second fuse. Only men who can throw well and are used to the stuff will touch it, though. One stick exploding on this flat could kill or maim a dozen of us."

"What if they throw dynamite up here?"

"You'd best not let 'em come that close—after the first action."

"And what'll that be?"

"You'll see, Major Slocum. A pleasant surprise for the enterprising foemen." He walked across to the front and scanned the broad street in both directions, came back and said, "Nothing yet. God, if they don't come!" A fist smacked a palm, the loudest noise they'd made yet. "If Schmidt sees through the bluff! But he can't, he won't."

"He's no dunderhead," said Beeman.

"No, but I think the Texas Ranger story will push him past his limit."

"Are there Rangers coming?" asked Stewart, the Australian ex-highwayman. "I'm wanted pretty badly in Paso."

"Neither Rangers nor federal marshal. There's only this group of men here."

"Jesus! The gall," muttered Stewart.

171

"Now all of you string out, pick your wall, and sit down behind it. Don't show yourselves till you have the order. Sharpshooters to the front barricade. What's your monicker, hunter?"

"Lighter Johnson," said the big man gruffly.

"You take the front of the wall by the chimney with that poison-slinger. You're worth ten pistoleers to me."

"Twenty." A statement of honest belief in his own value.

"Major, you watch for them. Nobody talks, smokes, or stands up." He laid his hand for a second on Slocum's shoulder. "You must protect the door."

Slocum nodded. He went over and blended in with the brick chimney, jamming his hat down over his brows to block out the moon. The town lay all about him: silent, motionless, dead under its coating of white. On either side the hide-and-pole shanties stretched out, lumps of drifted snow with dark holes where the doors, or skin-flapped openings, would be. Several hundred feet away to the west was the brothel. About the same distance east sat Bob Cook's timber restaurant, its roof stacked with one big sloped drift, smoke and steam rising from the tin stack together. Slocum's breath fogged out thinly. He could see everything that went to make up the ramshackle hamlet, even the five or six small respectable houses beyond the thicketed rise. He stared at the second one of the cluster. There was movement in front of it, sudden, ominous. Slocum grinned. The word had been passed. A small figure came out of another house and ran to Schmidt's, fell on the ice, clambered up, limped on. The little black manikins fanned out and came toward him.

He turned to look down past the two-story hotel—damn, if the bastards thought of it, they could fire onto this roof from that second floor, although the range was far enough to make a hit just lucky—and saw a blotch of darkness in front of the Earthquake that must

172

be thirty men or more. They weren't moving. Waiting for their orders. They probably had to get orders from Schmidt to visit the privy.

Stores, big barn, buff-hide shelters, jail, billiard parlor, undertaker's, cribhouse, saloons, dens, everything counterpaned with the snow. Dimly discerned, a thin trail cut through it going north from behind the livery barn: Kiwanwatewa's? Not made going out through the norther, but much later. Maybe he'd made it there and back. Slocum hoped. He scanned the land again. More men waiting across by the telegraph office now; they'd come out of nowhere. No such place as nowhere, unless it's where I'm going when I croak. Tonight? Who knows?

Silence.

Motion. The men coming over the rise. Those from the Earthquake headed this way now. They carried a log, six to a side. Hell of a big log, gnarled, humpbacked, but as good a battering ram as you'd want. Bunch from the telegrapher's coming kittycorner across the road now. Another lot, looser and more numerous, from The Bull's Pizzle.

"Enemy advancing," he said calmly.

A man was moving in the shade of the front parapet. Slocum whispered, "Who's that?"

Savage said behind him, "Never mind. No shooting yet." Slocum hitched up his Spencer and waited. The crouching man struck a lucifer and lit a length of tow yarn, the light eerie on his bare hands and face. Holding it low, he pulled on one gauntlet glove with his teeth and picked up a two-quart frying pan full of liquid.

"Wait for the ram." Savage's voice carried about a yard. The crouching man nodded. In the icy cold, Slocum saw sweat sheening his face; he was watching the burning tow in his bare hand.

The mob came together. Christ, two hundred was

173

conservative. They hung back in the middle of the road. The log was brought through. Slocum could hear little grunts and gasps. The thing weighed as much as a freighted ox-wagon. He wondered where they'd found it. Maybe it had been kept for just this minute, maybe for years. One carrier slipped and fell. The log jerked and was righted, somebody cursed. The man rolled over, whimpering. Broke his leg, most like. They kicked him out of the way. Even hurt, he was too frightened of Schmidt to cry out. He clawed away.

The log was held a few yards from the door. He could see the men tighten up, preparing. Nobody looked up. "In a second," he said, having grasped the intentions of the crouching man above the door. Then, "Here they come," he said.

The man stood up—it was Andy, the guard—and flicked the burning tow over the surface of the liquid. It was coal oil, half a gallon. It flared up with a muffled whoosh, the fire licking at Andy's face. He leaned over the low breastwork and with a powerful swing flipped the stuff out and up, then reversed the skillet so that every drop poured down on the men rushing at the door.

There was a yell that broke the night wide open, as the throng saw splashes of flame raining from the sky. Andy jackknifed and came up with a second enormous pan, lit the kerosene, flung it straight out. Screams like scarlet bolts jagged up across the crowd's roar. Slocum eased sideways and saw the log fall. The men dropped away, some running, their clothes and hair afire. The screaming was awful. It warmed his heart.

"Now," said Savage.

"Fire," Slocum barked, and put four spaced shots into the mob, trying to aim where his slugs would go through one man and hit another. Beside him Lighter Johnson leveled his Big Fifty and let her go, cutting a path in the thick of the bodies. Andy toothed off his

174

gauntlet glove and poked a shotgun nearly vertical over the wall and ventilated three or four skulls with the broad scatter of the buckshot, one barrel and then, higher, the other. Rifles cracked along the parapet. Savage called from the center of the roof, "Every other man to the front!" They were shoulder to shoulder now, firing into the black of them. Someone was crushed under the ponderous ram and screeching his guts out. The Sharps boomed again. Slocum saw men fall backwards in a fresh-sliced path halfway through the milling gang.

The slaughter was terrific. Nothing had been expected from the roof; they were all supposed to be huddled inside the hall downstairs. A few pistol shots came up at them, badly aimed, too fast: the amateurs and hotheads of the bloody crew, scared out of their minds.

Slocum, firing, reloading, looked for Tucker. No sign. Either he'd come in a darker coat or he wasn't even there. Likely he'd taken Schmidt's money and holed up. Skunk. He saw out of the corner of his eye that Andy was down. He shot three men in quick angry succession. Then the street had almost emptied, leaving only the wounded and the dead. The man pinned under the log was calling for help in a hoarse, agonized voice. His clothes were on fire and the great tree trunk lay across his groin. Slocum shot him.

"Back to your positions and sit down," said Savage. "The four in command to patrol their sides. Reload." He chuckled, a glacial trickle of sound in the night. "That medieval trick caught them, by thunder! How's Andy?"

A black man was rolling him over. "Took one between the eyes."

"Bring him to the middle, where he won't trip anyone. Damn," said Savage, "he was the best faro banker I ever knew."

"Movement over this way," said Barney laconically. "No, never mind. It's the Injuns is all." Slocum looked; the inhabitants of the pole-and-hide shelters were running across the frozen wastes, past the back of the restaurant, toward the rise, to hide in the snow-laden thickets. Of course they had no idea what was happening in this white man's warfare, or who the ultimate targets might be. The squaws carried bundles and babies, the braves unencumbered ran ahead. At least they were all wearing everything they owned in the way of clothing. But some of them could freeze to death if the battle went on all night.

Slocum eyed the street. Men were coming back, congregating between jail and billiard parlor, afraid to step into the moonlight. "Johnson, let's take us a few." The buffalo hunter stood up and rested his big slinger on the log coping. He and Slocum shot together, aiming into the middle of the group. Confused movement followed. Slocum shot twice more, Lighter once—he had to reload his one-shot weapon—before the enemy vanished, leaving bodies behind.

Lighter tore off a mouthful of Wedding Cake plug tobacco. "I make that thirteen down," he said, counting forms. "Some kilt."

"About right. Nice shooting."

"Calves in a bunch," said the hunter scornfully. "Thisyere girl will put a bullet through two old bulls. I figure that equals about eight men, if I could get 'em to line up."

A rifle cracked and Slocum felt a tug at his hat brim. He dodged into the shadow of the warm chimney. "That un nigh taken off your topknot, sonny," said Johnson, going to ground. "But them critters knows about as much o' shooting straight as a pig knows about a sidesaddle."

"Wait a while," said Savage. "There are bounty hunters and Kentucky riflemen out there."

176

The white snow was a boon; Slocum watched the mob edging back between the low buildings, nerving themselves for a charge. A voice called loudly, "Go on, you damn cowards, that Palace bunch is so ladylike they gotta sit down to piss!" Another answered him sourly, "Tell that to them dead men!" Then they were coming fast in a ragged line across the road, converging on the door.

"Up and at 'em," said Slocum, beginning to shoot. The trick of aiming downhill came to him gradually, as usual when there'd been a long spell since he'd done it. He fired at one man three times before he catapulted him backwards. Then he had it. He shot till the carbine was empty, then reloaded. He could hear the thunder of the buffalo gun and the crackle and hammering echoes of the line of Winchesters. Several men reached the log, then more; they heaved it up. Savage bent out over the wall and let go both barrels of his greener. It left two or three men, who couldn't hold the huge ram and dropped it, jumping away fast as it crashed to earth.

A spark of flame appeared toward the near side of the street. Slocum saw a man lighting the fuse on a stick of dynamite. He waited till the yahoo had lifted it to throw, then shot him in the belly. The dynamite rolled away. Some fool grabbed it up and Slocum took him out too. Then there was a hell of a blast, and everyone on the roof instinctively ducked. Men writhed and screamed on the packed snow.

"Dynamiters here," called the lunger joyously. He might have been announcing the arrival of a friendly battalion. "They're after the side door."

"It's blocked, but don't let 'em get close!" called Maynard Savage.

The rifles on the west wall opened up. There was another tremendous explosion. "That was three sticks wrapped together," said John Henry through the roll-

177

ing echoes. "Dumb yack." He leaned out and fired his sawed-off, then discarded it for a rifle.

Slocum and Johnson were working as a team, one firing as the other went down behind the logs. The more watchful assailants now had them located as the most deadly sharpshooters, and concentrated their fire on the chimney corner, leaning against walls in the darkest shadows and aiming in the moonlight when either one appeared. The slugs were too close for what Slocum called true comfort, but shooting was tricky in the milky, spectral, eye-foxing moonlight, and for a time they weren't hit. Meanwhile the road became a site of butchery. Two more would-be dynamiters were blown to pieces by their own explosive, and a phalanx of whiskey-bold attackers was opened up and scattered by Johnson's great gun. Then at last he grunted and touched his head.

"Them durn fools shooted off my ear lobe," he said, pulling out a dirty handkerchief for a bandage. "T'were my favorite lobe, too."

Slocum crawled down the line to where Littlefield lay dead, pulled him to the middle of the roof, took his place. His Spencer had jammed and he took a Winchester from the stack, with two boxes of cartridges. The pained screeching from below was horrible. If Schmidt had any military sense, he'd have the wounded muzzled or shot, or at least dragged out of hearing. It must be working hell on his men's nerves.

Savage was over beside John Henry. The life of a dynamite thrower being measured in seconds, and too much havoc being wrought in their own ranks by their own volcanic explosions, the attackers had quit trying for the side door. Only a token few were hiding among the abandoned shanties and trying to pick off the defenders.

There were seven dead men in the middle of the roof and three incapacitated wounded beside the heat-diffusing chimney. That left twenty-eight.

The firing dwindled and died. Slocum scanned the scene below, moving from wall to wall. Nothing moved except the wriggling, struggling wounded. Clouds of white powder smoke rose, hit the wind, and were dissipated. He saw one thin strip of light against the black hulk of the billiard parlor across the street, where a blind had not been closed entirely. Maybe that was GHQ. He took a stick of dynamite from a box, went to the near southwest corner, lit the fuse with a match, stood up and hurled it with all the strength of his iron arm. It struck the wall of the billiard room and dropped and went off with a flash and a roar. The front of the building, hardly more than a jerrybuilt shack, sagged and fell in. A lantern showed briefly and went out. Dark figures scattered, and he picked off three before they'd vanished. He hoped that he'd got some of the bosses. A cinch they wouldn't be out on the street fighting.

"Everyone down," Savage ordered. They hunkered, and the slugs of the enemy marksmen whistled harmlessly overhead. One or two fellows hoisted the hats of the dead men on rifle barrels and a flurry of shooting followed. Slocum went to the water barrels and dipped out two long drinks; then he joined John Henry at the bourbon kegs, and they toasted each other with tin cups sloshing full. Johnson, the kerchief tied to his torn ear with a whang string, came over on toes and knuckles.

"Lemme a cup o' that scamper juice. I'm a wounded man and like to die of the gashly pain."

Slocum gave him a cup. "You've been hurt worse with a skinning knife," he said.

"How'n billy-be-shat you know that fact, sonny?"

"You're missing the top joint of your left thumb."

"Right, it *was* a skin-knife, too," said Johnson. "First buffalo I ever tried to get the hide offen by myself. Sliced her like she was a sausage. See how you knowed—a sight of us has hacked their hands up when

179

we was learning the trade." He threw off the whiskey in a long swallow. "Not bad for civilized lemonade, long's you can strain it through a chaw of baccy. Gimme one more." Slocum dipped him a second. "You're all right, sonny. Some bosses think the milk o' the wild mare spiles the shooting eye, but that's wrong and you know it." He looked around, pressing his wipe against the bleeding ear. He'd removed his Mexican hat, a distinct target. "We got us saddled with a dead nag, gents. We ain't downed but half o' them punks, and there's mebbe an hour of light left. They got the sense of a turd, they'll wait and come in the dark."

"We'll be ready," said Slocum. "But let's try and draw 'em."

He crept to the front of the platform and slid upright next to the chimney and reconnoitered. The mortars hadn't been brought up; maybe they were mythical. The crowds were gone, perhaps behind the stable or the general store. Only an occasional flash of black powder showed that the snipers were still posted. As he was scanning the ground, he heard the whump of a slug hitting flesh and someone bellowed his agony. Slocum turned and saw Barney, the croupier, both hands clutching his face, spin around on his heels and pitch over the edge backward. *Twenty-seven,* he thought. He bent toward the street and let out a Blackfoot war whoop—a terrifying, screaming yodel of racket that carried across the town and the prairie.

Colonel Savage said, "Lighter, take command of the east wall."

Johnson said, "Yup," and strode over to where Barney had stood and gave an Apache whoop, a little different from Slocum's and just as horrible. Then they both gobbled, long and deep-throated and challenging.

The whoop and gobble, as every Westerner worth his keep knew, meant that somebody was due to cash in his chips. It was a defiant challenge: in words, it

180

meant "Come out and fight," and not to answer was to brand yourself a rank coward.

Some of the opposition took the bait. They couldn't help it. Even some who *were* cowardly and set high values on their useless hides came running toward the Palace, their muscles responding automatically to the threatening summons. They fired up wildly as the defenders rose behind the barricade and shot down at them. *"Vengan, hombres, muerte los!"* yelped a Mexican *bandido* just before Slocum blasted him in the guts. His *sombrero* fell off, its gold braid shining dully in the moonlight.

A big man as wide as a door, whom Slocum remembered from the Earthquake, came pounding unscathed through a hail of bullets till he'd come within a dozen feet of the door. He pulled a stick of dynamite from his hip pocket. "You're all gonna be blowed into the middle o' next week!" he proclaimed, stentorian as a rutting bull. He scratched a lucifer on sandpaper glued to the explosive. Slocum shot him in the head. The match fell on one side, still burning; the dynamite fell on the other. A man dived for the match and incredibly snatched it up before it went out. "No peckerwood gobbles at me!" He was groping for the deadly stick when John Henry let him have a skullful of buckshot. At last the match went out.

A man in front of the jail was trumpeting "Come back, come back, you damn fools!" Chris Adams. So the strategy was to wait for dark. Slocum drew as careful a bead on him as he'd ever drawn in his life, and the fucking cartridge jammed. He threw the rifle aside with a wordless roar, drew his second-best sixgun because the thumb-buster was for close quarters, and slammed both hands on it to steady it. He stood spraddle-legged and sighted and fired and knocked Adams back flat, which papered him on the wall, from

181

which he slowly glided down and made a dark puddle on the snow.

"Kinkaid!" he howled, brimming with violent, unthinking hatred, no longer cold and steady. "Come out, Kinkaid, you shit-brained immigrant!" Then he cooled a shade. "Ain't you man enough to answer the whoop and gobble? You gonna stick behind your wall and let your men die for you?"

One of the attacking runners stopped in his tracks and whipped around, back to the Palace. "Yeah, Kinkaid, McTaver, Floyd. Where are you lousy cunts?"

"For God's sake, don't shoot *that* man," Slocum ordered.

Some of the adversaries went crazy about the same time that this idiot had. The full moon had been working on their shallow minds all night, and now they turned from driving greed to unreasoning indignation. The street was full of wrathful yells, and four or five men emerged from the telegraph office, dragging a fellow who struggled and screeched. It wasn't Kinkaid, but it had to be a big shot. Slocum took him.

Then Long Slim was beside him, lighting a stick of dynamite. "I used to be good at this," he grunted, and threw the thing far out, turning end over end, across the street, to land on the roof of the telegrapher's shack. It rolled a little way and detonated. The shack went to pieces. A few men crawled away or floundered like fish tossed on a riverbank.

Someone shot the man who had yelled for Kinkaid. Most of the riflemen were lining the front parapet, pumping lead. There was an ear-shattering devil's tattoo over the town, a blend of voices in rage or in hellish agony punctuated by the steady rattle of the rifles and the great rich boom of Johnson's Big Fifty. It went on and on and then it was nothing but retreating echoes, the street cleared, nothing in sight worth shooting; and Slocum turned to count their own losses.

Worse this time. Too much excited exposure in the

heat of the fight. Reckon the moon works some on everybody, not just on the low primitive thugs out there, he thought, watching the dead put down in a row and the badly wounded carried to the chimney. Christ!

Of the thirty-eight men who'd been alive within the Palace walls not so long ago, twelve were on their feet; and Chicago Ed and Ambrose down waiting behind the door made fourteen. Seven were wounded badly enough to be out of commission. Seventeen were buzzard beef.

Slocum walked over to the lunger. "I always heard you bore a charmed life." They were both untouched.

"Yes, that's my curse," said John Henry lightly, reloading his sawed-off greener. "Have a stogie?"

"Makes a man too good a target. There's some snipers in the hotel now." Slocum got himself a drink of whiskey. It went down raw; his throat burnt from powder smoke and the delirium of fighting, from long breathing of the damn icy air and a lot of half-conscious yowling. It tore your gullet to give a real Blackfoot whoop, too. He got himself a dipper of water and then enjoyed more bourbon.

Colonel Savage, looking unruffled, checked on the wounded and told Slocum that three might live. Scarborough had a chest wound that had missed the lungs and might heal. Blue Davies, the bronc peeler, had a shattered forearm that would come off when they had the opportunity; his days with the rough string were finished. Slocum knelt beside him; the cowhand grinned. "What the hell, I asked in—and nobody lasts much longer at my job than I have, anyhow."

"What'll you do?"

"If I don't go over the range? Mebbe be a real mean chuckwagon cook. I make a good stew. A belly-cheater don't need but one arm and a hook, and that's what I aim to have."

"You'll have one thousand dollars in gold to start in with."

183

"Shit, I'll blow that in three nights in a fancy house."

Slocum went back to the colonel. "We lost Beeman, O'Kelly, Stewart, Daley, McBride, four others on that raid," said Savage. "I hope to God it was worth it."

"We took better than fifty of them with the whoop-and-gobble bait, if that's what you're being so frosty about."

"No, it was a good play. They were waiting to come after moonset."

"If Schmidt can bully them into coming then, what's left of them, we're mutton."

Savage tugged his gray mustachios. "Don't be too certain, Major. The old wolf has a trick or two left." He went to the hatchway and called down to Bertha. "Is that kettle of tallow on the stove?"

"It's bubbling," she shrieked back. "What's going on up there?" The women must be dying of curiosity, Slocum thought.

"We're watching the stars. They're superb tonight," said Maynard Savage, and walked over to the bourbon kegs. Slocum went with him, crouching a little. "They haven't recovered from the first setback, Major. They firmly believed they'd be fighting us in the building and have it over with in twenty minutes. Did you hear Schmidt yell when they brought up the battering ram?"

"No, I never."

"He was out there someplace then. I know that oily voice. He cried out, 'For God's sake don't bust the big mirrors!' Still hoping to run my place, the swine. I wonder how he expected to get the blood off the rugs?" He stood holding the tin cup like a crystal goblet, staring at his force. "A dozen. I wonder if I'd better bring Chicago Ed and Ambrose up? Not much sense sitting at the door when most of us are down." He went back to the trapdoor.

Slocum knelt by Lighter Johnson. "How's the ear?"

"Got enough varnish in this old hide by now to make

184

me think I got my lobe back." He was swabbing out the bore of the big rifle. "Reckon they'll come again, sonny?"

"Toss-up. We'd better be less brash this time."

"Yar, lost some good old boys useless-like. Killing gets in a man and he thinks puny."

Slocum sat down by the south rampart and loaded his fresh Winchester, then his Colt. The war languished. Time stretched out, the moon sank and touched the jagged white hills. A flurry of gunfire broke out somewhere to the west. Slocum couldn't tell just where because he couldn't see any powder smoke, and the echoes drumfired among the buildings. Chicago Ed, who had come up with black Ambrose, was sent down again on an errand, and returned carrying a huge copper kettle, as heavy as a three-month colt, from the way he staggered under it. He set it down at the wall above the door.

That stunt again, Colonel? Never work twice, thought Slocum. Ten feet away he could feel the heat radiating from it. Chicago Ed took off the thickly padded gloves and descended once more, to bring up an armful of sticks wrapped with tight rag heads, like giant lucifers. Torches, sure; Slocum could smell the kerosene above the stink of the kettle's liquid tallow.

Maybe it would work. When they came, they wouldn't be carrying lanterns. They'd have sighted on the log and the door, estimated the distance, then they'd advance by thin starshine. He wondered if they'd be visible from up here. As black blotches against the hashed-up snow, possibly, but not clear enough for good shooting. Slocum looked at the hot tallow, its steam rising through the air that was almost cold enough to rigidify his trigger finger. The three wounded men who could sit up were huddled against the bricks of the chimney; Ed had kept up the hearth fire all night.

The moon set, after a last grin at them.

The men had been stationed moments before, two to each of three walls, seven at the rampart fronting the street, Savage behind them prowling up and down. No shots had come from the hotel for a quarter-hour. Slocum speculated uselessly on who'd been firing at what, over west there.

Slocum thought about the skillets of coal oil, and the bubbling tallow. Hell, there's no rules when you're outnumbered. Nor when you're fighting foul refuse like Schmidt's crew—child-murderers, rapers, mass killers, *scum*—

But what a miserable death. Worse than buckshot in the face.

We gonna come through this alive? Lighter and John Henry and the Colonel and me? he mused.

Taking too long. Hate to stop and think in the middle of an engagement, he worried. He peeled off his gloves, massaged his frost-bound hands, wiggled his fingers, inched over and put them on the warm brick of the chimney. After a while they felt pretty limber. He edged back.

"No more movement," said Savage quietly. "Nobody budge. Nobody speak or cough. Just listen." His shadow loomed up between Slocum and Johnson. "Listen for any sound at all."

At the cue, there came a distant bark, like a booted yellow dog's, rising higher and higher as though the throat that sent it out was trembling; it was one of the saddest sounds in creation, till it hit its peak and held the tone like a golden bell struck in a temple, on and on, then dying, falling to a moan and a faint noise like a lady's sigh.

"Coyote," said Lighter, and was hushed for his pains.

Real coyote, too, unless the Apaches were attacking. They could imitate the brute's howl to perfection. No one else could. Real coyote. Bewildered in the cold and white and silence, lonesome maybe for a frozen mate.

186

Slocum eased his breath till it wasn't much more frequent than a corpse's.

Some foot hit wood down there, an awning post at the undertaker's or part of one of the shattered plank huts. A voice grunted a couple of words, not on the Palace roof.

Silently Chicago Ed and big Ambrose came to the kettle and lifted it with their padded gloves and set it on the coping of the log parapet. Savage, hatless now, leaned between Slocum and the hunter and thrust his head forward till it barely cleared the wall. Smart. Yacks looking up could see heads against the stars.

Footfalls, heavy, laboring. Scramble. Grunts. A word, another, husky and low. Steps, boots squeaking on ice. A rifle levered. Scuffling sounds. All from below, the roof a tomb.

Then the goddamnedest crash under heaven, louder than a thunder-crack, and the Palace of Mirrors shuddered under them like a stricken saddle horse, or so it seemed to Slocum. He almost leaped to his feet. But Savage reached out to either side and moved his hands up and down—still, be still. His authority held; a man trusted by his men. No one moved.

A long silence from the road. Then voices mumbling together. Slocum thought of the heavy oak door and the two immense planks that barred it. They'd stand another stroke of the ram, maybe even two or three more. Savage wanted to wait. Right.

A cool, purposeful, alert rage built in Slocum's chest and head. He tasted like blood; that was imagination, but he savored it. *Here comes the last big fuss.*

Grunts from men lifting something heavy. They must have backed off and dropped the log after that one incredible slam at the door. Scrabbling noises of clumsy steps in the snow, on the squealing ice. Then Savage was gone, and Slocum turned his head and saw the gray man strike a white phosphorous match on his thumbnail, in the fashion of John Henry, and touch it to the head of a coal-oil torch. The roof lit up like the stage of a big-town theater. Dead men, wounded, crouching fighters, water barrels and dynamite boxes were illuminated by the spitting brilliance. Savage swung it underhand and let it fly, out over Slocum's head toward the street. Slocum got to his feet, Savage again beside him. The Retch road was a scene out of Hell: dead men, dynamited holes in the ice and earth, knots of waiting enemy, and the titanic ram being carried full tilt for a second assault. Startled open-mouthed faces looking up from black-suited, overcoated men in a huddle beside the door, ready to be the first invaders into the Palace.

"Tallow pot," said Savage calmly, like a railroad engineer talking to his fireman. Chicago Ed and Ambrose tipped the kettle gently outward. A stream of reeking fat poured down onto the group at the door, splashing out farther as they moved the big copper vessel forward. Slocum, staring down, saw the terrible rain hit faces and backs. In the sputtering glare of the single torch on the ground, he thought he saw the flesh melt off the fronts of grinning skulls. It was no illusion; the noise those men made reinforced it. He knew he had seen Pony McTaver and Jim Kinkaid waiting in that bunch, confident that they wouldn't be fired on by the remnant of the defenders as they stood so close to the wall, confident of the awful force of their battering ram. He also was certain he'd seen Kinkaid take the jolt of the boiling-hot tallow right in his upturned face. No man ever deserved such a death more richly.

Another torch went whirling out, then a third and fourth. The kettle of tallow was emptied and set down behind them. Chicago Ed Sealey went to the dynamite boxes, pulling out a pocket match case with a candle set well within it—a patent lighter whose flame was almost windproof. He lit a match and ignited the candle, then began loading his left arm with dynamite sticks.

Slocum turned and drew a bead on the farthest man he could see and dropped him.

Savage had planned well, saving the liquid tallow for the time when the leaders of the attack would be oversure of their safety, after moonset. With that formidable shower he had taken out most, if not all, of the bosses, and left a leaderless rabble without real grit in their gizzards. Now the thing to do was kill as many of the remaining foes as possible, so that the handful of Palace men would be able to walk the streets in comparative safety. The whang of slugs still rang over the roof, but far less often than before. There were three or four times as many men dead and dying on the road than still stood or ran there. Slocum picked off the distant ones; so did the buffalo hunter and Long Slim, an expert rifleman. Sealey, at the right-front corner of the barricade, was throwing lit sticks of dynamite at any congregation of three or more. John Henry squatted behind the parapet and casually picked off the enemy riflemen one by one. Savage flung more torches, themselves as good as weapons, their glowing, flaring fireball heads creating panic as they came down like comets, here and there setting men alight. Every defender who could stand was at the front row, firing, firing, reloading, firing.

Revulsion caught at Slocum's throat without warning. Too much killing, too many men dead. He swallowed it. Those weren't men; they were mad dogs, skunks with hydrophobia, butchers without bowels of mercy. He shot until his rifle was hot to his gloved hands, and slid back and got another and more cartridge boxes.

"Panther piss!" Johnson growled. "This lad's outer bullets." He reluctantly picked up a Winchester. "Dumb fool toy gun," he said, filling its magazine. "Bets I she won't carry across the street." But she did, and then some.

Havoc ruled the dying Retch. The noise was indescribable. Between the massed firing and the dynamite, Slocum felt he was going deaf. Savage with his cannon-stunned ears must be almost entirely so.

At last everyone broke and fled, and Chicago Ed put away what was left of the dynamite, while the riflemen picked their targets fast but carefully. It was one of the very few times that Slocum had ever shot men in the back.

All in a good cause, he told himself. Most of them were heading for the western end of town, where a hundred or more horses stood in the livery barn, dozing or fidgeting at the noise.

"Let 'em go," said Long Slim.

"Drop every one you can see," Slocum yelled at him. "They'll be after the horses!"

"Jesus, yes." The men crammed on either side of the open trap door, firing at the small running figures.

Then there was the bloody loudest blast that John Slocum had ever experienced, and from being balanced with one foot on the roof and one on the outer coping of the log rampart, he felt himself flung straight out into space, the Winchester dropping from his hand, his body spreadeagled, aware of nothing else but falling. He smashed flat on his face and thanks to whatever quirky fate watched over him, it was a deep snowbank heaped against the western side of the casino. He sank about a foot into it and never even struck the killer ice beneath. After a minute or a day or seven years, he didn't know how long, he struggled up, shaking uncontrollably, all his senses concussed, and looked around and discovered that there were a lot of corpses here but nothing moving in the range of his blurred vision.

"Where'd they all go?" he demanded aloud, voice very wavery, as fluctuating as Brandy's. "Where's Savage?" No one answered him. Then he got oriented and weaved to the street and down to the front door and hammered on it with both fists. "Lemme in, goddamn you," he yelled, "it's Slocum!" He thought, his

brains clearing. "Jesus," he said, "I been dynamited."
He ran on wobbly pins to the east side of the building.
Across the snow-covered flat, beyond the hide shanties,
he saw a horse and rider trotting away as quickly as the
deep snow would allow. The range was almost 200
yards. Slocum pulled his .45 and aimed with both
hands, the sight elevated till he was pointing the gun
about eight feet over the man's head. He fired once,
blinked, fired a second and a third time. The horse
screamed and bucked and the rider was thrown hard.
Slocum slogged like a mad elk toward him, fumbling
out his good thumb-buster, holding both lead-chuckers
in his hands, panting and batting his eyes to get back
his vision as sharp and clear as he could. The man
thrashed in the snow, got up on one knee, drew a gun
and blazed away at him. Slocum, breathing through
his mouth and still tasting fumes of the explosion, kept
coming. The downed rider emptied his revolver harmlessly, and as Slocum came near, drew a hunting knife.
He was a tall skinny cuss that Slocum didn't know, and
he was down because his leg had been snapped in the
fall from the saddle. Slocum walked up to him and put
a slug into the middle of his face. Then he shot the
dying horse, and went floundering back toward the
Palace.

That bastard had had his share of guts. He'd found
himself some dynamite, God knew how much, got up
and stood on his horse's saddle and tossed it with a lit
fuse onto the roof, fourteen feet above the ground.
Everybody on the opposite side, shooting at the last
of the mob, never dreaming that one enemy would have
the intelligence and the nerve to sneak around and do
such a thing.

Well, the war was over, and for all he knew, Slocum
was the only man left alive on one side. But then he
heard more shooting down toward the livery barn. God's
best cuss on the worthless waddies if they killed the

191

old man, what was his name, Rascoe, and stole all the cayuses; that caballada included Slocum's good long horse. But the firing went on, so they hadn't done it yet.

He got to the door again and hammered on it with the butt of his empty Colt, hoping that someone was alive to hear him. "It's Slocum, goddamn you deaf bastards, lemme in!" The three women might hear him, but they'd be too scared to come. Slocum commenced to say every ornery word that he'd ever learned, at the top of his now-cleared lungs.

He heard the planks being taken down. He shut up and waited. Chicago Ed opened the door.

"You're alive," they both said at the same time, and then laughed at each other. Ed looked hale enough. "I got him," said Slocum, walking in.

"I saw you," said Colonel Savage. His coat was kind of burnt-looking but his face was untroubled. "That was fair country shooting, Major."

"Luck. Who's alive?"

They trooped in then from the gambling room: big Ambrose, John Henry, Long Slim with a smashed nose that bled unnoticed down his chin and shirt, Lighter Johnson, and the trio of ladies all fussed and fearful at the rear. "Is this all?" Slocum asked.

"Davies made it, but that arm still has to come off. That's it."

The buffalo hunter, cradling his Sharps, said, "Feller dropped a stick of blast-'em right over the edge of the wall. If he'd thrown it two feet farther, we'd all be crowbait. Them piled bodies and the distance saved us, but sonny, I wouldn't want to go through that wild gust again, not for another thousand in gold! And it played hell with the whiskey kegs, too."

"How come I was the only one got chucked off?"

"You were leaning out, we weren't," said Slim, grinning through the blood and showing the gap where his two front teeth had been. "I was flang on my face on the damn planks."

"I can see that," said Slocum. "Man alive," and he began to laugh again, "what a finish! Just when we figured we'd done for them."

"We did. We stood our siege and defended the right, and by the Lord Harry we won," said Maynard Savage. He looked around. "And nothing broken down here, either."

"A sight of lives paid for them pretty mirrors," grunted Johnson.

"No, for the lives of a multitude of future victims. We've cleaned up Schmidt's dry-gulchers for good. They'll scatter now, and in twos and threes they won't be much threat to honest men."

"Scatter!, Holy shit!" said Slocum. "There's a fight at the stable. They're after the horses. I forgot."

Savage said, "Johnson, your gun's empty. Stay here and guard the girls—get yourself a Winchester, they'll show you where. Come on, the rest of you." He hefted his silver shotgun, its mother-of-pearl cracked and its polish smudged with black. "We can't lose the horses."

They piled through the door, just half a dozen men, checking their guns as they ran, patting pockets that still bulged with cartridges and shells. The road was strewn with bodies and pieces of men, gored with frozen blood, dented and torn with dynamite; running was a risky affair. They heard a rifle crack, and the sound repeat into quiet in a dying rat-a-tat that told them it had been fired within the barn.

They went past the outfitter's and saw that the small front door of the barn was closed. "Must be at the double doors," said Slocum. "Right around the corner. Spread out and come in a rank, like we had more behind us."

They filed out to each side of him and turned the angle. The remnant of the enemy was there all right:

thirty, forty men, dim figures in the starshine, several at the big doors, one of which was partway open. One saw their party and said, throttled, "Oh fuck 'em, they're here!"

"Fire," said Slocum. It didn't occur to him until much later that he'd taken over command from Colonel Savage. He simply knew what to do and he did it. He hadn't taken many orders since the War, anyway. Two rifles, two shotguns, two hoglegs roared. The volley wouldn't have passed muster in a military academy, but it was satisfactory in Retch. "Fire," said Slocum again, and the weapons spoke. "Fire at will," he yelled, and emptied both his guns into the black of them.

The slugs tore into bellies and chests, and the head-less rabble faded off, oozing into darkness like the craven varmints they were. A few showed fight and went down with their death wounds in front. The rest were slaughtered from behind. Smoke rolled up and flame spat from guns into the night and only the fastest runners saved their lives as they went to the ground behind white lumps that were cholla thickets and cactus and rocks, far enough out to be impossible targets.

There were more bodies sprawled around this end of the barn than the half-dozen men had accounted for. "Who in hell's been defending the stable?" Slocum said, reaching up to shove back his hat and discovering that he didn't have it. He leaned over and picked up three or four from the corpses till he'd found one that fit. He loaded his .45s and stuck them in their holsters. "Let's go see. Hey, in the barn! This is Slocum and Mr. Savage and some o' the boys! The Schmidt gang's gone! Can we come in?"

"Yes, please," called a voice like a brook running over smooth stones.

"Jesus Jumping Christ!" said John Slocum.

Slocum, Long Slim, and Lighter Johnson had had among them a good deal of experience at doctoring wounds in various places far from the beaten track and farther from qualified physicians. They pumped Blue Davies full of whiskey till his eyeballs rolled back in his head and he passed into dreams. Then they cut off his right arm below the elbow, cleaned it up and sewed it together. They used all the antiseptics they could find room for, and bandaged him good. When he came out of the whiskey-faint, his first words were, "You got my hook ready?"

"That'll come later. Meanwhile, Mr. Savage will look out for you," said Long Slim. "Nothing to stew about."

"Lost a gallon of blood, I reckon."

"Easy."

"Bet I'm pale as frost on a bleached lily."

"You look like a rain-washed skull lying at the end of a bloody shirt, but you'll do."

"Damn right I will," he said, and went to sleep again.

Johnson shouldered his Big Fifty. "Gonna go loot the general store. I seen they'd busted into it, but they wasn't no Sharpses in that crowd and mebbe I can find some ca'tridges. See you lads." He went out.

Slocum went into the gambling room, where the fire had been built high and the survivors were lying on sofas or slumped in deep chairs, except for Savage who had put on a fresh pearl-gray suit, shaved, and was sipping at his brandy up on his stool; evidently it was where he felt most comfortable. When he saw Slocum he saluted gravely.

"A good night's work, Major. I thank you. Retch is dead."

"Sure is. What will you do?"

"Send Ed to Tombstone for freighters. Take my equipment and furnishings back to Kansas City and build a bigger house next to my old one. Care to come?"

"Still the answer's no, sir. I'm a traveler. Wasn't born to light long." He sank into a hard oak chair that suited his tired back. Amelia Schmidt, sitting primly beside her fiancé on a couch opposite, looked at him with a wistful shine to her green eyes. Slocum crossed his legs, tilted his own John B., which he'd found on the mangled roof, over his eyes, which were likely just as shiny. Brandy sat in the farthest chair, scrunched up, looking forlorn, and watching Slocum when she thought he wasn't noticing. Tucker in his big-medicine albino buff coat, even in the heat, stood talking quietly with the ancient Navaho, Foot in Grave, who had come back from Tombstone just in time to barricade in the barn with the other defenders. He and Old Man Rascoe, Tucker and Bill McGunn, and the oddly matched pair of girls had lasted out their minor siege there, armed with all the rifles and shotguns from the sheriff's office, as well as their own weapons. They'd come through unscathed because they'd gone to earth behind bales of hay. The men who'd wanted to loot the horses hadn't realized what a tiny force opposed them there in the black cavern of the stable. Total loss to the defenders had been one expendable jugheaded pinto, gutshot, whose screams had slowed down the attack because the Schmidt mob hadn't wanted to kill all the mounts with blind firing. They'd been nerving themselves to rush in when Slocum and his five comrades had appeared. Luckily, the other horses had been so desensitized from the cold that even the wounded nag hadn't spooked them.

Amelia had never fired a gun before. God knew if she'd hit anyone, but she was all keyed up even yet and every few minutes busted out in a gabble of mainly senseless chatter until Bill could hush her up. Her principal topic was what had happened to her father. McGunn hazarded a dozen times that he must have run when he saw the fight going against his horde of low-grade bandits. Slocum knew better, but he wasn't saying anything. Amelia need never find out that her daddy lay dead outside the stable doors, with another bastard's coat flung over his face so that nobody else would recognize him. He'd been blown away by a shotgun, his intestines sagging out of his middle and his expression hideous, frozen in terror of the death he'd probably felt for a couple of seconds before it took him down to his niche in the devil's brimstone pits.

"What will we do with all the b-bodies?" Amelia asked abruptly.

"Nothing. By the time the spring thaw comes, Retch will be empty of humanity," said Colonel Savage, "and the animals will clean the place."

"But they should be buried—a Christian burial—"

"Not a Christian in that whole congregation, Amelia," Slocum told her. "But I take it our boys will get a burying, Colonel? They deserve it."

"I doubt that even a pick would dent this frozen earth, Major. We'll gather them over to the south, where there's a lot of rock and rubble, and put a cairn over them that'll keep out a grizzly. Even the hard characters who came to our aid at the last minute, Scarborough and O'Kelly and that squad, who redeemed themselves." His steel eyes hooded. "We lost thirty out of thirty-eight. A very large cairn to erect. Perhaps the local Indians will help us do it, especially when we tell them they can have anything they want from the other corpses; that'll be wealth to them, all the money and weapons and clothing. I hope they've gone to their shelters by now."

Kiwanwatewa, who had been jawed at by Tucker for half an hour without uttering a syllable, said, "My sister she tell 'em. Go into bushes, say go home."

Slocum was anxious to find out what the old man had learned in Tombstone, if he'd made it that far, but didn't want to ask now.

"I shot two pistols at once!" said Amelia, and started to weep. McGunn comforted her. Slocum looked at the ceiling and thought his private thoughts. Two bounty hunters, a greenhorn, a girl who scarcely knew butt from muzzle, an old white man and an older red one, and they had held off a pack of maniacs who *had* to have horses and were driven on by a man whose word had been law to them, whose urge to escape the town must have been wilder than theirs, who when thwarted must have turned into a screaming human tiger. It was as amazing that they'd all survived as it was that eight men had come through the siege of the Palace of Mirrors. Sometimes things worked out. Not too damned frequently, but sometimes.

"There may be men suffering out there from wounds," said Amelia. Her brimming eyes accused Savage.

"No, my dear, the cold has taken them all by this time."

"Where's Ed Sealey?" asked Slocum.

"Keeping Rascoe company, in case someone wants a horse badly enough to come in from the desert for it."

"Good thought," said Tucker. Slocum looked over at him and saw that the big man was eyeing him carefully. He unfolded himself from the chair.

"See you outside a minute, Charlie?"

"Sure."

198

Brandy bounced up. "Not unless I go too!" she screeched.

"What in hell you think we're gonna do, *both* run out on you?" said Slocum levelly. "Sit down!"

When she still stood there, the shortened scattergun in its sling protruding from her heavy coat, Savage said, "Sit down!" and moved his own terrible weapon around in her direction. "I suffer you in this place against my will, Miss Brandywine. You will obey my commands."

Brandy cussed under her breath, shifted uneasily, and sat. "Johnny, watch yourself," she said, and glared at Tucker.

"Just a word between gentlemen," said Tucker, smooth and easy.

"Sure," said Slocum. They went to the front door, which wasn't barred or even locked any longer. "After you."

"No, after you."

Slocum grinned. "Such fucking oily politeness, old hoss," he said, and opened it and went out onto the untidy street. "You got to do it with one shot," he said, and whirled and skinned his thumb-buster and cracked it twice. Tucker had already drawn but was bringing his Colt .44 up to let Slocum have it in the face, which was as foolish a thing to do in a toe-to-toe gunfight as pissing against the wind was on a flat prairie. Slocum's two slugs took him in the paunch and Tucker keeled over backwards, like a heavy oak sawed through at the roots, straight and unbent till he hit the road and began to writhe in on himself, a wounded rattler. Slocum thought he was going to bite himself. Then Tucker's left hand came out of the fancy coat with his second man-stopper and Slocum shot fast from the hip and splattered that hand into sinews and smashed flesh and shards of bare white bone. Tucker screamed and cursed and begged for Slocum to finish him off. Slocum said

199

no. Tucker's right hand, still holding the first gun, edged out from under the big body and its muzzle spat death that whipped by Slocum's neck, slicing the collar of the elkskin. Slocum let go another slug into the man's chest. Then Tucker collapsed and his limbs went slowly out away from the torso till he was lying in a kind of mock crucifixion pose, dying fast, and he said clearly, "Thanks, I never hankered to go out from a belly-shot. Too damn slow." And he shuddered and died.

Slocum holstered his Peacemaker and went into the Palace. He thought he heard both girls sob with relief as he entered the gaming hall.

"Kid Slocum's dead," he announced.

Maynard Savage lifted one brow. "*He* was Kid Slocum?"

"Sure. I'd have guessed it before, but the mustache foxed me. Then when I saw Chicago Ed sticking on a fake hank of hair, the notion started working at me. That was all that separated Tucker from me, that long set o' stallion-tails. Why couldn't they be just as phony as the shag that Ed used to disguise himself when he went out hunting information yesterday? And Tucker was always smoothing and preening at 'em; I thought he was vain, but he was simply scared they'd come loose, especially in the snow. Didn't trust the stickum to hold."

"That was an artificial mustache?" McGunn exclaimed. "That great thick killer longhorn set wasn't real? Why didn't anyone recognize it? Artificial mustaches are for the stage."

"No, because it was made of real hair, Indian hair most like, as coarse and black as his own. You'll see." Slocum went back outside and leaned over the dead man and ripped at one long heavy side of the thing, as thick and tough as a rope. It tore away, bringing bits of skin with it: that glue had sure been the most pow-

200

erful stuff that Tucker could lay hand on. He carried it inside and held it up like a brave with a scalp. "Each hair's been pulled through this piece of gauze and knotted on the inside. It's a real mustache as long as it's on." He tossed it to the old Indian. "Souvenir of your hard trip, Kiwanwatewa." Switching to Navaho, "I am sorry you walked so far and so coldly for nothing."

"Not for nothing, my brother. There is proof that Tucker and not Slocum was indeed the murderer and thief. It may be needed in Tombstone."

"What is it, brother?"

"Everyone who spoke of the man who robbed the bank who said he was Kid Slocum, spoke of his eyes." The thousand wrinkles bowed up in a broad grin. "Eyes of pale blue like the summer sky. Not Slocum's eyes, *aiee* no! I had my deputy's badge and a warrant from McGunn. One man, suspicious, looked at them and then at the poster. He was the best—puffing up with excitement. He said"—the old man went into English— "'that's the bastard. I'd know them blue eyes anywhere!' So I knew. And I bought a bottle, not so good as you gave me, and another horse, and came back."

"Kiwanwatewa did well. It was the act of a brave young warrior, not an old man."

"That is because Kiwanwatewa is not an old man yet, nor for many years. And it was to repay Slocum's kindness to Spring Fawn."

Slocum held out his hand. The Navaho clasped it firmly. "If Slocum ever wishes any other small thing done, let him send for his friend."

"I will," said Slocum, "I surely to God will." He translated the blue-eye business for the others. His own dark eyes held them all. He noticed that Brandy didn't look especially surprised.

"And that's why I just killed Tucker, even though he was behind me and should have fired first," he said.

"He went for my face, like the essentially dunderheaded duffer he was, because he knew he had to obliterate my eyes before he took me in for the reward. Never occurred to him that he could have shot 'em out when he'd finished gutshooting me."

"With all that bank money, he was after his own reward too?" gasped Amelia.

"Some men are plumb gluttonous when it comes to money," said Slocum, "and others are a little bit worse."

"Yes," she said, her eyes puddling up, "like my father. I wonder where he put *his* money."

"We'll find out," said McGunn gently.

"We won't bother. *I* surely don't want it! Let it rot, wherever it is."

"That's a waste," said Savage. "I'll look into it. If I locate it—"

"Give it to charity!" snapped Amelia, and that was that.

Long Slim, who had cleaned up his face and looked almost normal save for his missing teeth, waved a hand. "Something I don't savvy, John. How did Tucker know you were coming to Retch? I had the whole story —at least, what was known then—some days ago from Colonel Savage. We couldn't think why you'd turn up here after a man calling himself Slocum had said he was aiming this way."

"That's about the last mystery I can't fathom, either," said Bill McGunn. "A slew of bounty hunters came to town practically on your heels, even before Tucker arrived. Oh," he said, blushing like a kid, "I know you don't think I know much of anything, but I've been talking to people since you, ah, put me straight."

Slocum sat down with a bottle handy, poured himself a glass and built a smoke. "I always had the feeling I'd seen him before, some damn place or another.

Without his mustachios just now, I saw why. He looks a lot like me. And I saw him in Tucson, where I was laying around and playing a little poker and wondering where to go next. Someone talked about Retch being hell with the lid off and the fires stoked, and I said I thought I'd laze down this way next. Tucker was there, not talking, but listening. I knew his face when I saw it naked. 'Course he wasn't wearing that white buff coat then, or I'd have remembered right away."

"He must have ridden to Tombstone, waited a day or two establishing that he was you, then robbed the banks when the payrolls were in and come to Retch— taking his time—to see that his plan worked. If he could get you himself, he was another $2000 to the good; if someone else did, then he could light a shuck for Texas, or Old Mexico, or even back East, and never have to worry about the law searching for a man of his description." Brandy was sitting up stiff, almost bouncing. "Simple and practical."

"And abominable!" said Amelia, flashing wrath. "He was a hateful man!"

"A very mischievous galoot," nodded Slocum soberly. "Bill, you and me are gonna take back that bank money, along with the late lamented, who ought to keep nicely at this temperature, and you are going to collect the reward."

"I didn't earn it!"

"No, but you earned something for saving all our horses, and you're going to need money to start farming again. And *I* don't need it. I got a stake that'll take me to Frisco or New Orleans or Persia if I want to go." He saw Amelia start looking agog. Oh damn. Yearning to follow the man with the itchy heels. "But I'll likely go to Boston and become a haberdasher," he said. "Bill, go out and search Charlie Tucker. Whatever's on him, if it isn't bank cash, is yours. Hurry up before some crook sneaks back and gets it."

McGunn looked uncomfortable. Long Slim gave him a push. "Go on, pard," he said, "Slocum's right. I was raised a farm boy too, and I can tell one at a mile. It's where you belong. Get a grubstake here while you can. There's good bottom land in Kansas going for four dollars an acre, but there's good country to the north, too. Don't be a contrary clodhopper! Slocum's being damn generous—accept it like a man!"

Bill McGunn looked at Amelia. "Well, the reward, if you really want me to, but I can't rob the dead," he conceded.

Slocum swore. He stamped out and searched Tucker's carcass. He came in and dumped a wallet of old greenbacks, a leather sack of double eagles, and a handful of cartwheels into Bill's lap. "Hear me, McGunn," he said harshly. "That's yours, and the reward; you change it at Tombstone to a Wells Fargo receipt, and have Amelia sew that receipt into the lining of her bustle where nobody's gonna look but you; and when you come to a place where you want to live, take the receipt to a bank and they'll transfer the gold there for you. Got that?"

"I can't take a dead man's money."

"It's my money. Take it."

"Your money?"

"Shit fire, man, I robbed him, didn't I? And I'm giving it to you because you played square with me— took my word and let me walk free while we waited for Foot in Grave. I don't know now if that was your good judgment or blind instinct or just lack of sense, but you did it and I owe you. With this little bit of cash and the reward, we're even. You think I want to roam around beholden to some farmer? Or maybe you want to draw on me and make me take it back?"

"Don't shame me in front of Amelia," Bill said coldly. "You know I'm no gunman. I'll accept the money."

"It's for Amelia too, mind. You're gonna marry her in Tombstone. Ain't you?"

"He is," said the girl. "Now you stop bullying him, you generous man."

"I'm not generous, I just hate having too much money." Slocum went over to Brandy and dumped four irons in her lap, all of which he'd thoughtfully unloaded outside. "Here, you can sell the real article for a change. The shortly-to-be-notorious Charlie Tucker's quartet of lead-slingers, with his own goddamn notches carved on 'em."

"Thanks, Johnny," she said carelessly. "You think the old man would let me stay here tonight? I don't like to sleep in that hotel alone—not every throat-cutting bandido's dead."

"You can stay. Go get your tack."

"My, but aren't you the grand boss these days," she said. "You taken over?"

"No, but Savage owes me."

"You're a little shy of being half-baked," she said quietly, "giving all that money away. It's the kid, isn't it? You're in love with your lost innocence."

Sometimes she could strike too near the truth. Slocum kept his mouth thin and hard. "It's what I said. If it wasn't for McGunn, I might have landed in jail and been shot there. Get to hell to your room and collect your gear, or I'll have you locked out."

"I'm going!" She flounced out, and Slocum relaxed. He went over to the stool. "I know it's against rules, Colonel, but I'd like the woman to stay here overnight."

"Yes, such a dainty dove shouldn't be at the mercy of what dregs remain in Retch. This is your house, Major Slocum. Bring in William Tecumseh Sherman if you like."

"No, there I draw the line," grinned Slocum, and went to take a bath. When he'd finished, dressed lightly in pants and shirt, and looked out the front door, the dawn had come.

He said to Bill McGunn, who was still sitting there looking confounded, "This time tomorrow, when we've all had enough sleep and got our possibles together, you meet me at the livery barn with the two or three best carriages that the gentry owned. Have all the widows and orphans collected, and whoever wants to leave town—that'll be Cicero Welch if he's alive, and Bob Cook and a couple more. One of Savage's men will be going too, to arrange for freighters to come for all this ornamentation and frippery, and your deputy and his sister. They're gonna work for you on your farm."

"They are?"

"That's part of the deal. They're good people and I won't have them left here to starve on greasewood sap and cactus juice."

"Glad to have them if they'll come."

"They will. You think a real man like Kiwanwatewa would have stuck with you through all that bullshit for the money? He takes to you. And Spring Fawn's older than your grandmother, but she works like a team of bullocks." He sighed. "Got all that, son?"

"Got it. Thanks."

Slocum went to his room. Brandy was already in bed, playing with the sheets. "Look," she said, "real cotton sheets! Better than what we had before."

"Did you take a bath?"

"Your three girls insisted on it, but I was going to anyhow."

"They ain't my girls. I got no girls." He stripped off his clothes and crawled in.

"You got me." She stared at him, uncertain and showing it. "I washed very well, Johnny. He was nothing to me. Nothing but a cock to make me forget I didn't have you anymore."

206

"If you'd had your way you'd have had me, stiff as a plank with a slug in the back."

"I'm sorry. I was wrong."

"You were. Brandy, you weren't too damn amazed when I gunned Tucker a while back."

"I was going to myself. So I was sore at you, but what the hell, you deserved to take him. Kid Slocum, the bastard."

"How'd you find out?"

"Figured it, slow, too slow, but had it by last night. See, when he—you know—when he did things to me—"

"When he fucked you."

"Yes. Well, he wouldn't kiss me. And I kept wondering why."

"A man doesn't generally kiss a whore. And that's what you were playing at. You rolled in the soogans with him even before I'd left you, while I was up at Schmidt's that night. I knew something was wrong when I came back, but I'd had my head broke and didn't know up from sideways and couldn't guess what. Afterwards I knew."

"I wasn't married to you!" she flared. "And I woke up alone and was lonesome, and he came hunting you."

"You're right, we weren't married. I just reckoned you to be my girl for the time being. What about him not kissing you?"

"He kept pushing at his mustache. He didn't even realize that he did it so much. And I remembered an actor in St. Lou that used to do that on the stage all the time. And I figured—"

"You figured that with the kind of kisses you hand out, the glue on his handlebars was likely to come unstuck from the slobber."

"Yeah. I begged him, just to show I was no bought cat, but he seemed *afraid* that I'd kiss him, and he sure wouldn't do it to me. Even a couple of loose hairs would have tipped me, I see that now. But at the time, while——"

"Never mind all the coy little details. He's dead and I'm alive."

"And he was never half the man you are, Johnny. Honest."

Slocum thought that over, and believed it. He saw no sense in false modesty.

"Besides, I get the impression you're pretty lovesick over little Miss Angelcake."

"That's horse crap. I'm not sick about anybody, including you."

"But we have had some good times?"

"Not bad."

"And we can have one or two more before you pull out?"

"After I've caught up on sleep. You know I was blowed off the roof with dynamite?"

"Oh God, no. Go to sleep, Johnny. I'll be quiet as a sphinx."

Growing drowsy even as he talked, Slocum found a moment to recollect that Brandy had once been an educated and decently reared girl. A Virginia lady. He thought maybe he'd ask her after one of their sessions about how she'd become a bounty hunter. Only bounty hunter in the Territory who knew what a sphinx was.

He wakened ten hours later, when Bertha rapped and brought in supper, looking all prissy and peeved at the sight of Brandy in bed with him. He woke her and they ate, and did what they did best together, and she was gentle and vicious and loving and violent and all the different women rolled into one big-titted package that he remembered. He fucked her damn near all night and only got another hour of sleep before Bertha came tapping again to tell him it was almost daylight.

They hugged and kissed and she made him admit that he held no grudge against her for Tucker, and maybe someday they'd meet again and have a time. They stood there on the rug stark naked, Slocum fondling her breasts and she holding tight to his manhood, which he'd never cram into his Levi's at this rate. She said softly, "But if you ever *do* bust the law too hearty, John, and they put a high enough price on you, I'll come after you same as I would any man."

"I'd expect that. That's all right, honey."

"The reason I was gonna back-shoot you—I didn't want to take you in alive because they'd have hanged you, and that's a mean way to die."

"And naturally you couldn't let me go."

"No. It's how I earn my living, Johnny."

He kissed each big nipple in turn. "And you got to live."

"Right."

"Mind telling me why you live the way you do?"

She thought, holding his cock and rubbing the head absently against her vulva's wet lips. "Next time I will. When we're better acquainted."

He couldn't think of a thing to say. So he banged her against the wall, standing up, and then they dressed in their trail clothes without bothering to wash, and wolfed down the breakfast that Bertha had brought, and gathered their gear and looked at each other.

"I'll see you again, Johnny dear. I swear to God, you're the best there is."

"I'll try not to gather any rewards on my head before that."

"If you do, I promise I'll buy you a tombstone out of the bounty. Not wood, marble; Italian marble. I even thought up what it'll say. *'Sub hoc conditorio situm est corpus Johannes.'* I think that's grand. It's Latin. It only means 'Under this stone is laid the body of John,' but it's so simple that it's impressive."

"I'm impressed," said Slocum. "But I don't plan to stick up a stagecoach just for the simple honor of some Latin plunked over me."

"You have to admit it's a sweet-thought," she said seriously.

Slocum stared at the lady with the hay hook. At last he said, "One of the nicest things anyone ever thunk up for me, honey."

They left the room. Slocum shook hands with Colonel Savage. "See you some time in Kansas City, Colonel."

"I sincerely hope so, Major. Remember me when you need a friend." He gave Slocum a wintry smile. "After all, we cleaned up a town together."

"Guess we did. Funny, I never did that before, and likely won't again, but it's not a bad feeling."

"It needed doing, and we did it." Savage handed him a new Remington and a sack of cartridge boxes. "Your thousand's in the bottom of the sack. I hope it doesn't offend you, but since I promised everyone—"

"Money never offended a man with anything better'n wool for brains, Colonel. Thanks."

He left the Palace of Mirrors for the last time, kissed Brandy good-bye on the street, and watched her trudge off eastward, Lord knew for what. He walked through windrows of frozen corpses and hashed-up drifts of snow to the big barn. He noticed that someone had dynamited the Earthquake, which lay in squalid wreckage with one lone leg sticking out from under a hunk of roof.

Carriages and wagons were waiting. Slocum went in, saddled and bridled his big gelding, fished the $8000 out of his oat sack and put it in his war-bag. He thanked Old Man Rascoe for taking good care of his long horse. "What's going to happen to all the others? Most of their owners are dead."

"Gonna drive 'em north and sell 'em in Tucson when the weather breaks. Mr. Savage, he says they're mine now, them as isn't claimed."

Slocum mounted and rode out to the caravan. Chicago Ed greeted him, and said that Lighter Johnson had just left on a good horse, not his own but with a bill of sale from Rascoe, with his $1000 gold and all the Sharps ammunition Retch had left. "He said to say so long to the big young feller. I suppose that's you."

"That's me."

"McGunn is going to report all this," Ed threw his arm wide to take in what was left of the town, "to the marshal in Tombstone, or to a federal marshal if there is one. Mr. Savage briefed him completely. There'll be no trouble."

"And I imagine that the Colonel's reach is even longer than a fake sheriff's. You have your horse ready?"

Chicago Ed looked abashed. "I never learned to really like one, Major. I'm riding in one of the carriages."

Slocum nodded. "I'll break trail with another rider. We'll follow the Indian's; since he came straight from Tombstone and knew what he was doing, we're less likely to fall into a wash full of snow. Hop in, Ed, I want to get started. Ought to make Tombstone by evening." He surveyed the travelers. There were Mc-Gunn and the two old Navahos; Amelia who twinkled with happiness, in spite of having lost a father, and smiled when she saw him till he felt silly before Bill; Cicero Welch and his wife and two kids; a couple of orphaned tads of De Moss's; the widows of Red Bass and Sam of the Earthquake. There was large greasy Bob Cook in a wagon of his own, piled with his frying and stewing paraphernalia and his big cookstove and drawn by rawhide-shod oxen. "Bob, you'll never keep up with the horses," said Slocum.

"Don't matter, I can last overnight on the plains with all this lard on me," grunted the cook. He uncoiled a braided bull whip twenty feet long and cracked the buckskin popper. "Can't leave my stove, after all,"

211

he said, "and there wasn't no use in staying. You put one too many leaks in my restaurant, and the customers went elsewhere."

Slocum rode down the line, chuckling. He said howdy to the rickety, enduring Indians and passed words with the bewildered batch of children. It looked as if everyone was here.

Christ, everyone was riding in vehicles, and he needed another man on a good horse to help break double trail for the wheels. He was about to lean on Bill McGunn, as Bill was better than nothing, when another rider came out of the barn. It was the lunger, muffled up so he looked almost half-healthy, coughing as the icy air struck into his chest.

"You're coming along?" Slocum said diffidently.

"Retch is played out, and I believe Tombstone will have calmed down enough to tolerate me again. You haven't forgotten anything, have you?" he asked. He pulled off a glove and extracted a cigar from his silver case, then offered Slocum one.

"Such as what?"

"Oh, Tucker, for instance."

"God Almighty!" said Slocum. "What a jackass!"

"From the racket I heard through our mutual wall last night, you had other things on your mind. She gives good worth for her pay, Miss Brandy."

"I never paid her!"

"You didn't suggest that?" He pointed. Slocum looked down the road. Brandy had found herself a big flatbed wagon somewhere and hitched a double span of mules to it; they were standing patiently watching her as she went from frozen carcass to frozen carcass, rolling some over, scanning the faces, occasionally riffling through a thick sheaf of fliers.

"I didn't have to suggest it," said Slocum. "That girl thinks of everything under the sun that'll make her a dollar." He watched her wrestle a grotesquely curved

212

corpse and heave it into the wagon. "She'll wind up with forty or fifty wanted men," he said, "and haul 'em to Tombstone and collect on 'em. Then she'll sell the guns to greenhorns with affidavits that they all belonged to Wes Hardin or Hickok or Masterson. See, she's even *searching* them she ain't taking!"

"Simply practical. I admire the lady."

"I better pick up Tucker before she lands him," said Slocum.

"I have him." The lean consumptive snapped his fingers. Rascoe led out a big roan stallion. Tucker was strapped over the saddle, toes down. "His own horse and saddlebags. The bank loot, by the way, is in them."

Slocum felt like the damnedest lamebrain in Arizona, and said so. He watched Brandy at her gruesome work. He'd miss her. The treacherous bitch. She was going to make more money out of the fall of Retch than all the rest of them put together.

Well, she had to live.

"You and I can keep an eye on the saddlebags, and tell McGunn about them at the first chance. I think his mind's otherwise engaged too. That's a plump little partridge he's snared." He lit their cigars. "Help you break trail?"

"I'd appreciate it." Slocum sat his long horse for another moment. Far off to the east, over the ridge, a woodpecker began banging on a dead tree with a deep, hollow drum-sound. Thank God, everything hadn't died in the norther.

He faced his companion. "John Henry, we came through a passel of hell together. Do you mind if I call you Doc?"

Doc Holliday laughed, choked, and said, "Guess it's all right now that I'm not on the dodge. What shall I call you?"

"Anything but Kid," said Slocum.

J.D. HARDIN

"THE MOST EXCITING WESTERN WRITER SINCE LOUIS L'AMOUR"

—JAKE LOGAN

___ 16840	BLOOD, SWEAT AND GOLD	$1.95
___ 16842	BLOODY SANDS	$1.95
___ 16882	BULLETS, BUZZARDS, BOXES OF PINE	$1.95
___ 16843	FACE DOWN IN A COFFIN	$1.95
___ 16844	THE GOOD, THE BAD, AND THE DEADLY	$1.95
___ 16799	HARD CHAINS, SOFT WOMEN	$1.95
___ 16881	THE MAN WHO BIT SNAKES	$1.95
___ 16861	RAIDER'S GOLD	$1.95
___ 16883	RAIDER'S HELL	$1.95
___ 16767	RAIDER'S REVENGE	$1.95
___ 16555	THE SLICK AND THE DEAD	$1.50
___ 16869	THE SPIRIT AND THE FLESH	$1.95

FOUR SWASHBUCKLING TALES OF THE HIGH SEAS

BY C. Northcote Parkinson

WAR BOOKS FROM PLAYBOY PAPERBACKS

A MARVELOUS SELECTION
OF TOP-NOTCH MYSTERY THRILLERS
FOR YOUR READING PLEASURE

Charles Alverson

____16530	GOODEY'S LAST STAND	$1.95
____16603	NOT SLEEPING, JUST DEAD	$1.95

Margot Arnold

____16639	THE CAPE COD CAPER	$1.95
____16534	EXIT ACTORS, DYING	$1.75
____16684	ZADOK'S TREASURE	$1.95

Michael Collins

____16593	ACT OF FEAR	$1.75
____16812	THE BLOOD-RED DREAM	$2.25
____16551	BLUE DEATH	$1.75
____16672	THE BRASS RAINBOW	$1.95
____16773	NIGHT OF THE TOADS	$2.25
____16822	THE NIGHTRUNNERS	$2.25
____16525	THE SILENT SCREAM	$1.50
____16855	THE SLASHER	$2.25

Phillips Lore

____16694	THE LOOKING GLASS MURDERS	$1.95
____16652	MURDER BEHIND CLOSED DOORS	$1.95
____16587	WHO KILLED THE PIE MAN?	$1.75

781-2

MEET
CHRISTINA
IN AN EXCITING
SERIES OF
ELEGANT EROTICA

THE BEST BUSINESS GUIDES AVAILABLE TODAY FROM PLAYBOY PAPERBACKS

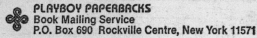

GREAT BOOKS
OF ADVENTURE
AND SUSPENSE